The BONE DIVER

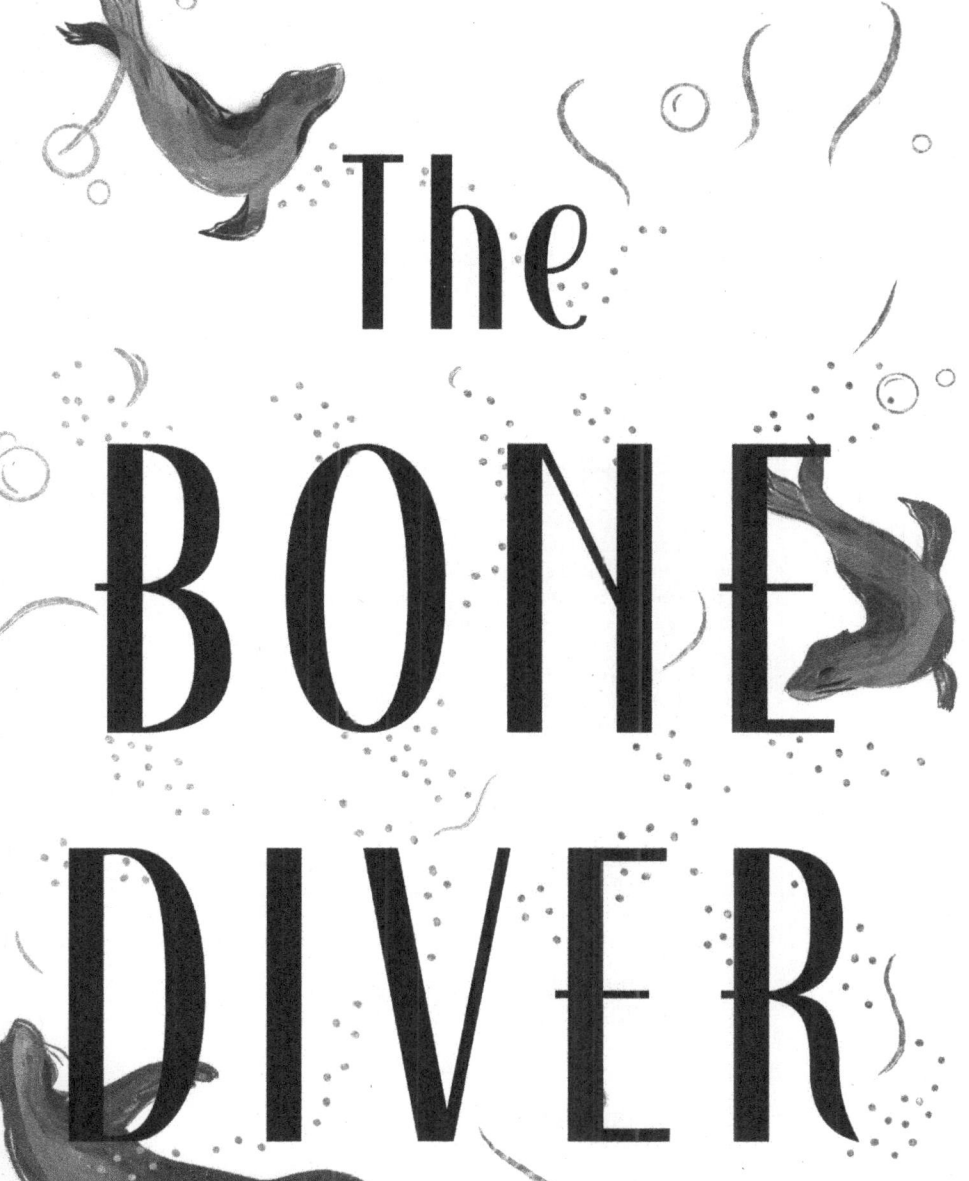

The BONE DIVER

ANGIE SPOTO

Black&White

First published in the UK in 2024 by
Black & White Publishing Ltd
Nautical House, 104 Commercial Street, Edinburgh, EH6 6NF

A division of Bonnier Books UK
4th Floor, Victoria House, Bloomsbury Square, London, WC1B 4DA
Owned by Bonnier Books
Sveavägen 56, Stockholm, Sweden

Copyright © Angie Spoto 2024

All rights reserved.
No part of this publication may be reproduced,
stored or transmitted in any form by any means, electronic,
mechanical, photocopying or otherwise, without the
prior written permission of the publisher.

The right of Angie Spoto to be identified as Author of this
work has been asserted by her in accordance with the
Copyright, Designs and Patents Act, 1988.

This is a work of fiction. Names, places, events and
incidents are either the products of the author's
imagination or used fictitiously. Any resemblance to
actual persons, living or dead, or actual
events is purely coincidental.

A CIP catalogue record for this book is available from the British Library.

ISBN (HBK): 978 1 78530 660 0
ISBN (TPBK): 978 1 78530 662 4

1 3 5 7 9 10 8 6 4 2

Typeset by Data Connection
Printed and bound in Great Britain by Clays Ltd, Elcograf S.p.A.

www.blackandwhitepublishing.com

To Harris

1

MY EARLIEST MEMORY IS OF A SEAL. Not a slick, grey head bobbing in the waves. Not a shadow like an arrow shooting through the murk. Not the stone-still heft of one sunning itself on a rock.

I remember the scarlet puppet of meat, its skinned body, all broken veins and black blubber. I remember the clicking sound the dripping blood made on the stones, as my father hung its still-steaming pelt. Mostly, I remember the way the dawn clawed its way across the rocks, tugging the sea with it, and how the whole sea sparkled. Sparkled and laughed, right in the face of death.

We are the Sealgairs. The seal killers.

My mother used to be a herring girl, gutting fish in two quick strokes. Maybe that's why my father fell in love with her the way he did – sudden and fast and without a glance backwards. Maybe he saw the fierceness in her fingers as she cut the life out of a dying thing and loved her for it.

My family are seal killers, but I am not like them. I don't mind the stench of blood, or the knives that are always glinting in my mother's fingers. I can sail the boat better than most, throw a spear almost as deftly as my father. I would be the perfect hunter, if I could kill anything at all.

But I cannot kill. That is my curse and, like most curses, I have brought it upon myself.

That's why I'm out at low tide, collecting driftwood from among the rocks and stinking kelp.

I feel sharp little claws digging into my jacket, a pressure on my shoulder, whiskers tickling my ear. Dratsie has her nose pressed against the soft skin below my jaw. She's chittering away, almost as loud as a magpie in swooping season. I reach up and stroke her back. 'Shhh,' I say. 'You noisy thing.'

'What's that?' Fie asks. He looks up from the tidepool he's crouched beside. I know him well enough to know he's searching for anemones, his favourite sea creature. I joke that of course he'd like something that looks like a pincushion among anything in the whole glorious sea.

'Not you,' I say to Fie. ' I was talking to Dratsie.' I lower my arm, and the otter scampers down the length of it, landing effortlessly on the rocks.

'Hermit crab,' Fie says, pointing into the pool. I stand beside him and look into the water. We're both already a handful of years over twenty, but this doesn't get old, peering into tidepools, hoping to spot a bit of life. I've lived my whole life beside the sea, and still it amazes me. The tidepools are little windows into what hides beneath the waves. A wee hint at how much goes on under the surface.

I don't see Fie's hermit crab. Hovering like a ghost above the sea moss and snails is the reflection of a house. 'House' is the wrong word for what it really is – something more like a fortress perched on the cliff edge, streaked with sea salt, gables topped with spires as narrow as knives. Though it is just a reflection, I can smell the dank of it, the dampness that darkens its foundations, and it's easy to imagine the way footfalls might echo off the stone walls within. Like many houses here, it has a name. Not a charming name, like Listmore Cottage or Ashdale or Cora House, but one that sounds heavy to my ears. Sharp and shortish. Erskine Manor.

I touch the water with the tip of my finger and make ripples that break the image.

Fie overturns a rock, and we both lean close, hoping to catch a glimpse of a fleeing brittle star. 'Liv's working the pub tonight.' Fie sets the rock back into place. I see right through the casual movements of his fingers, the way he talks down into the water so I can't quite see his expression. I've known Fie since before he could even speak, when the world had its assumptions wrapped around him tight like tentacles. I was the first one to start prying the tentacles free. So I've also known for months now how Fie says Liv's name like it's an apple in his mouth, taking a beautiful, sweet bite of it every time.

'Is she?' The quivering image of Erskine Manor returns to the rockpool. I flick the water again to make it scatter, and I lean back. 'We should go tonight. I could do with a drink.'

'Why's that?' Fie doesn't miss a thing and gives me an appraising glance. Neither of us is very good at saying exactly what we mean, but I like to think it doesn't matter much. He knows something isn't quite right, just as much as I know he's falling in love with Liv. I'm not ready yet to admit what's got me out of sorts. I don't even know if 'out of sorts' is the right way to the describe it. I had a nightmare last night, but I certainly won't mention that.

'Something feels strange.' I rise, taking an empty limpet with me so I can run my thumb over its smooth inside. The sea is calm today, receding, leaving behind a myriad of little glass-like pools among slick, green rocks. They put me in mind of a lady's necklace that someone has torn from her neck, silver beads scattering. Pretty, but something left behind. I see Fie in my periphery rising and looking out towards the sea as I am. I feel the presence of Erskine Manor behind me, and I'm annoyed at letting it affect me. I think of mist rising from thick undergrowth. A dark forest. A gate that is rusted shut.

'What's that?' Fie's elbow brushes mine as he lifts his arm to point. We look at each other, obviously thinking the same thing, both of us launching forward. Dratsie follows, scampering across the rocks far faster than either of us.

This close to the sea, the rocks are covered in a slimy film of seagrass. Fie's stick-thin and nimble, but he's a tailor's son, not the daughter of seal killers. He lives in the town in a flat above the tailor shop and didn't spend half as much of his childhood darting across these rocks as I did. I'm taller, heavier, but I'm faster than he is, and I reach the child first.

It is not a child.

What I saw for hair is black curls of kelp. What I thought was a child's torso is a bloated, chewed-up carcass. Of course, I recognise what it is immediately. 'It's a seal,' I shout back to Fie, so he doesn't hurt himself to get here for nothing. Insects flit around the seal's body, and the flesh stinks of rot. The seal's pelt is useless, chewed through by worms and brine. My heart squeezes a little at the sight of it, at the waste of it.

Fie makes a disgusted noise and doesn't come as close as I am. 'I thought it was a bairn,' Fie says, his voice muffled. He must be holding a hand against his mouth, but I don't look at him. I'm still staring at the guts of the seal. Something feels strange. It's been feeling strange for a while now, and I haven't said a word to anyone. But my parents are gone longer these days, out hunting for hours, and my father speaks less. Usually, he loves to talk of the sea. Its colours. Its mood. He hasn't spoken of it for days, and I've felt the absence of his stories, like a clenched fist hiding something. Something is strange about the dead seal, but it is only a feeling. It looks just like something the sea would give up, retch onto the shore as a sort of sacrifice. There's no shortage of dead things on the shore.

'Good thing it isn't,' I say, finally turning away.

2

By the time we leave the shore behind, the tide is rolling in again, slapping against the rocks. We turn our backs on the sea, both of us glad to be rid of it. The dead seal has left a sour taste in my mouth. We reach the coastal path and follow it into town, while Dratsie stays behind on the shore. She likes town even less than I do.

Fie's mood improves rapidly, and it's not long before he shucks off his careful gait for his usual, loping walk. He likes the sea well enough, but you can tell he prefers the town. I don't understand how he can feel so cheerful with houses rising around him and the horizon nowhere in sight. Walking into town always makes me feel like I'm about to be swallowed whole.

'Fie!' The butcher is leaning in the doorway of her shop. She's got bright black eyes and ruddy cheeks that often are smeared in blood. 'How's the dress coming along, then?'

'Beautifully,' says Fie, winking at her in a way that I suspect makes most people's heart jump a bit. I don't know where he got it from, that wink, but it's the perfect icing on the cake for

Fie. The last little thing that endears everyone to him if they didn't like him already. 'No one will have a dress as beautiful as your daughter's. The groom won't know what to do at the sight of her.'

'Oh, I think he might,' says the butcher, shaking her head.

'So it's almost done?' I say when we're out of earshot of the butcher.

'Hardly.' Fie pulls a face and shrugs. 'Can't rush beauty.'

'You can if the wedding's in three weeks.' A Midsummer Eve wedding. Everyone's looking forward to it. There'll be a ceilidh in the town hall after the ceremony, dancing and drinking to the couple's good health. The best way to ring in the shift in the season is piss-drunk, surrounded by friends.

'Plenty of time,' Fie says. He waves at someone else who's shouted a greeting at him.

'I can't wait to see the look on the bride's face when you present her with the prettiest dress you've only half-finished.'

'Still would be better than anything else she could get around here,' says Fie, and he's right of course. I've never been able to muster up much jealousy for Fie, but every once in a while, I feel a pang of it. Fie may not have been born into his name, but he was born into his family with a thimble on his thumb. He took up the family business as if it were as natural as breathing. He's so good at what he does that he's almost more sought after than his father. If I didn't know Fie as well as I do, if I didn't know that even he hasn't had an easy go of it, jealousy might have killed our friendship years ago. Fie has everything I'm missing. This ought to make me hate him, but it doesn't. Some people stick in your life and stay there, constant as sunrise.

By the time we reach the pub, the sky has grown a deep, hungry red. It's not long until Midsummer, and the days are long now. When even the midnight sky is soft around the edges, you get lulled into thinking the long summer nights will never end. They do, of course, and the winter darkness feels that much thicker for it.

The Corbie's Nest has always looked as if it were a hundred years old. The windows are warped and streaked with grime. The sign that swings above the door creaks even in the gentlest breeze. The pub smells of hops and fish and the sea, probably from all the fisherfolk that congregate here whenever they return to shore. The Nest is a coming-home sort of comfort, not quite as strong for me as the pull of the water, but nothing else on land comes as close.

Fie and I step inside and are hit with a fug of warmth, fisherfolk scent and, very faintly, the floral undertones of Liv's perfume. She's behind the bar, pulling pints. Her fair hair is swept up into a pile atop her head, and every so often she blows her fringe away from her eyes. I see why Fie loves her. She's always kind, never bitter, even when dealing with an aggressive drunk. She could calm a shark with just a touch. But she is no pushover. Her kindness has a fierce edge. A sense of justice. From what I've observed in the pub over the years, she doesn't always play by the rules, if she thinks the rules are no good.

Fie, for all his external confidence, is skittish like a colt, and it would do him good to have a woman like Liv at his side.

This is my mission for the evening. To set these two finally on their course.

I know if I were in the same position, dragging my feet about a woman I secretly loved, Fie would be there to push me along. But I'm not and never have been. This town is too small for me, and I know everyone too much to be falling for anyone here. I'm not saying there aren't girls pretty enough to fall in love with, but I just doubt any would be interested in returning the favour.

I steer Fie towards a table. They're all beaten up, full of nicks in the wood, knifed with initials, stained with drink. From here, we have a clear view of the bar and Liv behind it. I've still got my net full of driftwood, and I stash it under the table. A thing like that might be out of place in another pub, but not the Corbie's Nest. No one would bat an eye at a net full of scallops, or even a basket of still-flapping fish, let alone a meagre collection of driftwood. I kick it further under my seat. I'd rather it were a basket of fish, but I'm no good for fishing either. Killing is killing, no matter the creature, and my curse doesn't discriminate. I can't kill – not a seal, not a snail, not even a spider when it crawls into my bed.

'You going to order?' I ask.

'Last I remembered, you owed me a round.'

'Is that right?' I lean around Fie and look pointedly at the bar. To Fie's palpable discomfort, Liv catches my eye and nods. I hold up two fingers. She raises her eyebrows in acknowledgement.

'Yeah, well.' Fie leans his elbows on the table. He keeps his top two buttons undone, the rogue. 'What did you get up to this morning?'

'Bit of diving, swimming. Not doing any good for anyone.'

Fie huffs. 'You don't always have to be *doing* something. I only sew because it's like how diving is for you. I can't *not* do it. It's a kind of breathing.'

'Lucky your breathing has a purpose.'

Fie opens his mouth, but Liv is suddenly here, placing two slick pints onto the table between us. We both lean away, look up towards Liv. She's not looking at me, so I settle back and observe the flicker of panic on Fie's face. 'Anything to eat?' Liv asks.

'No, thank you,' says Fie. 'Beer's enough.'

Liv cocks her head. 'You know how to sew a button on, don't you?'

'I should hope so,' says Fie, winking. I have to hold in a cough that would obviously be construed as a laugh. He holds the pint glass but doesn't lift it up. I take a long sip from mine and watch him from over the rim.

'Then you could show me the ropes.' Liv lifts her wrist, showing where a button is missing on her cuff. There's no way she even uses that button. When I first entered the Nest, her sleeves were rolled up.

'The thread, you mean,' says Fie. 'I can show you the thread.' He clears his throat and finally takes a drink. 'You know—'

'I get the joke.' Liv nods and her lips twitch into a smile. 'My shift's over in an hour.' She laughs and turns away, swooping across to a busy table to clear away their empty glasses.

I clench my teeth and suck in some air, but Fie points a finger at me and swallows a gulp of his beer. 'Yeah, I know. Not very smooth.'

I hold up my hands. 'A little rough. But an easy sail's a suspicious one.'

Fie looks despairingly into his pint. 'My brain seems to slip right out of my ears.'

'Maybe for the best,' I say, and he kicks my shin so that my beer sloughs onto the table. After that, we settle into the comforting murmur of the pub. A few drinks make Fie's worries soften, and even I'm feeling lighter. The unsettling feeling I had at the sight of the seal seems silly now. I'm reading into things that aren't there. I'm making the worst of a perfectly natural occurrence. The sea is fickle. Anyone who lives by the shore, who makes a living from the water, knows that. The sea may be sparkling and calm one moment, dazzling you with its beauty; and in the next moment, it's throwing brown water against the rocks, revealing its dirty innards. That's just the way the sea is and always will be.

Life and death mingling together in the vast, deep depths of it.

3

An hour goes by in a soft haze. I'm not quite done with my drink by the time Liv is untying her apron. I've been nursing my third beer for a while now, contriving a good excuse to stay behind, when Fie rises from the table. 'Go on,' I say, then nod towards my drink. 'I'll finish this and head off.' To drive the point home, I take a sip, swallowing the warm beer with only a slight grimace at its taste. Like that, Liv and Fie are gone, and I'm alone at the table.

The pub is still full and crowded enough to feel cosy. A large group of fishermen, some standing, some sitting, congregate around one of the bigger tables. I've gathered from scraps of conversation that this is the crew that's been out to sea, just returned with a haul of fish. I've also gathered, from how quickly they got drunk, that the catch wasn't a bountiful one. They've gone out further than usual, hoping the different waters would bring more fish. But sometimes breaking from the usual isn't worth the trouble. By now, their disappointment is masked by laughter, but I see the worry tugging at their smiles. I see it and wish I had another drink to help me forget my own disquiet.

'Did you say you saw a mermaid out there?' one of the fishermen says, jabbing his companion in the ribs. 'Was she one of them with a fish's head? Or did you get lucky, catch a flash of some pretty sea flesh?'

'It was just a seal,' the man says. He leans on his elbows, takes a drink.

'A seal with a lady's face, then, huh?' the first fisherman says. 'You said you saw her pretty lips.' His companions don't mirror his grin. I sense the whole group heading down the other side of the night, the best beers behind them, entering a different kind of drunk. One where the darkness feels sharpened. Unsaid things coming to the surface.

'Wouldn't be a mermaid, then,' says another man. 'We call those selkies.'

'Nothing pretty is lurking in those waters,' another man chimes in. 'I swear, something is down there, eating all the fish.'

'It was just a bad run,' the cheerful man says, but I see even in his smile a hint of unease.

I lean back and take a long drink, finishing my pint. *Eating all the fish.* And the seals have been harder to find lately, too. I keep my family's books. I know we're heading for a hard winter if the hunts don't become more fruitful soon. Like I often do, I think of what it used to be like out on the boat with my parents. The rolling water beneath us. The spear in my hand, knife at my belt. My eyes trained on the water, looking for a stroke of black. They're out tonight, and I should be there with them.

I'm lost, daydreaming into the bottom of my empty glass, when a name makes my ears prick up. Erskine. The fishermen's conversation has changed, as it inevitably does, to the town's most favoured source of gossip. A good story doesn't need much. In fact, just a handful of delicious details and you're off to the races. The broader the strokes the better. Harder to tell a story when you know all the mundane details of a person's life. Much easier if all you've got is a manor house on the edge of a cliff surrounded by an estate no one has managed to enter for generations. Years ago, when my great-grandmother was young, the Erskine estate was known for its lavish parties held in the great hall of the manor house. They said the lord and lady at the time were generous hosts. The drinks flowed and the food was plenty and anyone lucky enough to be invited to an Erskine affair spent the next day sore in the shins from dancing. But those are old stories, and there hasn't been a party at Erskine Manor for many years.

We know the house isn't abandoned because, once a month, a servant or two appears in the town. They collect enough provisions for a decent-sized family, but no one has ever managed to get more than a curt reply out of them. The Erskine servants are closed books. The Erskines themselves are mysteries – blank pages on which everyone in this town likes to scrawl a tale.

'Just women in that house,' one of the fishermen is saying. 'Five beautiful young women, locked away by Lord Erskine. That's why there are five towers. One for each pretty girl.'

'Mairi said they get a regular order for scraps of meat. Huge quantities of it. Not very ladylike, that.'

'That's for the monster,' another man says.

'Aye,' the first man says. 'Lord Erskine himself. He murdered his wife. That's why the wall's got claw marks on it. He chased her right to the edge of the estate before cutting her down.'

'There's no claw marks,' another man retorts.

Erskine Manor is encircled by grounds that are choked with forest and brambles. The closest you can get to the house is by standing on the shore, looking up at the cliff it is perched on. Even then, it's still a fair distance. If you're brave enough, you could swim until you reach the cove beneath the cliff on which the house sits, but no one's that mad. The waters around that shore are dark, as if they're always reflecting a great storm cloud. They're rougher, too, always choppy with white-peaked waves, and there are currents that most definitely are rips. A boat would never make it into that cove without getting smashed on the sharp rocks. Superstitions hold a lot of sway in a fishing town like this, and there's a belief that anyone who goes into those dark waters won't come out.

Like most stories, it's a mix of truth and lies. Some if it's true, some of it's naw.

Erskine Manor is just as impenetrable by land. There are two gatehouses, one to the north, one to the south, but they are always shut. The entire estate is surrounded by a dark stone wall, in places heighted by iron bars. Beyond the wall rise trees that obscure any view of what's beyond. Brambles crawl over the wall, and trees stretch over it like people desperate to get out. You know you've nearly reached the southern gate when the trees thicken, growing so close together that shadows clot even on a cloudless day.

Like most children in the town, Fie and I tried many times to catch a glimpse of someone in those gatehouses. They're the places adults go when they're drunk and feeling like kids; somehow, the glass in the gatehouses has remained unbroken, despite all the rocks thrown at them. Sometimes, someone tries to scale the wall. No one, as far as I know, has ever managed to get into the estate. Except me. But I've kept that story wound tight. Not even Fie knows. After all these years, I'm not even certain it happened at all.

I was fourteen, and Fie had just turned fifteen, so we weren't kids anymore, but it felt like it that day. I was riding the thrill of a good hunt, having killed two seals just that morning, and things were better now between Fie and his dad, just enough that even I felt like a weight was lifted and we could breathe again. I don't remember what sparked the idea to go to the estate. I don't know what set us on the path out of town, into the countryside. I do remember the mist, how it crept upon us slowly. At first, just wisps of it hovered in the dips between hills, but by the time the great dark wall loomed beside us, the mist had started to lift among the trees. It seemed the wall disappeared into nothing, for how thick the mist hovered above it.

'What do you think?' Fie asked, looking up at the wall. 'Any scary monsters on the other side?' The day felt like dusk already, though it was only late afternoon. From beyond the wall, I heard the chittering of magpies.

'You mean the guardians?' I said, raising my eyebrows. It was one of the stories my dad liked to tell about that place: that creatures guarded the house, preventing any trespassers from getting close. 'Like the horse with pike's teeth. Faster than any horse, and it's always dripping wet. If you hear the sound of water splashing, you ought to run.'

I hopped up and tugged at a branch of a tree that leaned over the path. Its roots were firmly in the Erskine estate. I pulled leaves from the branch, scattered them on the ground.

'A wet horse ...' said Fie, watching me. 'Sounds terrifying.'

'Would be, if it were chasing you,' I insisted. 'You know what I think?' I said, feeling the roots of a new story taking hold. 'I think there are no wild creatures guarding the estate. In fact, it's the opposite.'

'What do you mean?' Fie asked.

'There's a reason why we never see the Erskines. It's not because Lord and Lady Erskine look down on us all – it's none of that what people say.' Here, I lowered my voice. 'They're protecting us, that's what.'

'From what? More wet horses?'

'From their children, of course. *They're* the monsters who roam the estate.' I looked up as I spoke, spinning stories into the branches above. 'The sons have long claws where they ought to have nails. They curl all the way down to their toes. And their eyes are huge and round without any lashes, and they can see in the dark. Perfect for stalking the shadowy pine forests. The daughters have long flowing hair, all the way down to their knees, and it's so smooth and soft, slick as oil, it distracts you from everything else about them. They seem like normal girls from the back, but when they turn around, you see their mouths full of needle teeth and skin made of glass, clear enough to see all their blood and insides and their little black beating hearts.'

Fie punched me in the arm. 'All right. You still going in?'

I pressed my palm against the wall. I noticed something carved into the stone I'd never seen before. A face. What looked like a man with wild hair, his mouth wide open in terror.

'Clasp your hands and give me a punt. I'm sure I could reach the top.'

Fie shook his head. 'Not a chance, Kier. Let's try the gate.' Fie pulled something from his pocket. A sewing pin flashed in his fingers. 'I reckon I can pick the lock.' He grinned, and I shook my head, but I followed him.

We reached the northern gatehouse. Just beyond the iron bars of the gates squatted a dark stone building, apparently abandoned and hardly cared for, with dust clinging to the windows from the inside and an overgrown garden with a few choked rose blooms.

'That thing looks rusty,' I said, making a face at the huge double gates. A massive lock secured them, but it was covered in rust. Flakes of black paint peeled away like dead skin.

'Nothing I can't handle.' Fie already had the lock in his hands and was fiddling with the pin. I turned away and pressed my face against the bars of the gate. Oddly, one of the gatehouse windows was clean, and it seemed as if I could see right through it. I stared at it, willing someone to walk by, for a silhouette to appear from within. And then – a flurry of something dark made me draw breath. There in a flash, then gone. I blinked, thinking maybe something had caught in my eyelash, but there it was again, a frantic blot of shadow disturbing what little light managed to leak through the gatehouse's windows. It wasn't human, wasn't big enough for that, and it was moving up and down. Fluttering. Flying. I caught the curve of a white breast. My fingers gripped the window frame as I tried to open the window. A magpie, trapped within. I could just barely hear its desperate warbling, and once I swear it looked me right in the eye, pinning me with its beady gaze. I tried again to open the window. The bird was out of sight for a moment, and all I could see were soft shapes across the gatehouse floor, a floorboard sticking up, the curl of wallpaper. I felt suddenly cold, and I looked down to see mist curling around my legs. The magpie slammed itself against the window. A shock of feathers, a splattering of blood. It fell onto the floor, out of sight. Through the blood-stained window, I thought I saw a shadow move.

It was only then I realised. The window. I was at the window. Beyond the gate. I tried to turn but I could not – it was as if the mist were holding me fast. My fingertips were baltic, my chest tight in fear.

I heard the sound of water dripping, and I'd never been so afraid.

Click, click, click.

But it was only Fie, still at the lock, fiddling in vain with his pin. And I was standing back at the gate with my face pressed against the iron bars. There was no mist at my feet. All the windows in the gatehouse were the same, none of them streaked with blood. My fingertips were cold, but only because I'd been gripping the bars so firmly.

'Ah, well,' Fie said. 'I give up. We'll never know what's on the other side of this wall.'

'That's fine by me,' I said, sliding my hands into my pockets, trying to look unconcerned. 'Can't be anything good.'

4

Dawn will always be my favourite time of the day. I like the way the sky glows, how it hints at the sun before the yellow ball of it emerges from the sea. I like the way the clouds gather on the horizon, shift and disappear if the weather is fair, clot in sodden heaps if a storm is coming. I always feel like the dawn is letting me in on a secret.

Today, the sky is empty of clouds. The sea is darker than the sky now, impossible to know if it's choppy or smooth. I take a few deep breaths of the sea air, let it clear the sleep from my lungs. A creak of the floorboards behind me, but I don't have to look to know who it is.

'What do you reckon?' my father asks. He's as tall as me, and we both have a girth to us that makes most people a bit wary. My father's a hunter, but he's only frightening to humans if you don't know him yet.

I suck in a breath between my teeth. 'Tricky one today,' I say. I tilt my head, feeling the wind shift against my cheek. 'Wind's northwest, so I reckon we'll have a choppy sea until noontime and then it'll be as clear as glass. No clouds. Not until supper time. A storm tonight.'

He huffs a chuckle. 'Always pessimistic. It'll be a grand day, only sun right till the moon rises. A calm night tonight. We might even keep the windows open.'

'You get that from a northwestern wind, huh?' I turn to him. He's shaking his head and turning away inside. The hob clicks and wooshes as he turns on a back burner. I heft the cast iron pan and set it atop the flames. We don't always get a morning like this, where he's not out on the boat, and we can guess the weather and make breakfast before Mum wakes.

He cracks egg after egg into the pan, filling the whole thing up. I get the bacon from the larder and start frying up some slices, filling another pan. As the eggs crackle, my father boils the kettle for tea and starts on the toast. We work in silence usually, moving about each other like clockwork. But today, the worry is back, scratching at my mind. I watch him tend to the eggs, carefully turning each one.

'What's wrong with the sea?' I ask. My voice is raw, as if the words have fought their way out.

'What's that?' he asks.

'Something's wrong with the sea, isn't there?'

My father glances up at me. He's got green in his eyes mixed in with the brown. His brows furrow, just slightly before he looks back at the eggs. They have his whole concentration. Bacon fat leaps out of the pan and scalds my wrist. I take the cue to turn each slice, and they erupt into a furious crackling.

'Nothing's wrong with the sea, Kier,' he says.

As a kid, you get to know your parents' voices. Their barely contained anger voice. Their at-their-wits'-end voice. Their someone-has-died voice and they're waiting for the right moment to tell you. My father's voice doesn't match his words. It's his lying voice. Lying and he's going to be damn stubborn about it.

I turn away and start setting the table. Something is wrong with the sea, and my father knows. The fishermen last night knew, and my instincts have been shouting at me for weeks. Something is wrong, but I don't know what it is. And soon, after we've eaten breakfast, my family will be going out there, sailing right into the depths of it, going further and further to catch enough seals to keep the breakfasts coming. I won't be there with them, I never am, because I'll just be underfoot. There's not enough room on a boat my family's size for a person who can't kill.

I get the whiff of something starting to burn and manage to catch the bacon just in time. The kettle whistles.

'Just how I like it,' my father says, half-laughing, as I peel the crispy bacon from the pan and pile the slices onto a plate. I snort, and Dad nudges me aside so he can take up the kettle and start making tea.

'Lucky you,' I say. I add milk to the tea he's poured. Only one mug will have sugar. That's for Mum. I plop two brown cubes into her mug.

Dad sets the kettle down. I know the look on his face, and I start edging backwards. I should have had the foresight to snatch up two of the mugs to bring to the table, but Dad is too fast. He takes me by the shoulders and pulls me into a hug that nearly squeezes the breath out of me. 'Stop worrying about things you can't change,' he says. 'It's a bad season. We'll be all right by spring.'

His hug is quick, slightly painful and leaves me feeling just a tad bit better. A bit, but not much. 'I'm the best worrier in this whole house. Someone's gotta do it,' I say, trying to sound lighter than I feel.

Dad shoots me a good-natured accusatory look as he takes a seat at the table. 'I thought that was your mother's job.' Dad is under the impression that Mum and I are alike in more ways than we really are. Physically, we're hardly similar at all, since I've inherited the Sealgair height and bones, and Mum is short, lower to the ground, with an excellent sense of balance that makes her a fantastic sailor. We might share the same eyes and skills with a knife, but not much else.

Dad and I are already loading up our plates when the floorboard at the edge of the hall creaks.

'Morning,' my mother says, as she pulls out a chair at the table. Her voice is still edged in sleep. She's never been an early riser.

'It's going to be a clear one today,' Dad says, as he reaches across for more bacon. He and Mum's elbows brush and they look at one another. 'We'll have a better go of it than yesterday.'

'We'll go north, towards Inverwick,' she says. 'There's a herd that likes the islands, especially when the sun's out.'

Dad clicks his tongue. 'Sorted, then.' He looks at me, as if I'd have anything to add to their seal-hunting talk. Mum doesn't even bother and tucks into her breakfast. I notice she's only taken a single slice of bacon, and I can't help the irritation that curls inside my chest.

What was it like, before I went out onto our boat alone that night when I just turned fifteen? What would it be like now, sitting at the breakfast table, if I hadn't taken up my knife, if I hadn't tried that last, fateful kill?

Dad would say to stop worrying about things I can't change. I'm not sure what Mum would say. She's not one for much talk, especially to me.

My parents talk more about today's hunt, about the route they'll take if their first choice proves fruitless. They fall into an easy rhythm, a back-and-forth about weapons and sails, currents and tides. It feels like a long time before the breakfast is eaten and we're sipping the dregs of our tea.

The plates clink as Dad starts stacking them. 'Look at that,' he says, rising, looking towards the window. We look in the same direction to see the sun, huge and yellow, rising into view. 'A beautiful day.'

'Don't speak too soon,' I say.

Around me, my parents begin to put away the breakfast things. Dad shakes my shoulder as he passes and gives me an eyebrow raise that says, 'Cheer up.' The worry must be written on my face.

Dad taps the horseshoe nailed above the door before he leaves, and they're both gone before I know it. The empty house breathes in and out. They left the door open after they trooped out, spears on their backs, an eager brightness in their eyes. They were thinking of blood, of a spear sunk deep into a seal's back. The thought makes me dizzy, and I grab the doorframe. I'm glad they're not here to see me. I stand there, looking out at the shore and the sea until I think I see their boat, already just a speck. It seems to tip over the edge of the world and is gone.

5

THE HOUSE IS IN ORDER well before noon, and I've got the kettle on again for another cup of tea. I leave it to boil and climb the stairs. When I reach the first floor, where our bedrooms are, I keep going. The attic door is well oiled, and it swings open without a sound. With only one slim window, the attic is dark. I wait at the threshold until my vision adjusts, and slowly the pelts hanging from the eaves become more than just grey shadows. What at first glance looked like a repetition of the same grey skin reveals itself to be a collection of seal pelts, each as unique as the next. I walk through them, savouring their soft leather-like feel against my cheek. Flecked in black, they seem to shimmer as I walk past them, almost as if they are alive, ready to leap away. I breathe in their animal scent, the tang of the sea, the harsh burn of what was once alive. I hold out my hand and brush each pelt as I pass.

When I was a little girl, I loved this place, where the pelts hang before we sell them on. Where I could imagine what each one once was, a wild slick creature riding the currents. I would come here and daydream, thinking up stories of what it would be like to be a seal. I envied their freedom. The stupid, careless way they lugged themselves onto rocks and lolled their heads back in the sun. To be a seal seemed to be the most wonderful thing of all. Wonderful, until my family found them.

My father, with his arsenal of superstitions, believes the Sealgairs are so skilled at hunting seals for one simple reason: we have the flute. It is a small, unassuming instrument, made of seal bone, roughly hewn, without a swirl of decoration. When my father holds it, it's dwarfed in his large palm. The flute has always been in the possession of a Sealgair. First my great-grandmother, then my grandfather, then Dad. It should, eventually, belong to me, but I cannot imagine what use I would have for it. The flute, my father claims, calls the seals. Dad thinks the flute is why the seals are so comfortable around our boat. Why they are so at ease, even when we heft a spear or spin a knife in our fingers. Certainly, the Sealgairs are, and have always been, the most skilled seal hunters on this coast. No one else even bothers to hunt the herds. As a kid, I always believed Dad's stories about the flute, but now I don't know what is real. What I do know is that the hunts have been poor lately, and they need to get better soon.

A wind blows, and the hanging pelts gently sway. I no longer want to be a seal, but I still love this place. I can't kill, but the sight of the pelts doesn't bother me. It's the killing that makes the world go dark, not death itself. The act, not the result. The pelts are beautiful, a reminder that death isn't always ugly. This is my family's livelihood. It's what keeps us together, keeps us thriving. Without it, I can't imagine who the Sealgairs would be.

All the pelts are lovely, but there is one that shimmers more than the others. We do not keep it hanging in the loft. It belongs to me, and I keep it on my bed. I press my cheek against it every night. Whenever a Sealgair is born, we're given a seal pelt rather than a knitted blanket or a teddy.

The day I was born, my father was out at sea, and my mother was in her bedroom with the midwife. She'd gone into labour not long after he'd taken the boat out by himself. In the version of the story my father likes to tell, I waited to breathe my first gulp of air until he was back on land. He returned home in time to hold my mother's hand, bloody though his was, almost as bloody as mine before the midwife cleaned me up. Hearing my mother's screams through the thick cottage walls, he didn't have time to put his catch in the larder. Instead, he carried it right into the bedroom, and it lay on the floor beside the door. I think, maybe, it was the first thing I ever saw.

My father describes the seal as the most beautiful one he's ever seen. He calls it a sign, a gift from the sea. He says that when he saw it swimming beside the boat, he knew the sea was making him a bargain, threatening him. Kill the seal, or the daughter who hasn't yet breathed will never take a breath. He said he felt a need vibrating through his bones, and that if his spear didn't hit true, his life would never be the same.

But the spear did hit true, as it always does for my father, and he hauled onto the boat a large, beautiful creature with black eyes still open, pelt shining with seawater. I was born looking into those eyes and, that night, my father skinned the seal and gifted me its pelt. I've loved it ever since.

I don't think my family has ever killed a seal with a pelt that shines so much in the moonlight, that seems to come alive beneath my fingers. That, when I press my nose against it, feels like diving deep, so deep I'm no longer myself.

My father, as with almost anyone who depends on the sea for a living, likes his signs and portents. He's as superstitious as any sailor. That pelt, sliced from the body of that beautiful seal, could fetch us a small fortune. In fact, it ought to have, if my father would sell it. But he tells me he's afraid that if he does, something will happen to me, that the promise he made to the sea will be broken, and she'll get her vengeance. He always says this irreverently, like it's a silly belief, but I see the seriousness in the depths of his irises.

So he's refused to sell it for all these years. Not even to the Erskines.

I was wee, probably eight or nine, but the memory is fuzzy. I must have been at least eight because that's when my mother gifted me my knife. A beautiful knife that always balanced perfectly in my palm, no matter how much I grew. That night, I sat in the dark in my bedroom with the curtains open enough to let in the moonlight. *Thwick*. That was the sound my knife made slicing through the air. *Thwack*. That was the sound it made sticking into the wooden frame of my bed. At the time, I was under the delusion that my parents didn't know I had the habit of practising my knife throwing on the bed-frame, but it must have been obvious, all those little nicks in the wood. I was determined to be the best seal killer of all the Sealgairs ever born. I remember throwing that knife and imagining – *thwick, thwack* – killing a seal in one swift throw, using the same knife to skin it, slicking my hand in scarlet.

The knife, still vibrating, was in the bed-frame, and I was halfway across the room to yank it out when I heard the creak of the front gate. Our old metal gate always makes the same yawning creak whenever anyone pushes it open. My mother refuses to let Dad oil it. It is a warning, she says. Some folk have fancy bell-pulls. We have that old gate.

It wasn't a cold night – it was summer, I think, or very early autumn – but I scooped up my sealskin and wrapped it around my shoulders like a cloak. I felt like a real hunter then. A proper Sealgair. I yanked my knife from the wood and put it in the scabbard I kept on my belt. I was invincible. Even as I snuck out of my room and down the stairs, holding my breath, I dreamed of how I'd face the intruder. I didn't want to wake my parents. I wanted to do this on my own.

But my father beat me to the door. When I reached the bottom of the stairs, tucked away in the shadows, I saw him, his broad shoulders filling up the doorway so I couldn't see who was there.

'Come around back,' I heard him say. 'The order's ready.'

Whoever was at the door didn't say a word. The silence was thick. I held my breath.

There was a clink of coins, and my father stepped back to shut the door. I froze, expecting him to see me, but he didn't and instead headed for the back of the house. Gripping my knife, I followed him. But, in my determination, I'd forgotten about the creaky floorboard. It squealed a betrayal, and Dad turned around.

'Kier,' he said and laughed when he saw my expression. 'If you can stay quiet, you can come with me.' He turned around, and I followed him down the hall towards the back door. 'It's good for you to know how the Erskines do business. They're one of our best customers.'

Even at that age, I knew about the Erskines, but I hadn't known they bought skins from us. In fact, the Erskines have been buying sealskins from us for years, ever since my great-grandmother started hunting. They are not only our richest customers, but the most loyal.

Of course, we never saw Lord or Lady Erskine, only a servant, who was sent to collect the skins and always at night. There's no reason for the Erskines to be secretive about their custom, so we've always assumed it was just their way, that they're a bit strange and perhaps protective of their staff, who don't often get a good reception from the townsfolk.

When Dad opened the back door, I was surprised to see a small, plain woman standing in our garden. She wore a heavy-skirted dress, charcoal grey and of a fashion more suited to my great-grandmother's childhood than mine. Her skin was very pale. I noted it, thinking how it almost looked clear. Her lips seemed very dark in that white face. An eider duck come to life.

At the sight of her, I hugged my sealskin closer around my shoulders.

On his way through the house, Dad had fetched a bundle of skins, already prepared, and he handed these to the woman. She glanced at them and lifted a finger, pointing directly at me. My heart flew right to my lips, and I almost screamed, but I remembered at the last moment that I was a Sealgair and afraid of nothing.

Dad shook his head. 'Not that one,' he said. 'It's not for sale.'

The woman only nodded before taking the bundle of skins into her arms.

'Good night, then,' Dad said, and the woman said nothing in return.

When the door was closed, Dad turned to me. 'She was from the Erskine estate,' he explained. 'They buy skins from us every season. It must be very cold in that old house.' He laughed at his own joke, ruffled my hair and wished me a good night.

I waited until I heard the bedroom door click closed before I scampered up the stairs as quickly as I could without making a noise. When I reached the first floor, I stood on my tiptoes at the window that looked out into the garden. I leaned hard against the windowsill and squished my nose against the glass. I remember wishing silently to myself, fervently willing the woman to come this way.

There was a long moment, filled up with my growing disappointment, before I finally got what I wished for.

She came around the edge of the house, not following any path. She moved strangely, tilting forward as she walked, as if the ground were rolling beneath her. She didn't look around but moved forward with a hunter's determination. A little fear curled inside my stomach. My instincts whispered for me to come away from the window. My ears whooshed with the sound of my own blood as the windowsill pressed hard against my breastbone.

If I had looked away, I would have missed it. The woman moved swiftly, bending at the waist and plucking something from the grass. The thing wriggled in her grasp. A toad. I saw its two back legs kicked up, silhouetted in the moonlight.

And then I saw the woman open her mouth and bite the toad's head clean off. She swallowed, and I was certain I could see the lump of it going down her throat. Another bite and the toad was gone.

I had forgotten about my knife. I was unprepared, like a good hunter never is. The sealskin was heavy across my shoulders.

She turned her head, and she looked at me.

6

THE SEA ON THIS SHORE is cold all year round. I'd tell anyone I'm used to it, but it always takes my breath away. When I break the surface of the water, the chill goes straight to my bones. I've slowed my heart by taking long, deep breaths, but it still skips a beat. I'm addicted to that initial shock of panic, when my body and mind are not yet in agreement. I dive, feeling the currents dragging at my legs. Down here, the quiet is a comfort. I sink right into it.

At the bottom of this particular cove trundle massive scallops. The plumes of dust that rise up as they move give them away. I brush my fingertips over the back of any one I see. It ought to be as simple as plucking one from the sand and taking it back to the surface. It'll die all on its own before anyone cracks it open. It would hardly feel like murder, this passive sort of death. Scallops have eyes, but they are not like seals. They don't stare at you like seal pups do, all trusting and soft. They are ugly, and this is supposed to make them easier to kill.

My lungs begin to burn. I know I need to rise soon. I grab the nearest scallop and clutch it tightly, like it might fix me, like it might transform me into the person I was born to be. As I am rising back towards the surface, I imagine exactly how it should be: my knife hangs on the leather scabbard around my waist and, when I reach the surface, I slide it out and swiftly use the tip of it to crack open the scallop shell, revealing the white, wet muscle within. It should be that simple, that easy. I imagine it so clearly that, when I break the surface, I am almost surprised I haven't done it yet.

Even if I had a knife, I could not use it. When I hold the scallop out into the crisp air, the horizon starts to tip. A different kind of coldness coats my skin. Clammy, cloying, and my breath is gone, sucked right out from between my lips. This is not the first-dive panic I'm addicted to. The waves begin to sound like whispers, scratching in my mind, growing louder, and I can almost understand what they are saying but not quite, not quite ...

I let the scallop go. It hits the water with a tiny splash, and as it sinks to the bottom it grazes my leg, leaving a stinging cut. I'm treading water, more exhausted than I ought to be, as the world starts to piece itself together again.

My stomach is sour with disappointment. Just a scallop. I can't even kill an ugly mollusc. It's not that I don't want to; it's that I can't. Because I do want to. I want more than anything to be able to kill again, like I did when I was a girl, fearless enough to squash a spider with her hand. I want to be that girl again, who was supposed to grow up slaying seals, skinning them for their pelts. A hunter. A proper Sealgair.

My father was wrong. Clouds are already crowding over the sea, and the wind skims across the water's surface. The sky and the sea seem to melt together. The beautiful morning is gone, giving way to a gloomy afternoon.

Once my heart rate slows to normal, I let myself sink. I don't dive, I just fall, letting my body move with the sea. I feel the tug of the stream tide, at this hour moving south. I'm settling back into the flow of water and untangling the knot that holding the scallop created in my chest. It's unravelling. Maybe long enough beneath the waves and it'll disappear altogether.

I'm almost comfortable again – with my thoughts starting to drift to easy things like Fie and Liv, what time I ought to start dinner, if it might start to rain – when I see blood. A scarlet curl of it, twisting like smoke. It's strangely bright in the gloomy water. I reach for it, but it evades my fingers.

The blood dances in the water, and I feel the same strangeness that I felt when staring at the rotten body of the seal. Something isn't right. I turn around, and the blood turns with me. My breath is gone and I have to surface, but I'm right back under as soon as I take a breath.

The blood is mine. It swirls out from between my legs. Of course it's mine. What else was I thinking it could be? When I surface again, I tread water for a moment, feeling both stupid and unsettled.

I'm far from shore, but the stream tide is in my favour. I swim with it, letting it tug me along. I can swim for ages this way, and the ease of it I know is something of a trap. Even though I'm comfortable in the sea, though I've grown up almost more in it than without, I don't ever forget that the sea isn't my friend. It doesn't care if I live or die, if I'm ensnared by a rip or dive too deep. The sea will just as easily give my body up to the shore as it did the seal's. So I don't swim as long as I know I can. I don't push my muscles to the very edge of their limits. I flow with the tide, but I draw closer and closer to the shore until I feel the sand grazing my knees and I rise.

This far down the shore, I see the marked change in the water ahead, how it suddenly darkens. Erskine waters.

The manor house looks down from its perch on the clifftop. Gulls lift away from its roof, swirl in a broken white cloud among the gables. A light is on in one of the upper windows. Or it's a reflection because, when I tilt my head, the light is gone.

7

It takes a day for that northwesterly wind to properly bring the bad weather I predicted. It arrives the next morning, with clouds clustered low, threatening to burst. I've got my hood up already in anticipation of a torrent, which might unleash at any moment. It's early enough that the walk into town is quiet, with most of the shops still shut tight.

The tailor shop is on the high street, on the corner of what you could call the busiest street in town. 'Busy' being a relative term. Beyond the mannequins set up in the window, I see the shape of Fie's father at the sewing machine. The door is shut, but I can just about make out the clicking of the wheel.

'Gallach and Son', the gold lettering on the window says. The 'Son' was added a few years ago. A peace offering. An acceptance that still makes me dizzy with mixed emotions. Fie was supposed to be a girl, but that didn't work out. His father didn't know what to do, didn't react too well when Fie told him the truth. Fie's mother has been dead for years, and it was just his father, grappling with something he didn't understand. I saw the darkness inside Mr Gallach. I saw him when he was my friend's greatest fear, a nightmare come to life. But I also saw him change, becoming the man I suppose he is now. Even Mr Gallach has buried Fie's old name. He added 'Son' to the shop window. Even so, I still see those old days, and I can't help but think of him sometimes as a monster in fancy dress. I can't help but expect the mask one day to slide off.

Well, if Fie's happy, then so am I. I'll try my best to be, anyway.

The shop emits a honey glow, inviting in the gloomy morning. A bell chimes when I push the door open. Fie's father looks up from the sewing machine, which ceases its whirring.

'Miss Kier!' he says cheerfully as he rises. He's not much like Fie in looks, but it's clear where Fie gets his charm from. Mr Gallach is a barrel-chested man who always wears the same black trousers and starched white shirt, like he's ready for a special occasion. He has none of Fie's unique style, but his clothes fit impeccably, and you know in your bones you can trust him with a needle. 'Fie's just stepped out.' He stands behind the counter and leans his elbows against it, looking up at me.

'Thanks,' I say. I've wondered if Mr Gallach senses my unease around him. I like him, and it's hard not to, but that's where the problem lies. Everybody likes him, and he's always been a kind of barometer in this town. A lot of folk follow his lead, and for all the time he doubted Fie, it planted the same seeds of doubt in others' heads. It meant some people had the confidence to say whatever was on their stupid minds.

The bell chimes, and I look over my shoulder to see Fie sidling into the shop. 'Hey,' he says when he sees me. He's smiling in a way that I can tell isn't for me. 'I would have got you one if I knew you were coming.' He holds up the greasy paper bag he's carrying. It smells of bacon and egg.

'No, no, Kier gets mine,' his father says, nodding at the bag in Fie's hand. 'I'll get my own breakfast.' He flashes a smile. 'Need my dose of gossip anyway.' He squeezes Fie's shoulder before he leaves, and the bell chimes behind him.

'Everything all right?' Fie says, settling against the counter. His smile is gone.

I wave his worry off. 'We're not talking about me.' I knock my shoulder against his. 'What's the news?'

'There's not really much to say,' he says, but the smile is creeping back onto his face. He doesn't look at me as he fiddles with the paper bag, reaches in and pulls out a buttered roll filled with bacon and bright, dripping egg. He hands it to me before taking his own. Outside, it begins to rain. A flurry of raindrops spatter against the window, making us both look up.

'Really? Why're you grinning like that, then?' I say. The roll is heavy in my hands. All this is perfect. The warm tailor's shop. Fie finally getting the girl he's been after. A breakfast roll in my fingers, making my mouth water. It's perfect, but an annoying unease tickles at the back of my mind. I feel like I'm waiting for something. Not a good something, either. Outside the sky darkens. It feels suddenly like dusk. I can practically taste the impending storm.

'I had a good night,' Fie says, around a bite of his roll. 'We went for a walk on the shore. That's all.'

'You showed her how to sew a button?'

'Yeah.'

'Did you kiss her?' I ask.

Fie nearly chokes, and I'm about to make a joke, thump him on the back, when the door opens. The scent of rain unfurls into the room.

A woman stands framed in the doorway. She is tall and thin with black hair to her shoulders. Her hair is dripping wet, and I'm amazed to see no hat or umbrella in her hand. Around her shoulders is draped a beautiful sealskin cloak. The colours shift like oil on water, brilliant to look at, like watching the clouds shift across the halo of a full moon. The cloak is clasped around her neck with a gold chain.

Both Fie and I stand frozen as she steps into the room. Her dark eyes take us in.

'Can I help you?' Fie says, recovering himself and moving behind the counter. He adjusts his sleeves. I see his gaze darting over the woman's dress and the dark-blue velvet jacket with gold-laced ribbon up the front that peeks out from beneath the cloak. She is dressed unlike anyone we've ever seen in this town. Maybe she's visiting from the city, though it's miles away, and I've never known sealskin to be in fashion there. Maybe she's lost.

'Yes,' she says in a low, smoky voice. 'You may.' She catches my gaze. She does not smile or nod, only stares so intently that I nearly look away. But I don't back down easily. She is, perhaps, a bit younger than my mother, but her age is only present in the way she holds herself. Her skin is porcelain smooth, and even her hands are unlined. 'I am looking for fabric for my daughter's dress.' She looks again at Fie. 'Much like this.' She holds out her wrist. From beneath her jacket's cuff peeks out a silky green fabric. I notice, as I'm sure Fie does too, the mother-of-pearl button adorning the sleeve.

'May I?' Fie asks, hovering his fingers above the woman's wrist. She nods once, and Fie brushes his fingertips over her sleeve. 'That is very fine silk,' he says. 'I'm afraid we don't have anything quite as nice as that, though I can offer you what we do have.' He turns and looks at the back of the shop. 'One moment.' He disappears through the curtain behind me. The woman runs a gloved hand down the length of her hair and flicks the excess water from her fingertips. A drop lands on my cheek, icy cold.

Fie hurries back in with a skein of white silk in his arms. 'I would have to dye it,' he says, setting it on the counter. He shakes his head. 'And as I said, it's not like what you have there.'

The woman plucks off one glove. She rubs the silk between her finger and thumb. 'It'll do,' she says.

Fie looks uncertain. 'It'll be dear. We don't usually sell fabric alone. It might be more economical to go to a haberdashery. There isn't one in this town, but the next town over—'

The woman holds up her hand. 'I have no time for that.' She taps the skein of silk. 'Dye it blue.' She captures my gaze again. 'The colour of the sea at dusk. I'll have someone come to pick it up. How long?' She looks at Fie again.

'Three days.'

She nods once. 'How much? I'll pay it upfront.'

Fie still looks uncertain as he tells her the price, but she seems wholly unconcerned at the vast amount. Since she arrived, I've been silently spinning stories about who she might be. A city dweller who lost her way; but she is too certain of herself for that. A friend or a sister visiting someone from town; but no one in town has such glamourous friends – because if they had, everyone would know. That leaves just one option, though it is also improbable. That this tall, beautiful woman, who smells like fresh rain on stone, is Lady Erskine. Could she be? I have no way of knowing for certain, but I cannot imagine she is anyone else.

The woman pays swiftly and pockets her small purse.

'Do you need an umbrella?' Fie asks her as she begins to turn away. 'I think the rain's only going to get worse.' As if on cue, a gust of wind sends more raindrops against the front window. It looks miserable outside, the rain horizontal.

'No,' the woman says. 'I am not afraid of a little water.'

She is at the door, one hand outstretched, when she turns to look directly at me. 'One other thing,' she says casually. 'I am looking for a diver.'

Fie and I are surprised into silence. I wonder at first if I've heard her correctly. Did she say a diver?

'You are a Sealgair,' she says, as if it's obvious. 'You are always on the shore. You should know someone who is a strong diver. They must be able to hold their breath for a very long time, and they cannot be afraid of small spaces.'

I am caught completely off guard and am unsure what to say. Fie's stare is heavy; I can feel the weight of it. We are both thinking the same thing – how does she know who I am?

'A diver?' I ask, feeling like a dafty as soon as the words leave my mouth.

The woman's fingers brush against her cloak and she smiles, just slightly. 'Yes. Someone who dives in the sea.'

Oh, I know a diver. Someone who can hold her breath for a long time, who isn't afraid of small spaces. But an instinct keeps my mouth shut. The sealskin around the woman's shoulders shimmers unnaturally, in a way I've never seen a pelt do before. I know for certain who this woman is. She cannot be anyone else. This is Lady Erskine, and why she needs a diver I cannot imagine.

'No,' I say, my tongue thick. 'I don't know anyone.'

'Ah,' she says and lifts her chin. 'A shame.'

Rain flurries into the shop as she opens the door. A crack of rare thunder follows just before the door chimes, and Fie and I are left staring at the space where Lady Erskine once stood.

For a moment, it seems as if her shadow lingers on the shop floor even though she has already left – but I look away and, when my gaze returns, it is as if she was never here at all.

8

I can't tell if the rain has stopped, or if the sound of it against the roof is hidden by the snap and crackle of the onions in the pot. When I add the potatoes, the whole pot erupts even more fiercely, and I step back, fearing for my forearms. The house is filled with the scent of fat frying, and I imagine what it will be like for my parents when they step inside from a day out on the boat, that transition from brisk, sea air to the warm, hearty scents of home. The table is already set, and I get busy digging out the oatcakes from the cupboard. We're due a trip into town for groceries – hence the stovies and oatcakes – so I'll go tomorrow.

I try not to think about how much I'm wasted on all this. Of course, having dinner ready, doing the shopping, all that is important work and isn't to be discounted by any means, but it's just not me. I can throw a spear. Aim true with a knife. Sail a boat and swim for ages. I'm built like a hunter, and instead I'm at home, scraping together a meal. It doesn't feel right.

Aimlessly, I stir the stovies again and my gaze falls on the windowsill behind the sink. Three bones are lined up there.

Looking closely at them, I realise they've been switched out from the ones that sat there yesterday, and if that's not a sign my father is worried, then I don't know what is. Bones on the windowsill in our kitchen aren't surprising to me. Dad's been lining up bones there since before I was born. Always seal bones, and each one has a different purpose or meaning. I remember my grandmother telling stories about seal bones. Vividly, I imagine a tooth in her wrinkled palm. She believed, just as my father still does, that there is a bone for every problem. I've never been interested enough in the bones to remember what each one might be for, but I can guess that the three rib bones on the windowsill are meant to bring my family success on their hunt today. After a closer look, I notice there are marks carved into each one, likely my mother's doing.

The rising scent of cooking potatoes sends me back to the stove. The potatoes are sticking nicely to the pan, crisping up golden around the edges. I give them a stir, think about adding mince, but we've not got any. Instead, I get out some cold slices of herring. No one in this house ever said no to herring. I'm just setting the herring on the table when the door bursts open.

My greeting dies in my throat. It's not Dad or Mum who barge through the door but Archie, our neighbour from a few houses down who goes out on his boat each day to catch fish, bringing with him a rush of rain-scent and sea air. Archie's expression is a strange one. Not fear, but something just as elemental darkens his features. Before I can puzzle it out, Archie turns and soon he and Mum are shouldering their way into the cottage, with Dad between them, one arm across Mum's shoulders, the other dangling at his side.

I don't notice the blood until they are halfway across the kitchen.

A long trail of it smears across the floor.

Archie and my parents move swiftly, and I'm reeling at the shock of their unexpected force. My mind can't quite keep up – I'm caught in the scene that should have been. Of Dad, rowdy and good-natured from a successful hunt, smelling of blood and brine, greeting me with a grin and exclamation – *Smells braw in here, Kier* – and throwing himself at the table.

Not this – Mum's face set in shock. The blood on her hands. Archie clearing a path across the room like his life depends on it. And Dad – not my strong, tall father striding over to the stove to peer into the pot and give the potatoes an approving stir – but a broken man caught between Archie and my mother, something wrong, something wrong.

Everything as it should have been plays out across my vision, blurring reality.

An accident. There was an accident on the boat.

Archie knocks into the table on the way through the kitchen, sending a plate crashing to the floor. They're taking Dad to my parents' bedroom.

What happened? I say, but I realise I haven't actually opened my mouth.

I only move again when the stovies start to burn.

After I've got the stove off, I turn around, half-expecting to have imagined everything. The kitchen is a mess: so much blood, pieces of shattered plate strewn across the floor, the table askew. I didn't get a good look at my father's injuries, but he was walking, wasn't he? Or nearly so? He was conscious, at least, I'm sure of it.

The flute lies in a pool of blood. Unable to move, I stare at it long enough for the blood to seep into the floorboards. By the time I've unthawed enough to approach it, the blood is but a dark smear. My fingertips are tipped in red after I pluck the flute from the floor. I haven't held my father's flute in ages, and it's lighter than I remember, hardly there at all. I've left red fingerprints all along the length of it.

What happened?

A commotion from the hall makes me look up. Archie is hurrying into the kitchen, moving fast and with his gaze trained specifically away from me, so that I know I need to catch him like a fish before he leaves. He goes around the far side of the table, away from me, but Archie's not a young man anymore, and I'm far faster than he. I catch him by the arm. His muscles tense, but my grip tightens, and he doesn't pull away. 'Archie. What happened on the boat?'

'The doctor's on the way,' Archie says, only half-looking at me. The scent of him is strong; of fish, sea-soaked mud. 'His arm's in bad shape, but he'll be fine. The bleeding's mostly stopped.' He tries to pull away, but I don't let go.

'What *happened*?'

Archie's gaze flicks towards the door, towards the sea. 'I've got to get to my boat.'

'Yeah, I know that, Archie,' I say, my voice taut. 'But my father's blood is all over this floor, and seals don't usually bite. So what happened on that boat?'

Archie's throat works. He's been fishing on this shore for years, going out alone on his small boat for longer than I've been alive, and I would never think of him as a coward. But that look in his eyes is fear.

'What did you see?' I say, my voice lower.

'There was a mist,' Archie says. 'I don't mean the haar.' His gaze flicks again towards the door. 'It settled over the boat from ... from below. From the sea. I came close to the Sealgair boat on accident, could hardly see.' His brow furrows, remembering. 'I didn't see what happened, but right before—' He clears his throat, and when it's obvious I'm not letting him go anywhere until he continues, he does so. 'I saw a streak of dark in the sea. It was no seal, Kier, though it was as big as a bull. It was' – I feel the tremor in him, shivering my own bones – 'a thing of night, something that took the darkness with it, black wrapped around it like it was wearing midnight.'

Now, Archie's a fisherman. He's no poet. He can't possibly mean that he thinks he saw a creature in the sea wearing darkness like a cloak, but that's what I'm hearing. That's what he's saying, isn't it? Mist and a streak of black.

My confusion loosens my grip on Archie's arm, and he takes the chance to pull away from me.

'The doctor'll be here soon,' Archie repeats. 'I've got to get to my boat.'

'Archie—' I start, but I've lost him now. Already he's at the door, turning away from me so I can't see the fear in his eyes.

Archie leaves the door hanging open on its hinges. When I close the door behind him, there's the sea, beautiful and shining, as if it is laughing.

9

THE COTTAGE IS THICK WITH SILENCE. The doctor's been and gone, and I did what I do best these days – stay out of the way. The stovies were burnt black on their underside, so I scraped them into the bin. I put the herring away. I can't imagine anyone is in the mood for supper. The doctor gave me a curt report after she left. Dad's arm has been torn open where it meets the shoulder, requiring stitches. She mentioned something about a knife, which I don't understand. What knife? What does a knife have to do with the streak of midnight Archie saw cutting towards my family's boat?

I let the silence settle for a moment longer while I hesitate at my parents' bedroom door. I can hear nothing from within, and I think: this is what death sounds like. But I am being dramatic, aren't I? I knock on the door and, after I hear a muffled answer from Mum, I open it.

She's dragged the old armchair to the bedside. She sits in it, elbows on her knees, fixedly carving a piece of driftwood. The mess of pale curls at her feet dance as a draught sweeps in through the door I just opened. She doesn't look up at me or say a word; her blade drives into the wood in her fingers.

Dad's on the bed. His face looks sunken, drawn, and the blanket is pulled up to his chest so that his shoulder wound is not visible. His eyes are closed and, from the way his chest moves, he looks to be deeply asleep. I swallow the shock that shoots up my throat at the sight of him. To me, he's always been a force larger than life, always moving, always ready for a hunt, a big man full of life. The man in the bed looks like my father, but my brain can't quite believe it's really him lying here. He looks as if he's shrunken to half his size.

I've taken the Sealgair flute with me, and I place it now on the bedside table. The white shaft is stained red despite my attempts to clear the blood away.

Before I can say anything, Mum speaks, raising her head for the first time since I entered the room.

'Your knife was in his shoulder,' she says roughly.

My knife? I'd lost my knife when I was fifteen, the day I stopped hunting, the day I became afraid to kill. It is in the sea or else washed up on a distant shore. I haven't held the perfect weight of it for nearly a decade, but I remember it keenly. The beautiful, light-but-fierce knife my mother presented to me on my eighth birthday. With my initials carved into the polished wood. I loved that knife, and I always wished I'd find it again, that the sea would give it back. But not like this. What did she mean, my knife was in his shoulder?

'What?' I say.

Then, there it is between her fingers. The blade is a bright as it was the day I lost it; the wooden handle as smooth as if polished yesterday. 'Bury it,' Mum says after a moment, looking down again. 'Under the hawthorn in the garden.'

'I don't understand . . .' I say, even as I reach for it. My fingers cannot help themselves. They want it. I *want* it. It's a reminder of who I was, who I'm meant to be.

The knife is exactly as I remember it. When I take it from her, it sits so easily in my palm that it seems like I was never parted from it. There is no blood on the blade; she must have cleaned it.

My mother looks up. Everyone says we have the same eyes. Everything else, I've inherited from my father. Looking at her, I feel like I am staring at the person I am supposed to be. Who I could have been if my path had twisted differently. Sometimes, I notice that my mannerisms match hers. More so as I get older. She was my age once, dreaming of making more of her life than spilling fish guts all day. She was younger than I am now when she and Dad met. Twenty-two years old and she spent all those years right here on this shore. She says she had her bags packed and was ready to leave this place for good, until 'that seal killer' came hurtling into her life and suddenly this place didn't feel so small anymore. She always says that: he made my small world feel big.

We're both staring at the knife in my hand.

'How?' I ask.

She sighs. 'The sea doesn't follow reason.'

'But the mist. Archie said it came from the sea, and there was a black shape—'

She holds up a hand, silencing me. 'I don't want to talk of it.' Then I see it in her eyes, the same fear that sparked in Archie's. A cold fear of my own curls at the nape of my neck. I have never in my life seen my mother afraid. 'I don't know how it came back, but it doesn't matter. Bury it.' She glances at my father. 'The wound will heal by winter, if we're lucky. That's all, Kier. We just have to wait.' I wonder what she is lying about, which part of what she just said is an untruth. Because I know her voice, just like I knew my father's when I asked him about the sea. There is something she is not saying.

'I'll get cockles for supper,' she says. I don't mention that we have a bucket-full already. That isn't the point. She rises, setting her knife and half-carved wood on the table beside the flute.

'I should have been with you,' I say. My throat is raw, and I have to swallow my tears.

Mum shakes her head once, but it is not in disagreement.

'What can I do?' My voice sounds like a little girl's, and I am reminded of all the arguments I've had with my mother over the years. I want both to break down and cry and to scream in rage.

'I don't know, Kier.' She walks past me so that our arms brush, and I know this is the most she can give right now. As close as she can be. She shuts the door behind her.

I stand stewing for a long moment, hate making my guts burn. A kind of teenage hate, sparked by my mother, but I'm old enough to know it isn't her I'm angry at. I'm angry at myself. I notice the shutters are closed. Dad likes to keep them open because, from here, you can see a strip of the sea. 'I like to keep an eye on her,' he always says.

The shutters squeal as I push them open. I gulp in the sea air and let my eyes close for a moment. I want to curl up in my bed like a wee girl, press my sealskin against my cheek. I think about my family, about how we'll manage without my father to hunt. He will miss the entirety of the summer season. He may miss the rest of the year. Without him, none of us is fine. I know, because I sell the pelts at market and I do the shopping. I know just how fine we're cutting it, even now. My mother is a skilled hunter, but she is only one. I'm thinking this when my father speaks, shattering my thoughts.

'I see it.'

His voice is raw, surprising. I turn to see him struggle up in bed, grimacing in pain. He's suddenly, violently animated, shocking me into a run, and I press my hands against his shoulders to push him gently back down, but he is all force, resisting.

His eyes. They're not the ones I'm used to. A fierce spark ignites within them, reminding me of a spooked horse, startled whites with blood crimson in the corners. He is looking beyond me, through me. To the open window. Towards the sea, sparkling, ambivalent, on the horizon.

'It's coming,' he says.

I dart to the window. An instinct, a hunch, or perhaps just the continued, unspoken fear that has been growing within me for days, tells me to close the shutters. Shut out the sea.

And it works. As soon as the shutters bang shut, dimming the room, blocking the view to the sea, my father falls back, chest heaving. His shoulder is bandaged, and blood blooms through. I help him back against the pillows, and he is asleep again in a moment.

As if nothing happened. As if nothing at all is wrong.

10

Diving requires an intimate knowledge of the shore. It's not enough to see the sea only at high tide. You have to be there as it draws back, bares her naked rocks. You have to know where the currents flow. Which way the stream moves against the shore. You must know when the jellyfish bloom and where the terns make their nests. I know this shore, its timings and its landscape and the creatures that live here. I know everything about this shore, and I know which dives are dangerous and best left to a clear day. I know that the cliff edge I stand on now is one I've only ever leapt from once. The position of the rocks below makes it dangerous, especially when the tide is as high as it is, as the rocks are impossible to see beneath the surface. Making the jump safely is worth it, though, because of how deep the water is here in this cove. I dived here once and nearly broke my shoulder, and that was in daylight. Now, the moon is bright, but even a bright moon isn't enough to reveal every detail of the shore. It's dangerous, stupid, but this time I don't care.

A seagull shrieks just as I jump. The sound is whisked away from me as I cut through the air. I hit the water and slide effortlessly below the surface. I love this moment, the transition from air to water, sharp sounds to muted. I propel myself through the water, deeper and deeper, letting all the emotions that have built up in the last two days break free.

It is not only that my father has been wounded on a hunt. It is not only that my knife has returned like a ghost to haunt us. It is not even that I cannot see a way for my family to make ends meet before winter, with my father unable to hunt until at least the spring.

It is the sea.

The fishermen are right to be afraid, and my instincts haven't been howling at me for no reason. Something attacked my father on our boat, something that frightened even my mother.

Something lurks in the deep, and I am certain it is no coincidence that the seal herds have changed their courses, and the local fisherman have been returning home with increasingly empty nets.

What makes it all worse is that there is nothing I can do.

I dive deeper, imagining myself like a stone sinking.

Within a day of my father's accident, my mother was already out on the boat, hunting seals further down the coast. She knows her grief through killing, through the rush it gives her to end a life, to cut her grief into the guts of a fish. A herring girl still. I can't kill like she can. I feel my grief and worry building up inside me, churning with nowhere to go. I feel it turning over on itself, becoming a furious weel.

My lungs ache. I shouldn't go deeper, but I do. I take broad strokes, enjoying the way the water moves around me, how the creatures and kelp I pass shift in my wake. The moonlight grows dimmer. My vision becomes blurry, but the darkness below seems almost reachable. Just one more second, just one more stroke, and I might reach it.

A dark shape hurtles towards me. I reel back, instinctively hold up my hands. Dratsie. She darts circles around my head. It's enough to make my instincts kick in, my body finally winning out over my mind. I need breath.

I twist up and kick, propelling myself towards the surface. It takes a painfully long time, and I almost don't make it. I open my mouth just in time, swallowing only a little water as I break the surface. My legs are screaming, but I tread water as I gasp for breath. I can't stop moving, otherwise I fear I might sink, might be drawn down to that darkness again. The dark blanket of the sea stretches out before me. What is the water hiding? I turn and begin to swim for shore.

I look towards our cottage, my heart climbing into my mouth at the thought of going back there. Maybe one more dive before I go. Maybe one more will be enough.

I am about to turn when I see a figure at the water's edge. Too dark to know who it is, but surely a person. My throat tightens. They are unmoving, seemingly staring straight out to sea. Their stillness is unnerving, unnatural.

Staying in the shallows, I move towards them slowly. They should see me now, standing, taking deliberate steps through the water, but they do not move or turn their head.

Clouds shift, darkness deepens. When eventually the clouds move away, the darkness melts, and I am close enough to see who stands there.

She does not move, only watches, waits, standing on the shore. Her long, dark hair lifts in the wind. She wears a dark dress and the beautiful, sealskin cloak around her shoulders. The woman from the tailor's shop. It feels like an age since Fie and I saw her, dripping with rain in the blue of a morning storm.

She watches as I pull myself onto the rocks at her feet. 'You were under for a very long time, Miss Sealgair,' she says in a measured way.

My impulse is to snap at her, to accuse her of spying, but I don't have the energy for it.

'I'm used to it,' I say. I hesitate, but the words slide from my lips, lined in anger: 'How do you know me?'

I notice her feet are bare beneath the gathered hem of her dress. The dress is simple, with no buttons and hardly any darting. It ought to be shapeless and plain, but on Lady Erskine it is striking.

We are the same height, and I realise it unnerves me to be stared at so directly, unflinchingly.

'I know the Sealgairs. They've hunted here for many years.' She pauses, does not blink. 'Your father is unwell.'

'He'll heal.'

She almost seems to smile. 'Eventually.'

My hackles raise. I am certain she is Lady Erskine, though she hasn't introduced herself. There is simply no other explanation. A woman in such a dress, a cloak like that, barefoot on the rocky shore. She stands here as if she owns the place. As if everything around her is hers. Even the sea. Erskine Manor is a black shape on the horizon, watching.

From the corner of my eye, I see movement among the rocks. Dratsie has followed me to shore. Afraid of most people, she won't come near until I am alone.

'As you know, I am looking for a diver,' Lady Erskine says.

I know Fie would be appalled that I'm about to march indignantly away from the woman who no one in the town has ever seen, who is the source of so many stories, even my own. There is so much I could learn in just a short conversation. Fie and I would have something to talk about for years to come, as we dissected every detail. But I am not curious or intrigued. I am cold and soaking wet, afraid of returning home to the silent cottage.

'For what? Scallops? I'm no good for that.' I stride past her.

'You should listen. I pay well.'

That makes me stop. I do not look behind me when I bark out, my throat burning, 'How much?'

I turn, and she is still looking out across the sea. A silver chain glints around her neck. I catch sight of it there in the pale triangle where her hair parts to lie across her shoulders. I feel pressure at my feet and look down to see Dratsie. I bend and let the otter brush her sharp whiskers against my knuckles. I imagine drawing something like energy from Dratsie – the soul of the sea, you might say. I've always done this, carried this strange superstition that Dratsie can channel the sea's energy. She's the sea's messenger, after all, and my grandmother always talked of the sea having a soul. Nothing like a human soul, of course, not a sentience. But present as much as the haar is – surely there but impossible to bottle, impossible to examine in any detail. A feeling, really, but something more than that. Often the sea does seem to have a mind of its own.

Lady Erskine flicks her fingers, beckoning me. Dratsie shoots away as I move in her direction. She steps forward so her feet are submerged, the hem of her dress lifting and falling as the tide breathes. I watch as she bends and plucks something from the water. A silver fish, a whitebait, wriggles in her fingers. She looks at me as she squeezes the fish until red guts spiral from between its broken scales. The little fish's eyes bulge.

Finally, she answers my question. 'More than what your family would make in an abundant summer season. You will not have to be away for long, no later than Midsummer.'

Her words strike up a ringing in my ears. A good summer season's profits would usually last us until late spring.

'Don't worry ...' She looks down at the fish, so my gaze returns to the dead creature in her fingers. Her fingers move, and the fish is lost in the palm of her hand. When she opens it, a flash of silver almost makes me jump. The fish is alive, wriggling fiercely. Lady Erskine bends once more and releases the fish into the sea. '... What I need you to find is already dead.' She looks at me again, her expression not necessarily friendly, but almost so. 'What is your answer, Kier Sealgair?'

I stare at her dumfounded.

'If you come tomorrow morning to the southern gatehouse, someone will be there. Bring your things. You will need to stay at the manor house while you dive for me.'

I want to say something else, to ask her questions, anything, but my mind is numb, my lips frozen shut. As I watch her walk away, I feel something like hope bubbling up in my chest.

Dratsie scampers up to me with a wee fish in her jaws.

11

I OPEN MY EYES AND ROLL over to feel the softness of my sealskin against my cheek. I was dreaming again of dark water and mist. A new nightmare, one that's been making a more regular appearance these last few nights. I'm cold with sweat. This time, Erskine Manor was there, its windows like eyes watching me.

For a moment, I cannot parse reality from dream, and I wonder if Lady Erskine and I had truly met. If she had really offered me a job as a diver. A diver for what? I think of the silver fish, her cloak, her words, but I cannot piece the encounter together completely, as if there are gaps in my memory. Or, simply, it was so strange that I feel as if I must be missing something.

I close my eyes and take a deep breath, in hope I've still got enough sleep to hold onto, enough scraps of it to drift off again. A sound makes me tense, and that scrap of sleep is gone, replaced with a rigid awareness. The sound is like an animal in the garden, scratching in the dirt. Nothing much unusual in that, but I'm still tense from the nightmare and before I can try to resist, I'm up out of bed, fumbling for my slippers, tugging on a jacket. I go to the backdoor and notice as I near it that it's open just a crack. The moon is shrouded in cloud, hardly enough light to see by, but there is the scraggly mass of the hawthorn and a dark shape beneath it.

The scratching continues. The shape moves in time with the sound. A fox, I imagine, or a dog.

'Hey,' I shout. I move nearer, intending to scare the creature off, but I'm the one who is frightened. When my father looks up, the moonlight catches the whites of his eyes. His face is cut up by shadows, harsh and unfamiliar. He does not seem to see me and returns to scrabbling in the earth.

He digs with his one good hand, scooping up clods of dirt and tossing them in haphazard piles around his knees. I smell it. Overturned earth.

'Dad?' I say quietly.

He continues digging, so I settle down next to him. I put my hands over his to get him to stop. 'Kier,' he says. 'You need this.' Ever since the accident, I've found it harder and harder to recognise my father. He is changed, either by the pain or the medication or, perhaps, from what he saw out on the boat. His usual joy is gone, replaced by an urgency that has nowhere to go.

'I don't.' I try to stop him again, but he shifts his bulk, nearly knocking me over. 'I don't want it. Leave it.'

He stops digging and reaches into the hole he's made. My knife is in his fist. He holds it up and though it's grimy with dirt, the sharp point of it shines.

'Dad,' I say, wrapping my fingers around his fist. He looks at me then, and I'm so relieved when he doesn't look right through me but seems to hold my gaze, properly.

'Don't lose it again,' he says.

I shake my head. 'We have to put it back,' I say, but when I try to force his hand downward, my father resists, and he is stronger than I am. 'I don't want it.'

'Doesn't matter, Kier. You need it.'

A door creaks. I look towards the house, where Mum is standing at the backdoor. She's like a rabbit caught in a sudden light. Frozen and staring with surprise at me and Dad.

Dad presses the knife into my other hand and pulls away from me, and the sudden weightlessness makes me sit back. I stare at the empty hole in the ground, at the disrupted dirt all around. Mum is helping Dad up, and I should put the knife back, cover it up as if none of this happened, but I cannot. I can't let go. My father's words whisper through my mind. *You need it.* It is the last thing I need, but I cannot put it back. He will only come back to dig it up again.

'What happened?' my mother asks from the doorway, after she's led Dad into the house. Her expression is stormy, and I feel blame thick in her gaze.

'He wanted me to have this,' I say. I feel myself shrinking, as if she is the taller of the two of us, the more substantial. 'He dug it up.'

'You should put it to use,' my mother says before she turns away.

I watch the back of her and feel the anger rising up. 'What do you want me to *do*?' I bark after her.

She turns, and I see that her anger matches mine. 'Try, Kier,' she says. 'I want to see you *try*. What more reason do you need than this?' She gestures towards the hawthorn behind me, the scar in the earth.

'I do,' I say, hating how quiet my voice has become.

'Try harder. You're a Sealgair.' Her gaze flickers to the knife in my fingers, the knife she made for me. 'Try to fix yourself.'

Her last words are spoken low, but they are the most powerful. I feel their resonance long after my mother has turned away.

12

It's pissing rain by the time I'm sure that my parents are asleep. I eat a few cockles before I go, and the briny taste coats my tongue. I walk along the shore for a while, hoping to spot Dratsie so I can say a proper goodbye, but she must not yet be awake.

I've never bothered with an umbrella; there's always a wind on the coast, and if it's raining you can be certain it's not a gentle breeze that's blowing. Instead, I've got my rivlins and my rain mac made of waxed sealskin. Rain rolls down the glossy surface and away, leaving me dry. The rain today is mostly vertical, which is as much as you can ask for.

The sun isn't up yet when I reach town. The streets are silent, and I like the way my footsteps sound louder in the emptiness. I have with me a rucksack filled with some clothes, my sealskin, a few bits and pieces, and my knife. The rucksack isn't heavy, but I feel strange wearing it.

When I left home, I wrote a note for my family, feeling foolish and cowardly, as if I were a little girl running away. But I couldn't face either of them again, not after what

Mum finally said aloud, what she surely has been thinking all these years.

The tailor shop is dark, and the window is speckled with rain. I have a key that Fie gave me ages ago that I never thought I'd use. The shop smells of starch and wool, and the scents seem stronger in the darkness. A clock ticks. A floorboard above creaks. Fie and his father live in the flat above the shop. They'll be sleeping, like most normal folk, but I didn't want to leave without speaking to Fie first. I don't usually make big decisions without him.

I'm just pulling aside the back curtain, when a figure startles me.

'Kier?' Fie turns on a light, and all the dark shapes in the room become familiar again. The sewing machine. The reams of fabric. Clothes hanging on a rack. And Fie in his pyjamas, which he must have made himself given their vibrant green pattern and the polished buttons.

'What's going on? Are you okay?' He notices the rucksack.

'I'm fine,' I say.

'Okay.' He pauses. 'I came round yesterday but you weren't there.'

'I was diving,' I say flatly.

Fie plays with his cuff. 'How's your dad?'

'He's not good,' I say. 'He can't hunt.' I leave it at that. Fie and I haven't properly spoken since the accident, though I know he's tried. I just don't want to talk about it, not even to my best friend.

Fie looks thoughtful, his mouth quirking up on the side. 'Do you want ... I mean, I could speak with Liv and see if they're needing help at the pub.'

'And what would I do in a pub, Fie?'

Fie spreads his fingers helplessly. 'Anything, Kier. You could do anything. I'm sure they'd be happy to—'

'I don't want to do just *anything*. And I especially don't want anyone giving me a job just because they feel sorry for my family. I couldn't make enough in a pub to cover what my father would make in a year, so what's the point?' My voice has risen and has an angry edge to it. Fie will know what I'm not saying aloud. That I'd be too embarrassed to work in a pub, that it would make my family think even less of me. I am a Sealgair. There's a pride that runs in our blood. We've been hunting seals for generations, living on the edge of the shore where the living isn't easy. We have a reputation that I've already done enough to tarnish.

'All right, I get it,' he says. His words drop away to silence.

'Anyway,' I say, less loudly now, 'I've got something else lined up.' I hike up the rucksack on my back to emphasise my point.

'What?'

'Lady Erskine offered me a job.'

'You spoke with Lady Erskine?'

'She came to the shore.' I shrug. 'She needs a diver, and it's the one thing I'm good at.'

Fie's frowning, looking at me like I've lost my head.

'What?' I ask.

'How often does she need you there? That's a long walk every day.'

'I won't have to walk there. I'll be staying in the house.'

'In Erskine Manor?'

'Yes, Erskine Manor.' My anger's back, directed at Fie, though it ought to be directed at myself.

Fie's silence speaks for itself, but eventually he says, 'You can't do that.'

I stare at him, not sure what to say, sensible enough to know anything I could say would be coloured too much by my anger. So I keep my mouth shut.

'Your family needs you. Right now, especially. What good will you do for them in Erskine Manor?'

'Good enough to keep my father heading back on the boat before he's ready. Good enough that they won't have to worry about him being unable to hunt and earn money. That's more than what I can do staying here, getting underfoot, being useless, more than useless. I may as well go. I *want* to go. It's only until Midsummer.'

Fie looks away, studying the rack of clothes. 'You're wrong about that, Kier. Your place is on the shore.'

'I'm not leaving the shore,' I say.

'You know what I mean.'

'I don't, actually,' I say. My anger is white-hot now, and my voice is flat and low. How does Fie not understand? Why doesn't anyone want to admit what no one will say aloud? I'm useless to my family. I'm useless to this town. Erskine Manor is a fresh start, at least. A chance to prove myself. I realise that I *do* want to go. I want this change.

'Kier, don't go,' Fie says. He rubs the back of his neck and looks at me in a way that reminds me of when we were kids. I was there for Fie when things were rough for him, and I know he's here for me now, when my life is falling apart – but I don't want him to be here. *I* don't want to be here.

'I have to,' I say.

'Hi, Kier,' a voice says and, from behind Fie, I see Liv emerging from the stairwell. She's wearing a lovely blue nightgown, which I suspect she hasn't owned for very long. Her hair is braided and pulled up and away from her face. It's a bit messy from sleep, but she otherwise looks bright-eyed and happy.

Almost as if it's second nature already, Fie reaches behind to wind his arm gently around her waist. Fie's mouth twitches as he supresses a smile. I don't know why he has to be this way, dampening his joy just because I've not got any. It annoys me, and I feel that kind of sticky feeling in my heart that makes me want to run straight into the ocean.

'Sorry,' I say quickly. 'I was just leaving.'

'Kier,' she says, in a way that makes me fear she's going to spew some platitudes about my father. She unwinds herself from Fie and comes towards me. 'Come to the Nest sometime. I owe you a pint.'

'For what?' I ask.

She smiles and shrugs, but I know what she means. For Fie. I notice that she is wearing a pendant around her neck. A stone with a hole in the centre and a chain wound through it. A hag's stone. I've never seen her wear it before. I realise I know very little about Liv, and that I've probably only got to know one version of her, the Corbie's Nest version.

'All right,' I say, feeling like a liar because if all goes right, I will not be going to the Corbie's Nest for a long time.

'Good.' She touches my arm, a soft pressure. The kindness of it almost makes me break down, almost makes me spill out all the worries and fears I've been harbouring for days. I imagine what an ugly, ungainly mess that would be.

'I won't be gone long, okay?' I say to Fie, but he keeps his lips pressed together.

When I leave, the door chimes, and its high, tinkling sound makes me want to rip it from the wall. I pull up my hood and head off into the rain.

13

THE RAIN IS STILL COMING down in torrents, but by the time I reach the outskirts of town and head into the countryside, it begins to fade into a light mist. I push my hood down and enjoy the feel of the misty rain on my cheeks. Questions dart through my mind like minnows, but I catch none of them, letting each one wriggle away unformed.

The landscape of the Erskine estate is strange compared to its surroundings. A winding coastal path leads from our cottage into town, where there's not much except for a high street and a town hall, and a few pretty houses the next street over with views towards the sea. There's the harbour, where boats lay stuck in the mud at low tide, and the fish market after that. Then, the landscape changes, draws upward and becomes steep cliffs covered in flattened, coarse grass. The coastline is treacherous for boats, filled with rocky coves and small bays where I love to dive. On one of these cliffs perches Erskine Manor, but the house is unreachable from the shore. You have to go through town, keep walking along the shore, but inland a little, until the town drops away and you're surrounded by countryside. Everywhere is fields with sheep and windblown grasses, except when you approach the Erskine estate. That's when the trees rise up – dark, thick, pungent pines. They form shadows as thick as velvet.

I reach the gatehouse expecting to see one of the Erskine servants waiting for me. No one is here. The gatehouse is as shadowed as usual. For a while, all I can hear are the sounds of the forest behind me. Birds, raindrops scattering down in flurries as the trees shift in the wind, small creatures scuttling through the undergrowth.

Crossing my arms, I lean against the gate with my back to the gatehouse, trying to muster up some confidence. My stomach twists with worry. Everything ahead of me, down the path towards town, is something I don't want to think too long on. Mum, Dad. Fie. Our fight. I hate when we fight. Doesn't happen often, but when it does, I feel its resonance for days.

I turn around suddenly, wanting to put all that behind me.

I'm almost scared right out of my skin.

I'm no longer alone.

A woman stands on the other side of the iron gates.

The maid is quiet as a mouse, and I wouldn't notice her if I wasn't so alert already. I'm as tense as if I were on a hunt, but with none of a hunt's thrill, none of the invigorating chill of a sea breeze. I swallow the strangled sound of shock I nearly make at the sight of her. I know that face. Those huge, dark eyes. The maid who visited our cottage years ago. She looks hardly a day older than when I saw her last, gobbling up a toad in my family's back garden.

She says nothing as she takes a key ring from her belt and begins sorting through the keys. When she finds the one she's looking for and slides it into the lock, I'm astounded that the gate opens for her. It was rusted shut, as long as I've ever known.

I step through. Gate's closed. Then I'm following my silent guide as she leads me into the forest.

I'll admit I was expecting something different once I got across the wall. A manicured path, perhaps. A clearing cut through the woods and undergrowth. There is no such thing, only a slim deer path that winds deeper into the shadows.

My guide stomps through the undergrowth, apparently impervious to the sting of nettles. The plant is prolific along the path, and I stay well away. I like nettle soup well enough, but their stings are insufferable.

The trees are close around us, and undergrowth curls over the path, catching at my trousers. I feel claustrophobic here, so far from the sea, so enclosed. It's not the darkness that bothers me – after all, the depths of the sea are dark – but how stark and loud everything is. Birdsong, the chittering of magpies, my own loud movements.

The woods do not thin as we walk, and time feels warped, confused. I cannot tell how far we've gone or for how long we've been walking. The landscape hardly changes, though of course everything is unique, every moss-covered tree, the lichen dripping from branches, the way the light lattices down from the canopy.

As if my eyes are adjusting to the details of the forest, I start to notice things I hadn't at first. Stone peeking out from between leaves. A boulder that at second glance is covered in carvings. A grey hand reaches from between two trees, and I catch a glimpse of the weathered face of a statue. But my guide does not pause; in fact, she seems in a rush. I have long legs, a long stride, but even I am lagging behind.

The trees are no less dense when I hear a rustle that makes me look twice over my shoulder. The maid plods on, ever moving forward, but I stop, peer into the trees. I think, if I am not imagining it, that I hear breath. Not my own. And a quiet trickle of water. A creature bursts onto the path, and if I had blinked I would have missed it – a beautiful silver horse with a black mane and a man astride it. I grasp only pieces – the man's dark hair, the shine of his riding boots, what might have been a grin – before they are both gone.

I realise that, instinctively, I've taken out my knife and am gripping it as if I'm poised to throw it. As if I even could. I adjust my grip on it and relax my muscles. I do not put it away. Not yet. 'A horse,' I say, running to catch up with my guide. 'I saw a horse.' Of course, the maid says nothing in reply.

I'm surprised when suddenly the woods end, and my guide and I step out into rolling fields. The grass here is tall and unkempt, and just like that I can smell the sea. The landscape consists of small hillocks so I cannot see far ahead in any direction. The path begins to widen and soon connects with another, broader path that looks like it once was well managed. Certainly it looks more deliberate than the path we've been treading, as this one is made of stone. We join the new path, and I feel an unnerving, building dread at the nape of my neck. Somehow, I sense the imminent presence of Erskine Manor, and my instincts are right because there, without preamble, rises the dark shape of the house.

I recognise the silhouette of the house but not much else. The gables and roof I could see from the shore far below, but I could make out none of the details. Though it is still a bleak place with dark stone and black slate, the details reveal an extravagance I've never realised. The stonework is carven, seemingly on all surfaces, with curling shapes and designs. The massive double front doors are painted a glistening black, and the door pulls are bright silver. Though the stone path under our feet is broken and choked with weeds, the steps leading up to the house are clear of undergrowth and almost shine, as if recently cleaned. In fact, they appear wet. As we approach the house, I realise that the stone with which the house is built is darkened by water. It seems Erskine Manor is soaked to the bone. Close now, I can feel the dampness, the cool breath of water, the suggestion of rain.

I'm surprised my guide leads me straight up the front steps without a knock or greeting. She handles the huge doors easily, without much apparent effort, and holds one open for me to step through. A wall of cool air rushes over me. The house feels as cool as Midwinter, as if it has forgotten Midsummer is just around the corner. It is dark inside, but not in a suffocating way. The ceilings are huge, taller even than the town hall, which is the biggest building I've ever set foot in before now. The floor is polished wood, and the walls glisten as if made of mother-of-pearl, not a bright almost-white but the steel-grey of a mussel shell.

I am startled when the door snaps shut behind me. I look around at the great entryway, at the double staircase twirling upward. The air is thick, close as the feeling of a storm drawing near.

Somehow without me noticing, the maid has slipped through the door and past me. As she leads me into the house, I'm unable to take it all in and catch only snatches of the paintings in their silver frames and the banisters of the double staircase. My guide darts forward, leading me down an artery into one room and then another, which I take to be the drawing room. Or the reception room. I'm uncertain what wealthy folk call a room like this, with settees and armchairs scattered about. There is a low-burning fire in the grate, which does nothing to abate the chill.

She departs without a word, and I'm left alone with my pick of where to sit. Each settee and chair is upholstered with different fabric, sometimes studded with brass or embroidered with the same sort of curling designs as those carved into the stonework. I choose one that is a Beryl green with stiff-looking cushions. I move one cushion aside to sit more comfortably and try to settle in. My knife is tucked up my sleeve. I have the impulse to keep it near.

I realise, now that I'm no longer moving, how my body is tense with anticipation. I've been so preoccupied with observing this place, the oddly unused grounds, the unexpected beauty of the house, that I hadn't considered my own feelings. I reason that I can always refuse Lady Erskine's offer. I can always back out.

But I do not have much choice, do I?

My fingers are cold as I wind them together. I'm not nervous, not really, nor afraid, but I feel queasy with uncertainty. Whatever happens next feels desperately important.

A rhythmic ticking noise makes me hold my breath. I look towards the door, from where the sound comes. I cannot place it. A silver spoon rapped against a porcelain cup, perhaps? Then, I see the train of a bottle-green dress. Velvet with a lighter green gauze beneath. I see the polished length of a cane. A young woman stares at me from the slim opening of the door. One dark eye appraises me. I raise my hand in a greeting, and a flicker of a smile crosses her lips. I open my mouth to say something, but she is gone, replaced a moment later with the maid carrying a tray of tea things.

She clicks and clacks as she sets up the tea on the low table before me and is gone as quickly as she arrived. The tea smells something like the one we drink at home, but lighter, sweeter.

Maybe this sort of tea is more refined, but it doesn't go down as smoothly as the tea my father makes. I add in another lump of sugar, fumbling with the little silver tongs. The ends of the tongs are shaped like wee hands, and I feel giddy at the sight of them. Like I've never seen anything more ridiculous. I almost burst out laughing but manage to hold myself together and take a few respectable sips of tea.

Then I wait. I drink one cup of tea, pour myself another. I'm on my third by the time the tea goes cold. I sit there, drinking cold tea because I don't know what else to do, feeling more and more uncertain about what will happen next.

One moment, the room is silent save for my cup against the saucer. The next, Lady Erskine's skirts rasp across the floor, and she is breezing across the room towards me.

No greeting, no small talk. She goes to stand at one of the long windows and peers outside. I look over my shoulder at her. She wears a long gown like the young woman I spotted, but hers is blue-black and bares both her shoulders.

'I have asked you to dive for me, but I have not told you yet for what.'

She looks over her shoulder, one eye appraising me, much like the young woman's had. But there was a playfulness in the younger woman's eye, a twitch of a smile. Lady Erskine's gaze is stark in comparison. Not quite cold, but something else. Like she can see the inside of me, like my skin were made of glass.

'I want you to dive for bones.'

I rise partially in my seat. 'Bones? I don't—'

She cuts me off with a sigh. 'The sea is full of death. Sometimes, it gives that death up onto the shore, but sometimes it hoards it like a prize. There are bones in the sea, are there not, Miss Sealgair?'

'There must be,' I say, thinking of all the creatures that live and die in the water. I've seen bones often on the shore and sometimes while diving. But I've never thought to collect them. I can't imagine why you would.

'There are.' Lady Erskine turns away from the window. I feel the force of her coming towards me, and I'm pinned to my seat. 'I want you to find them for me. I want you to ask no questions. Can you do that?'

I open my mouth, intending to ask a question, but I'm not sure if her directive applies even to this very moment, and I find I cannot. 'I can dive for bones,' I say. I cannot kill, but a bone belongs to the already-dead.

'You will have to dive deep in places unfamiliar to you. I need many, and they will not be easy to find. The sea does not want to give them up, and she will try to stop you.'

Her words whirl through my mind, and though I cannot understand all of what she means, I sense the thread of foreboding running through them. All I have are questions.

'I will give you everything you need here, and you will be paid well.' An almost-smile. 'Until Midsummer. Do you understand?'

No, I cannot say that I do, but I understand what matters. Despite the strangeness of her offer, I do not think I can refuse. 'Yes,' I say.

'Good. But I am not offering this job without reassurance. You will dive once for me, now, and if you find what I am looking for then the job is yours.'

'Now?' I say.

She sweeps past me, towards the door. 'This way.'

14

LADY ERSKINE LEADS ME INTO the bowels of Erskine Manor. Though it is a grand house with high ceilings and rooms bigger than my family's cottage, the corridors are so plentiful and the rooms so many that I feel like we walk through a labyrinth. We see no one else. The only other faces we see are those of the oil portraits that hang on the walls. They are all dark-haired people, always well-dressed, often draped in furs. I wish I had a fur for how cold this place is, but I left my things, including my sealskin, in the drawing room. This place, and Lady Erskine herself, makes me feel forgetful.

Eventually, we arrive at the large front doors. The transition from inside to out is stark, like moving from winter to summer in a heartbeat. Lady Erskine doesn't bother to lift her skirts, which rasp against the stone pathway. I expect her to take me to the cliff, and I'm already imagining how we'll manage to make our way down the cliffside to the sea. But she does not lead me to the sea. Instead, she curves away from the coast towards the pine forest. I almost say something, but she has not looked at me since she turned away from me in the drawing room, and my mouth is too dry anyway.

Maybe there is a way to the shore that isn't apparent. Certainly, nothing here seems quite what it appears to be. When we reach the edge of the forest and, finally, she lifts her skirts to step right among the undergrowth, I choke out a half-formed 'The forest?'

'Yes,' she says, not bothering to hold back branches as we move deeper among the pines. I feel swallowed up.

The forest is much the same, repeated over and over, and goes on for ages. Without Lady Erskine, I would be utterly lost. There are no landmarks, no human-made paths, just tree after tree.

I stumble and look down to see a lichen-scored rock bursting from the earth. It looks, at first glance, like a skull with a gaping eye socket and elongated nostrils. The jaw is buried beneath the earth. I twist around to look at it, to confirm I'm not seeing things, but I only dare a quick glance, learning nothing. When I look forwards again, my heart leaps into my mouth; I have lost sight of Lady Erskine's dark skirts.

Gasping around my fear, I hurry forward. A shift in light. The branches move in the wind. I pass a large, mossy trunk, stumble right into a clutch of nettles. And then she is there, as if I'd never lost sight of her in the first place. I remain as close to her as I can and ignore any interesting rocks along the way.

We do not go much further. She stops, and I nearly tumble into her. We stand at the edge of a clearing. Can I hear the sea? I like to think so. It makes me feel less trapped.

Lady Erskine steps forward. She kneels at what I took at first for a swatch of black earth. But she dips her fingers into the darkness, making the whole thing ripple. A pool. Black. Blanketed in pine needles. Surrounded in places by the strange, dark rocks. Rocks like those that form the walls of Erskine Manor, I realise. They are carven, too.

Lady Erskine rises, scattering water droplets from her fingertips. The pool ripples again, and the needles shiver, drifting away to make odd shapes across the water's surface. I realise, looking down into the pool, that it is deep. Very deep, and this is where Lady Erskine expects me to dive.

'There are bones in the pool. Collect any you find and bring them to me. The pool is deep. I hope you have strong lungs, Miss Sealgair.'

She sweeps away, leaving me standing at the pool's edge with blood roaring in my ears. Or is it the distant sound of the sea? There is one moment where I consider turning back. It is fleeting, hardly there at all. It only takes the thought of my father, of the scar of earth where my knife was buried, for the thought to fizzle out.

'I do,' I say.

I strip off everything but my underthings, twist my hair back away from my face and secure it there. I take ten deep and slow breaths, feeling my stomach grow with each one, flexing my lungs, calming my heartrate. Then, with only a quick glance into the depths of the pool, I dive.

The water is icy cold, but I knew it would be. I swim beyond the panic, ignoring the little voice of betrayal that begs me to go back. The water is dark, but there is enough light yet to see the hazy shapes of my hands and arms as I swim. Below, something glows, and for a disorienting moment I think I am turned around, that I'm actually swimming towards the surface. Little specks of light twinkle like starlight. I swim towards them, and soon they surround me. Tiny creatures with clear skin and beating, glowing hearts. I've not seen anything like them before, but I have no time to admire their strange beauty. My leg grazes the side of the pool, and pain shoots across my skin. There may be blood in the water. The pool is narrowing. Searchingly, I stretch out my fingers and brush the wall. My fingers find the groove of a spiral. I am nowhere near the bottom, as far as I can tell, but there are ledges in the walls. Hewn from the rock. Nooks that were made for some purpose.

An instinct tells me to dive deeper, and so I do. The thrill of this risk, that maybe the pool goes on for ages and I am swimming too far, not giving myself enough time to surface if I run out of air, is intoxicating. It's all part of the thrill of the dive. Every dive is a risk, and in some ways this dive is no different. That my family depends on it only makes the thrill that much more intense.

The bottom of the pool, where I expect a bone is most likely to settle, does not come easily or quickly. I'm beginning to think my choice was a risk ill-taken, when something changes in the structure of the rock wall. The colour of the water changes, and I feel a cool current, tugging at my hair. Another choice – to continue on, hoping the bottom is near, or follow the current. I follow the current and am rewarded when it leads into an adjoining cave.

A pocket of air glimmers at the surface. I breach gratefully, sucking in long breaths. I am in a narrow antechamber. Above me, the rocky walls continue upward, and the roof of the cave melts away into shadow. It's impossible to guess how far it goes. Maybe there is an opening somewhere in the forest floor, buried beneath a thin layer of earth and undergrowth, that leads to this small chamber. Looking up at it makes me dizzy. The imagination is wont to run amok in a place like this, and not in a cheerful way.

My lungs replenished, I drop back down into the water. The only reason I can see anything at all is because of those strange, silver creatures. The sea is murky on a good day, but though this water is certainly salty here, it is clearer, clearer than it ought to be. Is this pool unique or are there others scattered throughout the estate, eventually leading to the sea?

I search among the nooks and crannies formed by the rock walls. I learn to ignore the glowing creatures and focus instead on the dark spaces between them, hoping to spot a gleam of dull white.

And I do. Inconspicuous, almost not white at all but dulled to a yellowish tint. A crunched-up twist of bone that looks at first glance like a sea-beaten rock. I am only certain it's a bone once I've got it in my fingers. It has a bone's lightness. I wrap my fingers around it protectively.

All at once the creatures' glow blinks out. Like a hundred little eyes shutting all at once. The cave is plunged into darkness.

Something brushes my leg, and I panic, slamming my head against rocks.

Bone in fist. Lips firmly pressed together. Lungs starting to protest. And a throbbing in my temple that radiates behind my eyes. Blindly, I reach forward, scrabbling for the way out, but I cannot find it. My fingers meet rock, rock and nothing else.

I cannot find the way out.

Somehow darker than the deep black of the water, a true-black ink splattered against a blue-black canvas, something moves. My head is hammering, and I'm light-headed in a way that frightens me. I need to get out. I don't have much time.

There's no point in fighting the panic. I'm in a dark underwater cave, deep beneath the water. The panic isn't going anywhere, so I don't fight it. I take it along with me, hoist it onto my back like my father might throw a dead seal over his shoulders. All right, I think, and I close my eyes.

This simple act puts me in tune with the water. The water that swirls around my feet is colder, flowing differently. I swim downwards and follow it. I half-expect to come up against rock, but I don't. The clicks and ticks of the water, the sounds of rocks shifting, creatures moving, sound differently now, too. I'm free. I'm out.

Once I am certain I am free of the small cave, my thinking mind folds itself up neatly. My body and my instincts take over. I don't remember the swim upwards. I don't perceive even the passing of time. All I can think about is that bone. The scrunched, measly bone clutched fiercely in my fist.

Then, the water changes. Light filters through. Surfacing is painful, a rush of noise and bright light. The chirping of the magpies is like children screaming. I haul myself over the stone lip of the pool and kneel beside it.

My hair has come undone and hangs in thick clumps around my cheeks, dripping water that makes my reflection shiver. My stiff fingers uncurl. A vertebrae, small enough to fit snugly in the centre of my palm. A vertebrae. A bone.

I recognise it immediately as belonging to a seal. I've seen many bones like this one, once the fatty flesh has rotted away.

The water in the pool shifts unnaturally, as if shivering, as if afraid. I look up, and there is Lady Erskine, looking down at me. No, looking at my hand, at the bone there, with rapturous interest.

'Ah,' she says. 'You've done it.' She plucks the bone from my palm, and I struggle to stand. Lady Erskine holds the bone with her thumb and forefinger and raises it up to look through its empty centre. As if it were a hag stone and peering through it could show her something from another world.

She holds the bone against her cheek, cradling it as if it were a dear thing. Her mouth moves, and a stream of almost inaudible whispers flurries out. I wonder why Lady Erskine reserves such a tender caress for something as mundane as a seal's bone. There must be hundreds of thousands of the very same in the sea. Why is this one important? Why should a bone be important at all?

'You've done it,' she says again. Her eyes glisten, almost as if she is about to cry. 'My bone diver.'

15

The maid shows me to a room. I try to remember my way, counting the turnings and the doors, paying particular attention to memorable things. A painting of the sea in the throes of a storm. A vase fashioned from a dark shell, the likes of which I've never seen on the shore. An ornate rug with deep gashes nearly severing it into pieces, as if a creature with great claws had sliced through the threads. So much is new and unusual that I find it hard to lock onto one thing, to remember where I am going, and by the time the servant stops, I feel certain I haven't memorised a thing.

The maid takes a heavy key from a chain at her hip and opens the door. I expect her to hand me the key, but she does not, and I'm soon alone with a hollow unease in my stomach. She is the same servant who brought me tea. The whole morning I have been here, I have seen only three people. The maid, the man on the horse, and Lady Erskine herself.

And, I remember, the young woman who peered at me from the crack in the drawing room door. Who could she be?

My things are already here, sitting in a heap on the floor beside the bed. I leave everything where it lies and explore the room.

It is large and smells not only of damp but also of dust. It's clear no one has occupied this place for a long time and that it had quickly, and ineffectively, been cleaned just before my arrival. The leather chair is stiff with age, but it looks hardly used. It's so different to the armchair my mother inherited from her parents; that one is made from the softest leather and feels as if you're sinking into wet sand as you sit in it. This one is rigid, the leather taut and shiny, but it has no life in it. Everything in the room is like this. Made of lovely material but lifeless. The curtains are damp and frayed at the bottoms where they touch the floor. It seems everything here is falling apart from the wet. I press my hand against the wall. The wallpaper is filled with air bubbles. I tug at a piece that has lifted away, and it comes off easily. The curl of paper in my palm is wet, too, and I wonder how no one here has died of pneumonia. Perhaps they have. Perhaps I will, too, before Midsummer is upon us.

I go to run a bath in the bathroom attached to the bedroom. Inside is a pale silver-clawed tub. With one hand already on one of the taps, I peer inside but come up short at the sight of the brown flesh of a mushroom growing from the drain. I lean in, the tub's side pressing into my gut, and peer at the mushroom. A cluster, in fact. Not the edible sort. I feel unmotivated to disturb them. No bath for me.

The prospect of spending until Midsummer here without even servants to talk to makes me almost sick with loneliness. I miss Fie already, and I saw him just this morning. Our last conversation lingers like a bitter taste in my mouth. I want to explain myself again, maybe tell him the whole truth this time, about the creature and the knife, but I won't get the chance.

I'll admit I'm feeling sorry for myself when I unpack my few things, wrapping them in my sealskin mac to keep them dry before finding a place for them in an empty drawer. The sealskin I take with me onto the bed. I wrap it around my shoulders and corrie myself under the covers like I'm a little girl. I wish Dratsie were here. Only once or twice she's dared to slip into my room through the open window, and both times she kept me up all night with her coarse fur and constant chittering, but I think of her now and wish I had her instead of sleep.

But I am alone, and sleep comes easily. I'm exhausted from the dive, and still cold from it, so that almost as soon as I pull the musty covers up to my nose, I drift off.

I wake at the taste of blood.

A warm, salty drop of it lingers at the corner of my mouth. Another flurry of droplets splatter against my cheek, one catching in my eyelashes, blurring my vision. I shoot up to sitting. I must have been asleep already for hours because the room is dark. In the crack between the curtains, I see a night sky, soft with clouds, a few stray dots of rain clinging to the window.

Another drop falls on the crown of my head. I look up to see a bloom of black on the ceiling. This time, I hold my hands out and soon enough a few drops fall into my open palms. Where I expect to see a streak of black-red, I see nothing. I get up from the bed and bring my hands, still cupped, to the window. Nothing but water, glistening in the life line that cuts across my palm. Not blood but salt water. Brine, as if from the sea.

The bloom in the ceiling seems to be growing, and my bed is wet where I touch it. Something in the room above me is leaking. I stare for a long moment in despair at the bed and the growing dampness. In a rush of inspiration, I strip the sheets and throw everything into a pile at the foot of the bed. I consider brandishing my knife, but realise how ridiculous that would be, carrying a knife through a fancy house like this, and instead I head out into the corridor with it tucked in my sleeve.

Alone in the vast, shadowed hall, I feel self-conscious, vulnerable. I wonder if I should take my knife out, after all. Holding a weapon has the positive effect of making one feel surer of oneself, or so I've always felt. At least as long as I'm not expected to truly use it.

It's even harder in the darkness to know my way. The only sources of light are the glistening of things – the edge of a frame, the shine of a mirror, the glint of something I cannot put a shape to. Eventually, I find the staircase, and I hope it will take me where I want to go.

As I climb the stairs, I listen for the sounds of water. Usually, the song of the waves, the trickling of a burn, the splash of a bird diving for a fish – all these would make me happy, would feel like home. But Erskine Manor has a way of twisting what is lovely. When I reach the top of the stairs, I do hear water, but it is not comforting. I imagine two hands dipped into water, swirling it around in a slow, methodical dance. A sinister sound. An unfriendly one. Certainly one that does not sound natural.

I do not know what to expect as I follow the sound down the hall. Every room along this way is closed and, as I pass each door, I listen for the water. I am getting closer.

The open door seems closed at first glance. What gives it away is the slight sheen of water on the floor, pooling out from the open crack. I'm usually not so hesitant but I find myself standing back, trying to peer through the crack in the door without getting close. I huff, imagining what my parents would make of me sneaking around Erskine Manor like this, as if I'm afraid of some shadows. The thought makes me bold, and I step into the doorway. I keep my stance wide to avoid the water, but I still feel the warmth of it against the edges of my feet.

Water sloshes as I step into the room, the door creaking wide as I push forward.

I am not prepared for what I see.

A white ceramic tub with clawed feet sits beneath an open window. The long, pale curtains flutter, lifting up around the tub in a kind of cloud. It reminds me of mist.

Languidly, water flows from the tub onto the ground. It rolls over the ceramic rim and cascades onto the floor to join the puddle spreading across the floorboards. At first, I think the tub is empty, that the bottom of a curtain has caught in the water and that explains the billows of white fabric floating within.

But then I see swirls of black hair, and the fabric drifts, and there is a face. A young woman, I think, staring straight up at the ceiling. I can tell by the dark line of her lashes that her eyes are open, and my instincts strike up, putting me even more on edge. Water splashes as I move across the room.

She is dead. She is drowned.

She turns her head and I freeze where I am. Warm water flows across my feet.

The eyes that stare at me are not human. I know those eyes. I've stared into them countless times, full of life before I released my spear, dulled with death while I drew it out. A seal's eyes. Black, round, unmarked by iris or whites.

Distantly, I hear laughing. And I run.

16

THE SUN SHINES BOLDLY, as if to tell me how foolish I am to be afraid. Outside the window, birds twitter, and I recognise the voices of magpies and starlings. I pull my knees to my chest and try to get the blood flowing through my limbs. I'm too tall to be able stretch out fully in the tub, as large as it is. Though I padded the bathtub with the sheets and covers and stacked two pillows beneath my head, I couldn't do much to make it feel like a bed.

Not that it would've mattered anyway. I've not slept, and I wouldn't have, not even if I were stretched out across the softest mattress. All night, I thought of the young woman with dark hair. Those dark, round eyes. The way the water fell to the floor in an arc of silver. Because I can't lock my bedroom door, I dragged a chair in front of it. It brought me only a little comfort.

Now it's morning, my fear has settled; and the sun is so bright and cheerful that I'm second-guessing myself. Did I really see a young woman look at me with seal eyes? I half-expect to find the real bed completely dry, to find that I had imagined last night's sighting. But my bed is wet, and the bloom on the ceiling is still there.

The fear is a hum in my chest that I try to ignore.

Maybe the loneliness is getting to me. I've always had my family and Fie and even Dratsie around me. I've never really been alone, even though for these last eight years I often felt it. Now I know what it's truly like to be alone, and I don't like it one bit.

I get changed and go out because when the sun shines, you have to make the most of it. It never really does stay for long around here.

There is no one else about, as far as I can see, as I navigate through the house. I stumble upon the drawing room where I took tea yesterday. The tray of tea things is still resting on a table, and I think maybe there really is only one servant here, after all – why else wouldn't it have been cleaned up already?

My stomach growls, and I realise I haven't eaten anything since yesterday morning. I make an educated guess that the kitchen is at the back of the house and wind my way through the halls until I find a back corridor that is shabbier than the others. A servant's passage, I assume. I'm so hungry that I'm almost contemplating eating my own hand, but then I hear the clinking of kitchenware and soon find myself standing in the kitchen doorway. The kitchen itself is old-fashioned, with a big brick oven and deep copper sinks. On a large table is spread a meagre breakfast of porridge and oatcakes, a teapot and one overturned cup. Mine, I assume, though I look to the maidservant who stands staring at me from her perch beside the sink.

'Morning,' I say in a strained voice that was meant to be cheerful.

She stares at me, and I hold my breath, waiting for her to blink, but she doesn't move an inch.

'Thank you for the breakfast,' I say, testing the waters and settling slowly into the chair beside the breakfast things. Not a peep from the servant, so I pretend to be enraptured by the food. A crusty layer has formed over the top of the porridge. I move it aside and make the most of the tepid oats beneath. The tea is about as bad as it was yesterday, but a few cubes of sugar give it a bit more life. There's no pot of jam or butter, which I find odd, but I'm reluctant to make a fuss. I swallow a mouthful of dry oatcake and turn to the servant. She hasn't moved at all and continues to pin me with a silent, unblinking gaze. I think of a toad's legs silhouetted in the moonlight and nearly choke down the rest of the oatcake.

'Does anyone else live here?' I ask her. 'Besides yourself and Lady Erskine?' I think of the young woman in the tub. Could she be Lady Erskine's daughter? The rumours in town often told of five beautiful daughters. Are there others, hiding in the dark innards of the manor house?

I don't mention the young woman to the maid because I can see it won't make any difference. She doesn't reply, and I turn back around to eat my breakfast alone. Her gaze on the back of my neck ignites an unnatural urgency, so that I end up eating far too fast. The whole lot sits like a stone in my gut, and I almost regret eating it, except at least I'm no longer tempted to chew my own hand off by the time I hurry back out into the hall.

It takes me longer than I'd like to find the front entrance, but eventually I make it to the double staircase, and a moment later I'm standing in the sunshine, feeling as if none of this is real.

The sun is gorgeous on my skin, and time seems stretched as I walk. It's easy to forget how lovely the sun is after a long spell of rain. I love the cosiness of rain and the scent of it, but the sun is something special, maybe because it's so fleeting. I have no purpose as I walk, only maybe to banish the loneliness that is creeping back in. The fear I felt last night is muted now, and I've mostly convinced myself it was all just a strange dream.

I thought, when Lady Erskine was leading me back from the forest, that we passed a walled garden. Leisurely, I seek it out.

The grounds are unkempt on this side of the house, just as they are elsewhere I've seen. If there is only one servant for this whole, vast place, it is no wonder. I keep an eye out for nettles and am so focused on evading them that I nearly walk right into the garden wall. It is lined with trees – more pines – and is so covered in moss and lichen that it blends in with the foliage around it. There is no obvious doorway, so I spend a while walking alongside it, searching for a break in the pines.

I do not find a gap among the pines, but I do spot an archway. Sunlight spills through it, and I can imagine it would be nearly impossible to find on a cloudy day. There is no door or gate, only an arch cut in the stone wall. Vines drape down from above and I reach up and touch the silky skin of ivy as I enter the garden. A mouth of ivy, I think, recalling one of my father's favourite sayings. The thought of him brings a pang of panicked grief. What am I doing, frolicking about in the sunshine while he's in bed, recovering from an attack that nearly cost him his arm? I may have a purpose here, but it feels as slippery as a fish. I've put my trust in a woman I know nothing about, save her strange obsession with bones.

A warm breeze whispers through the garden. A wind that warm cannot be coming from across the sea, and in fact it's easy to imagine the sea is a far way off. I cannot even hear it; it must be calm today.

Though the garden is as unkept as the land surrounding it, nature has thrived here. Roses and poppies push through the earth. They sway as if rejoicing in the sunshine. The faded imprints of paths wind among the weeds and flowers. This place once must have been an incredible sight. It has me thinking of the origins of Erskine Manor. How old is it? No one in town could tell you, and even though I've walked the halls, I couldn't even hazard a guess. Five generations? Maybe more? Strangely, the garden feels even older than the house itself, though surely it was not here before it.

Between the blooms and thorns of a rose bush I catch a glimpse of something glittering. I tramp through the bush to find an oval pool dug only just a few inches into the earth. The surrounding stonework is green with lichen, and algae blooms atop the water's surface. Rainwater, captured in a shallow pool, nothing special, but it feels suffused with life. The sight of it makes me feel less lonely. It is lovely, in the way so many things are here – past its prime, succumbing to the force of nature.

I crouch beside it, as if it were a tide pool. I can almost feel the presence of Fie beside me. I'm delighted to find little black shapes darting within the water. Tadpoles. Some already have their wee legs. I touch a finger to the surface and the whole pool ripples.

The tadpoles entertain me for a good while until I grow restless, wanting to occupy my hands. This spot in the garden is a suntrap, so I settle down with my back against a stone wall and pull out my knife. A pine branch, snapped ages ago from its host and now completely dry, lies in the remains of a rose bush. I pluck it out and turn it around in my fingers. The shape and feel of it conjures an image of a fish, a small narrow herring, and that's what I begin to carve from the wood. I'm just finishing it up, starting to feel like my cheeks might be burnt from the sun, when—

'Is this your beast?' a voice says from behind me.

In a rush, I rise to standing and turn to see a young woman standing beneath the arched entrance. Perhaps she is twenty or just over, tall and pale with an elegant air. And there is Dratsie, digging her little claws into the sleeve of the woman's dress. The bottle-green dress I saw a glimpse of in the drawing room. One of the woman's gloved hands grips a cane, silver-tipped and made of a deep, polished wood.

Dratsie chirps a hello, and her black eyes glitter. She scampers to the ground and comes over to me, spinning circles around my feet. I laugh and bend to brush my fingertips against her coarse fur. 'What are you doing here, you rascal?' I say.

I'm still smiling when I rise and catch the gaze of the woman standing there. My heart jumps. I recognise that face. She is the woman from last night, but now her eyes are like a human's again. Still dark, nearly black, but rimmed as they should be in white. She looks so changed in the sunlight. Her black hair has a blue sheen to it. I think of my sealskin, tucked beneath my pillow.

'I know you. You're the seal killers' daughter.' Her voice is low and quiet. Her gaze is very direct, and I notice that she hardly blinks. From the way she looks at me, I don't think she remembers our strange encounter last night.

'How do you know that?' I ask. Why do I feel as if something is missing? That I'm letting something slip through my fingers? I think I see a haze of white hovering over the small pool, but when I look at it properly, nothing is there. Only the sunlight sparkling across the surface of the water.

'I make Calder give me all the details of every person he sees. He sees you often, on the shore.' Her lips pull back into a delicate smile. 'He is very precise in his descriptions.'

'Who's Calder?'

She spins the tip of the cane slowly into the earth, and a bramble twists along with it. 'What is your name?'

'I'm Kier,' I say. I do not remember walking towards her, but I am close enough now to see the details woven into her dress.

'I am Breagha.' She holds out a gloved hand, leaning on her cane as she does so. I take her hand, but her fingers are limp and, instead of shaking it, I squeeze it once. She seems satisfied by this gesture and returns both hands to the cane. This close, I think I catch a glimpse of the silver top. A seashell, I think. A whelk.

Breagha is strange, but I like her. She is friendly, at least, and that is more than I can say for anyone else I've met here. Dratsie's claws dig into my leg and, startled, I look down at her. She's staring back at me with her whiskers twitching.

'Do you live here?' I ask, though it's a stupid and obvious question.

She tilts her head, as if contemplating whether to reply. 'Yes. Lady Erskine is my mother.'

I shouldn't be surprised to hear it, but I am nonetheless. What was I expecting? Of course she's an Erskine. She shares the same dark eyes and glossy hair as her mother. I ask the first question that comes to mind, that everyone in town has been wondering for years. 'Have you ever left?'

She laughs. 'Of course, I leave the house all the time. Whenever I like.' She looks away, in the direction of ... something. 'I never cross the wall, but now Mother is more preoccupied, I think I may do so if I want.' She has a strange way of speaking, a different lilt to her voice than most folk in town. I suppose the affectation might be a consequence of living your whole life in a manor house whose grounds you never leave. She taps her cane. 'You are not at all like Mother said you would be.'

'She told you about me?'

'No,' Breagha says curtly. 'Not you in particular.' She lifts a finger from her cane and gestures generally at me. 'People like you. People from the village.'

'What did she tell you about the people from the village?'

'Oh, you don't have to worry. I know everything, as if I've been there a thousand times. She's told us all the details, and Calder watches the shore, so we know even more besides.'

Half of what she says is nonsense to me, but she speaks so confidently that I half-believe it's just me being daft. 'You're not like what I expected, either,' I say.

'Oh?'

'You're supposed to be a monster.'

'Ah.' She seems to consider this. 'Why don't you ever join them?' she asks.

'Who?' Dratsie squirms out of my arms. To my surprise, she scampers up to Breagha and winds between her legs affectionately. I swallow a silly hiccup of jealousy. I trust Dratsie. She has good instincts about humans. There was a young man who came to town one summer. He used to wander the shore at midnight. I like a midnight swim if the moon's out, and I spotted him a few times, leisurely pacing the shore. I don't like to judge folk when they find themselves on the sea's edge. It's a place for contemplation and, sometimes, beside the sea, the dark thoughts we've been clutching to on land finally have the freedom to breathe. But whenever I saw the shadow of him on the horizon, Dratsie was there, furiously swimming circles around me and baring her teeth whenever she broke the surface. He was gone a few weeks after my last sighting of him, and not long after that the town was abuzz with news. He'd killed a girl two towns up shore. Drowned her, they said. Dratsie knew and, after that, I always trusted her.

The otter seems to have fallen for Breagha Erskine, and there's not much I can do about it.

'Your family. On the sea,' Breagha replies.

Mention of my family puts my back up. 'Who's Calder? Why is he spying on me and my family?'

Breagha is unaffected by the angry tone of my voice. She stands very still and hardly lifts an eyebrow as she speaks. 'My brother,' she says without elaboration. She lifts two fingers from her cane to gesture at the garden. 'Which is your favourite flower, Miss Seal Killer?'

'You can call me Kier. I don't kill.'

She smiles again. 'I know.'

I shrug. 'I like the blooms of the hawthorn tree.'

This time she laughs, and I'm almost caught in the current of her joy. I repress a smile. She says, 'There are none of those here.' Her eyes glint with mischief. 'But maybe somewhere on the grounds. The past likes to push itself through whenever it gets the chance.'

I haven't a clue what she means, but I realise that this is the allure of Breagha Erskine. She is so unlike anyone I have ever met – also so unlike how I imagined she would be. I tried to find the monster in her, to catch a glimpse of those strange eyes, but I cannot find it. She is elegant, certainly, but she does not speak to me like I am a servant, which I suppose I am of sorts. She talks like we are already friends.

She takes a step towards me, and my heart goes straight to my mouth, but she only brushes past me to the wall at my back.

'Look.' Breagha runs her palm against the wall. She does not tear the ivy clinging to the stone, but gently brushes it aside. I cannot see what she is referring to, and I think maybe this is another one of her odd comments. But then I see it. A design carved into the stone much like the one carved into the house. Breagha's smile is wide now, and she looks over her shoulder like a little girl about to reveal a secret. She smooths away the ivy until I can see another archway carved into the wall, etched with spirals and a stone door beneath it.

Breagha leans with one hand on her cane, the other hand pressed against the door. 'I could never open this. It's too heavy for one.'

'Couldn't you ask your brother?' I say. I wonder what Calder is like and how he knows me. Does he stay on the grounds, too, and if so, how does he manage to spy on the goings-on along the shore? Is he the young man I saw on the horse the day I arrived?

'Oh, no, Innes is no help. He and Lennox are thick as thieves, and Lennox tells Mother everything. Mother hates this garden. She'll get cross if she knows I'm here.' She must read my expression because she adds, 'You mean Calder.' She shakes her head. 'He won't come here.'

Innes, Lennox, Calder, Breagha. I say the names in my mind. Four children, all hidden from the world behind the great walls of the Erskine estate. Are they all like Breagha, or ought I be afraid?

'Well, all right. I'll help.'

Breagha utters a delighted gasp. I come up close beside her, a bit too aware of the differences between us, and brace my hands against the door.

'Go on,' Breagha says, and we push together.

At first, the stone does not budge, but then it begins to slide forward. Stone crunching against stone, the scrape of earth. We manage to push the stone door open enough for a person to squeeze through, but no further. A pine grows too close for it to open fully. This garden must have been here a long time to have been standing before the tree sprouted from the earth.

'A new escape,' Breagha says, squeezing through the gap. Dratsie darts after her, and I follow, having a bit of a harder time than those two but I manage it.

'Should we leave it open?' I ask.

Breagha considers the opening. 'Yes. I want to see what finds its way out.'

I look around me. We are hidden among the pines, but I am aware of the manor house not far away. Suddenly, I feel as if I'm doing something I ought not. Lady Erskine didn't mention her children, but if she wanted me to know them, wouldn't she have made a proper introduction? I feel as if the house is watching me, the windows her eyes, waiting for me to fail, to find any excuse to send me away. I cannot have that, not when she's my family's only hope.

'I should be going,' I say, not giving a good reason because the one I have is founded only on a hunch, a sense. Struck by a sudden inspiration, I hold out the pine-carved fish. It's very crude but looks enough like a fish, I think.

Breagha seems genuinely delighted when she takes it from me. She nods once. 'I have my own quest now,' she says in her odd way. She holds out her hand, and I squeeze it again, like she is a princess. 'Well then, Miss Seal Killer. I am delighted to know your name.'

'You could use it, you know,' I say. 'I don't kill, not seals or anything.'

'Kier.' Breagha looks intently at me, and my face grows warm from her unblinking stare. 'I will find your hawthorn.' With that, she slips back into the garden.

Dratsie is nearby, crunching on something with tiny bones. 'I better see you again,' I say, and I'm not quite sure who I'm speaking to.

17

Clouds have moved in, and the sunlight is softer now as it filters into the room. Thoughts of the garden keep me warm and remind me that although it feels like winter inside Erskine Manor, summer flourishes in the garden and beyond the walls.

For a while, I busy myself by tidying up the room. I scoop the pillows from the tub and hang the covers over the bedposts, so they hang like laundry on a line. Everything feels damp. I suspect I'm just going to have to get used to it, but I may as well try to make myself a bit more comfortable tonight. I go to the window to open it just as a bird alights on the windowsill.

A big, white-breasted magpie. Its wing feathers are a vibrant blue and its tail feathers a shimmering dark green. I fumble in my pockets, looking for something the bird might like. A button or a coin. I find a pin; one I'd probably stolen from Fie at some point. When I twist it between my fingers, it catches the sunlight. It may be shiny enough to appease the bird.

I have my fingers on the clasps of the window, ready to give the magpie my gift, when a thud makes me pull back. The bird drops from the sill, leaving behind a window speckled in blood.

'No,' I whisper to myself. I thrust open the locks and yank the window open. Leaning out, I scan the ground below. There is the bird, a feathered lump on the ground, nearly lost among the tall grass. A shaft extends from its breast.

My neck prickles. I sense someone watching. Dragging my gaze to the tree line, I see her. A woman, dressed in a green riding jacket with black leather boots, stands just out of reach of the sun. She holds a bow, still held aloft. She has straight black hair, like her sister and her mother both.

Lennox, I think. She is older than Breagha. I can tell even from this far.

She stares right at me, and I feel the threat in that gaze.

She does not stride towards the bird to pluck the arrow from its breast. She stares hard at me for a moment longer before turning away, dissolving into the shadows between the pines.

I set the pin on the windowsill, for want of what else to do, and think about what my father said once when telling me one of his stories. *Not all monsters look it so. Some keep their monstrosity cleverly hidden beneath a convincing human skin.*

18

Someone's hand is in mine, leading me from my room. I fell asleep early, with light still glowing from behind the edges of the curtains and birds conversing energetically outside. The house is dark now. Only one lamp light gutters its last breaths in the corridor. There is no one here with me, but I was certain someone took my hand. Certainly, I feel as if I am being led somewhere in particular; my movements are automatic, the turns I take deliberate, though I do not know where they lead. The halls are like tunnels carved from rock, narrowing, darkening, and I realise that I am not in the corridor any longer but in a passage that is indeed made of stone. My footsteps disturb a trickle of water that flows across the floor. I smell metal, rain, something like wet earth but richer, thick with decay.

The hand in mine is cold. Wet, I realise, as I hear the scattering of drops that fall to the floor as I walk.

'Wait,' I say, and I try to stop, but I am propelled forward. 'I don't want to go this way.'

I know nothing of what I am hurrying towards, but the closer I get, the thicker the air around me seems to grow, the louder the sounds of water moving across the floor, and through it all I hear a throaty laugh. I look down at the hand in mine, but there is nothing there. Something dark and slick coats my fingers.

The sound of scampering feet makes me look up. Dratsie runs across the ground, splashing water as she does, and I break into a run to follow her. There are no more turnings, only a door up ahead. The door is streaked in silver with a mother-of-pearl sheen. I do not want to open it, nor even to go near it, but Dratsie scrabbles at the door, digging frantically at its base.

I reach the door, but before I can open it, a boom resounds off the stone walls, and I turn just as a wave of water, white with foam, slams against the curve of the wall and barrels towards me. My hand is on the doorknob, and I twist it, but it is locked, and the cold, wet fingers are on my neck and a voice is in my ear, whispering, *Help me*. And the voice says this phrase again and again, not one voice but soon many in chorus, and I cannot tell where the voices end and the water's roar begins. The door is locked, the water fast. When it reaches me, I do not shut my eyes, but keep them wide open, right until the moment it swallows me whole.

The water slams against me, and I am thrown hard against the door at my back. The chaos of rushing water clears impossibly quickly. When I open my eyes, I do not see white swirls of water or rushing bubbles. Instead, I see clearly through the water. A long-fingered hand, tipped with talons, and a voice. That voice. Laughing, urging me down, beckoning me to the depths.

And although I'm beneath the water, I open my mouth to scream.

19

I WAKE TO A SODDEN BED.

The bloom of damp on the ceiling is still there, clinging, but no water drips down. My clothes and covers are soaked with sweat. I am the culprit this time; it is my own doing. A nightmare. Different than before, but familiar still, with the same resonating fear. Already, the dream is fading, but the after-image of it lingers.

I'm not interested in letting it return. I jump out of bed, peel off my wet clothes and get dressed. I am going out, I decide, as I pull the shirt over my head.

Something on the windowsill catches my eye. A hawthorn branch, blooming with white flowers. Hawthorns usually bloom just as spring turns to summer, but somehow this one is flowering late. I open the window and take up the branch, hold it to my nose, breathe in the scent of home. People don't often think of hawthorn when they think of flowers, but ever since I was a wee girl, I have loved the smell of them. It's the smell of magic, I told my father once, and he still pokes fun at me for it to this day. *Your magic tree is blooming, Kier*, he tells me every spring when the hawthorn's white buds opened.

Today, it smells like grief, and I don't think there's a difference now, between grief and home, the two are so muddled up.

'Thank you,' I whisper and shut the window. I'm unsure how it came to be on my windowsill, which is a storey up and unreachable from the ground below, but perhaps Breagha has a trick up her sleeve. She certainly seems like the sort of person who keeps secrets.

Carefully, I wrap the hawthorn branch in a handkerchief and place it in the inside pocket of my jacket. I feel compelled to arm myself against Erskine Manor and its grounds. A hawthorn branch near my heart, and I take up my knife, too, from where I've kept it in the bedside drawer. Both are a comfort, though not much use in any practical sense.

Armed with my knife, the branch in my pocket and a determination that Fie has noted more than once tends to get me in trouble, I step out into the hall.

I notice details I hadn't before. There is no paper on the walls, as there is in my bedroom. The corridor walls are made of brick, a dark stone, much like the one used for the outer walls of the house. Sometimes, my feet press into the softness of carpet, but the long, faded runners placed along the floor are rare; I guess they are more prominent in the corridors with bedrooms, but it is impossible to know what function each room serves. All the doors are closed.

Most curious are the fountains. I find one tucked into the shadows beside a stairwell. I think, perhaps, there are three floors to Erskine Manor, but I cannot find the stairwell to the uppermost floor. The fountain is made from smooth, black stone and looks like it belongs in a garden, not inside a house. Of course it is not working, and no water spurts from the figure in the centre. A carven fish with its mouth open, the depiction of waves around it suggesting it has just leapt from the sea. The fish stares upwards into the darkness, its mouth dry. There is a sheen of water in the basin. From the scent of it, I'd guess it is saltwater, but perhaps it is just so old it has begun to stink.

I find another fountain built into the wall at a kink in a corridor on the second floor. This one is also made from black stone, though it is less elaborate than the fish fountain. Some swirling designs are carved around the basin but there is no figure within. This fountain is completely dry. When I press my fingertips into the basin, they come back covered in dust. Then – a sheen. I swipe my palm along the basin, brushing aside more dust. The basin is covered in a stone or pounded metal that mimics the glimmer of the inside of a mussel shell. It has me thinking about this place and how it might have looked when the floors were polished and the curtains pounded of dust.

I wander down a staircase, to a corridor lined with portraits, though only the details of the nearest one are visible. The lights are so few and so dim I can only make out the features of the subject when I come up close.

An oil painting, a portrait of a beautiful young woman with the black Erskine hair and large, wet eyes stares ambivalently at me. She is draped in furs and loosely holding a hand mirror, which rests on her knee. I've seen other portraits like this around the house, the echoes of Erskines past. By her looks, the woman could be Lady Erskine in her youth, but I am certain she is not. The painter has captured a glimpse of desperation in the young woman's eyes, a yearning, and as I lean close, I think I can see dark waves depicted in the woman's pupils.

Leisurely, I walk down the hall, soaking up the stares from the rows of portraits on either side until one in particular catches my eye. A dark-haired Erskine. A young man with sallow cheeks and a tired look in his eyes. He is sitting very straight, looking directly at the viewer in a way that unnerves me. Like in the other paintings I've seen, the background behind him is dark, but I notice that it is not completely black. The paint strokes suggest the sea. Moonless, midnight, swelling in a storm. Other than this suggestion of the waves, the young man appears to be inside, seated and holding a silver comb, I think, though he grips it so fiercely, it's hard to know exactly what it is.

Astounding how all the Erskines are beautiful and seem always to have been so. I do not mean that their beauty is conventional. If you were to describe them, feature by feature, you would not paint a picture of beauty. But, on the whole, there is a glamour about them. I imagine how eligible the Erskines would be if they ever left their estate and ventured into town, how many suitors Breagha Erskine would have. Quite a queue, I think, but I leave it at that.

Water drips down the painting, tracing a pale gleam the length of the young man's cheek. I feel compelled to reach up and wipe it away, but I don't. The young man pins me with his weary stare. He is dressed in a dark suit, wears his hair slightly long but not down past his chin. It's impossible to guess the year the portrait was made. The dust caught in the dips of the elaborate silver frame suggest a long time, but everything is like that here. Dusty and damp.

Then I notice that a plaque is nailed into the frame at the bottom of the portrait. I tilt my head to look at it better. If I were shorter, maybe I would have seen it more easily. It is almost lost to the curvature of the frame.

With an apologetic glance at the young man, I swipe my thumb over the plaque to clear it of dust. The silver gleams, suddenly made fresh, though it is still mottled with tarnish.

Artair.

No date. No surname. Only the given name, Artair.

I look up at the young man again and form his name in my mind. Artair.

20

The morning air is surprisingly warm and feels properly like summer. The air out here is so much warmer than that in the manor house. The dampness is gone too, replaced by a soft breeze. Only a few grey clouds drift in the sky,

Now that I'm outside, the portrait hall feels distant, like an old memory. The house is a heavy presence at my back. I can nearly feel the weight of its history across my shoulders. All a mystery to me, something for Fie and me to mull over for the rest of our lives once I leave this place.

I am contemplating taking a wander through the walled garden, pretending to myself that a walk would do me well before I return to the cold, damp bowels of the manor house. The real reason flits in and out of my mind, so I have to keep batting it away. Thoughts of Breagha Erskine, details that I cannot help but dwell on. Her gloved fingers wrapped around the silver cane top. The silk hem of her dress catching on rose thorns as she walked. The sincere look she gave me when she promised to find the hawthorn.

Breagha is without a doubt the oddest person I've met, unlike anyone from my life back home. This must be why my mind keeps wandering her way. If she were woven into a fairy story, I'm not sure what part she would play. How would I describe her to Fie? Utterly unexpected.

My neck prickles, and I hold in a breath. A syrupy feeling of being watched slides down my back. I look towards the tree line, and I am certain, for a moment, that between the trees I see a tall, thin shape. Not a tree. A person, standing there. The figure is motionless. I see a shock of dark hair but can make nothing out of their features. Surely, though, they are watching me. I feel their gaze, even if I cannot see it.

'Hey!' I want to shout but don't, afraid that if I do, I'll draw notice from Lady Erskine in the house. She hasn't forbidden me from wandering the grounds, but she told me not to ask questions. Isn't poking around a kind of way of asking?

The figure raises a hand. A greeting? It feels like a warning, and I'm shocked into motion. I have the Sealgair instinct to run into a threat instead of away from it, so I bound into the forest towards the figure. As if without effort, they slide back into the shadows, and by the time I'm standing three trees deep in the pine forest, I see no trace of them.

'Fine,' I say, under my breath. The sensation of being watched doesn't go away, but without being able to see the person watching me, I can't really do anything. 'Do you want me to leave?' I ask. As if in reply, several magpies flutter from above and land on the lower branches of the pines around me. They strike up a conversation, chittering loudly at one another. A crow barks a reply in the branches above them, and I look up, startled to see the pine branches filled with an odd collection of birds. More white-breasted magpies, blue-black carrion crows, hoodies with feathers like ash and starlings, too, peering out at me from between the pine needles with their black, glassy eyes.

The sight of the birds sends a different sensation washing over me. Not just a feeling of being watched – because, clearly, I *am*, by a hundred little black eyes – but of something *not right*. A starling is no friend of a carrion crow, and their presence together is unnatural. I thought the discomfort I felt in the house had lifted when I went outside, but it has returned.

My knife is in my palm; I don't remember taking it from its scabbard. All these years without it, and it's still an extension of me. Brandishing it is as natural as lifting my hand to wave. But what use is a knife against a feeling? I can't cut away the sensation that something is wrong with this place – not just the house but the grounds, too.

The whole host of birds suddenly rise up. I expect them to scatter into the forest but, together, they fly forward only a short distance. Magpies, crows, starlings and even one fat young seagull, still mottled with brown feathers. They all fly a little way into the forest, settle in the branches or on the ground. After I take a few steps in their direction, they rise up in a flurry to fly only a short way again. It feels uncannily like they are leading me somewhere. They seem unafraid of me – only mildly interested, at best.

Why do I follow them? I guess because, even though I promised Lady Erskine I wouldn't ask questions, I still want answers.

The birds continue their unnatural progression through the forest. Flying, waiting, fluttering again. I'm only comfortable trooping through the forest because I'm so close to the edge of it that I can hear the sea nearby, the rush of the waves throwing themselves against the rocks and the roar as they pull back.

Then, the birds fly forward, each one disappearing from view, and when I follow them, they are gone, no longer waiting. But they have led me somewhere. A small building rises, half-hidden, from among the pines.

The stone structure is curved like a bee skep, with layers of dark brick coiling upward to create a domed roof. I recognise it as a dovecot, a place where pigeons are kept and bred for their eggs and meat. Pigeon isn't a very popular dish these days, but this dovecot isn't abandoned. The sounds from within echo and resound like the tide drawing in and out of a sea cave. It is filled with birds. I know where all my wee watchers have disappeared to.

Avoiding the prolific undergrowth of nettles around the dovecot, I get close enough to press my palm against the brick. It is shockingly cold, but, unlike the house, which weeps a constant damp, the brick is dry.

Am I daft? Maybe. Fie would say I am, but my best friend's not here to stop me from ducking into the small opening of the dovecot.

The bird noises are deafening, battering me before my eyes can adjust to the darkness within, and the smell of bird shit makes me nauseous. The dovecot's roof whorls above me and, just as you'd expect, the walls are lined with little square nooks. Each one houses a bird, and each bird stares down at me, blinking marble eyes in my direction. I turn in a circle with my head tilted back. Every nook is occupied. There must be a hundred birds in here, at least.

Suddenly, all the birds go quiet.

A figure darkens the small doorway. All I see are a pair of legs, black trousers and black shoes. The figure steps back and before I can launch myself from the dovecot, the birds do so first. A chaos of birdcalls heralds their sudden movement. I curl inwards, wrapping my head in my arms as a hundred birds rush around me, streaming through the small opening. Feathers brush against my hair, soft bodies slam into my back. To my embarrassment, I've shut my eyes, and only peel them open when the sounds quieten. I see the fat seagull streaming last from the opening. All the other birds are gone.

I clench my fist, ignoring the shaking of my fingers, and step through the opening.

The figure and the birds are gone. The forest is quiet and, not far away, the sea sighs.

I'm a Sealgair. I don't run from danger, but when my instincts tell me to do something, I listen. I hurry out of the forest as fast as I possibly can.

21

I'M GRATEFUL THE DOOR TO my room is in need of oiling. I wake to the sound of it creaking open, and when I scramble to sitting, I see the maid standing silent and still in the doorway. A knock would have been much appreciated. She appears unashamed at her terrible manners and watches me mildly, without a hint of interest.

'What time is it?' I ask. The room is still very dark, and outside, the sky is just beginning to brighten. The morning has hardly broken through the night, and the moon still shines.

The maid responds by lifting her arm and pointing out the window, toward the forest.

'Another dive?' I ask, and she simply turns away.

I make my own way through the house, out the door and down the slick front steps. When I see Lady Erskine standing at the edge of the forest, dressed in black with her face half-turned away in shadow, I almost shout a greeting, but it sticks in my throat.

At first, she does not see me, or doesn't seem to, and I begin to doubt that this is Lady Erskine, after all. Have her eyes always been so large and round, her skin pulled taut against her cheekbones, her hair – *wet*?

When she turns her head, the scant dawn light shifts across her face, and the strangeness of her features smooths away. She lifts one finger, motioning for me to follow.

Lady Erskine leads me along the cliff edge, further away from the house. The pines rise up alongside us as we walk; stick-straight, thick with shadows, smelling like winter.

We walk for a time, and there is not much to distinguish the landscape. It is always pines to our left and, to our right, short, windblown grass that grows right up until where the cliffs drop away. And after that, it is all dark blue sky and inky sea. The sounds from both mix; rustling of leaves blending into the roar of the waves. The path we take, which is no path at all but the naturally flat landscape of the clifftop, feels like a corridor between swathes of darkness. The sun is taking its time this morning.

Already, I brace myself for the dive. I breathe more deeply and focus on my senses so that after a short while I feel at ease among the birdsong and low rustle of the waves, the pine-scent and the twinge of salt on the air. Diving has always been something I've done purely for enjoyment, never with any purpose. What purpose is there to diving if you cannot collect scallops or anything else to eat? Treasure is far less abundant than stories might claim, though sometimes I'm lucky enough to find a piece of old pottery or a lovely, worn stone. Now, I prepare myself to search for bones, and I have to swallow down a coil of worry. What if, like killing, I suddenly can no longer dive? What if I fail at this, too?

I huff and flick the thought away.

Lady Erskine walks swiftly ahead of me. I could match her pace, but I have no desire to be close to her. She radiates a coolness I prefer to avoid. Not a crisp, sea-air chill but a flint-edged energy. I think, if I'm not careful, I may be cut by it.

Just as with the first dive, she leads me through the forest along a path that is impossible to follow. With the dawn just a pale blue strip in the sky, the forest is leeched of colour. The pine trunks are mere strips of shadow, and the undergrowth is a pool of ink. I grope for the closest pine, press my palm against it and seek out the next one, using the trunks like stepping stones. I am certain that if I must traverse the forest this way, I'll lose sight of Lady Erskine. Already, she's only a distant smudge of black. My mind is twisting over the options, weighing up how likely – or not – Lady Erskine is to try to find me if I lose my way. But then a prick of light appears ahead of me. It shifts, grows brighter, and my eyes adjust to make sense of what I'm seeing. Lady Erskine holds a lantern. It gives off a soft, blue light, like a concentrated orb of moonlight. Not particularly strong but bright enough to ward off some of the thicker shadows.

I stifle a grateful whoop at the sight of it. I follow the light deeper among the pines.

I have only a vague sense that, this time, we are going a different way. Are there more pools hidden, scattered throughout the forest?

My question is answered eventually, when Lady Erskine leads me into a small clearing, much like the first one. This clearing is different though, lined with larger rocks, some of which appear to have once been stone structures. The remains of buildings or monuments. They are streaked wet like Erskine Manor, though it hasn't rained since the day I arrived here.

The pool is different, too. Smaller, completely clear of pine needles, as if recently disrupted.

Just as she did before, Lady Erskine lowers herself at the pool's edge and dips her fingers into the water. The gesture feels ritualistic. I may be imagining things, but the air in the clearing seems to change as her fingers break the surface. An opening up, as if the wind inhales.

Lady Erskine looks into the depths of the pool, and I join her at the edge. Up close, it feels smaller than when I peered at it from the edge of the clearing. The pool appears to be completely ordinary, but I cannot stop the rushing in my ears. My instincts are telling me to step away. Panic quickens my heart and I breathe long to quell it. Panic during a dive can be dangerous. It can be deadly.

'The pool narrows quickly,' says Lady Erskine.

She does not elaborate, but any warning from Lady Erskine carries weight. I breathe into my worry, so it's only a light flutter in my chest.

'Take the light.' She hands me the lantern. It is lighter than I imagined, and I realise that it is made from bone. The flame within dances like a will-o-the-whisp, hopping up and down erratically, behaving like no flame I've ever seen before. She means for me to take it into the water. I'm too afraid of her to ask for clarification or protest. Surely, it will burn out almost immediately.

Impatient, Lady Erskine gestures at the pool. I don't hesitate. I strip down and lower myself into the water. Cold shoots pain through my feet and fingers, but they will numb soon. I am under in a moment, sinking, and then I begin to swim downwards. At first, the lantern feels like a burden. Its bulk in my hand changes the way I swim, makes my movements through the water feel stilted, but after a moment, I'm glad I have it. Its light doesn't go out. It continues to glow white-blue and bob like a tiny moon dancing to a selkie's song.

The water here is strangely clear, very different from the muddied sea I'm used to. Almost immediately, I am aware of how flippant Lady Erskine's words were compared to the truth – the pool does indeed narrow quickly, but that is not the only challenge. It is lined with rocks, sharp and crystal-hard, glistening with a fish-skin sheen. I swim towards the centre of the pool to be clear of the rocks, but though I have been under for only a few moments, already my blood swirls in the water. I've cut my palm, and my shoulder. The pain will sting later when my body warms.

The pool darkens as quickly as it narrows. The water is absent of life, at least so it first appears. No kelp or seagrass clings to the rocks, and no fish flit by, though surely the pool is deep enough for them to thrive here. Then, I notice little silver orbs glittering in the nooks and crannies. Though I shouldn't be wasting time observing the flora and fauna, I touch one as I pass. The surface is as hard as a shell and, when I touch it, a flurry of thin, pale tentacles erupts from within the orb, and the shiny creature scampers away, far faster than I can dive.

Bones, I think, trying to resist my curiosity. *Look for bones.*

My first dive proves fruitless. Shortly after discovering the creature, I have to propel myself back to the surface, earning another few nicks from the rocks as I do. But now I have a sense of the way, and the strange rocks and creatures are less strange to me the second time.

After swallowing several gulps of air, I am back under again. This time, I get further, and I search the rocks as I go, but I see nothing. The silver creatures frustrate my efforts. The pale lamplight in my hand reflects so many flashes of silver that look, at first glance, like pale pieces of bone. I have to return to the surface again, and as I dive for the third time, I am determined. This time, I will find a bone. I can only dive so long before I become exhausted, and I am certain the bone is deeper than I've already gone.

My eyes sting from the saltwater, but I keep them open and train my gaze along the rocks as I swim deeper and deeper. The water is dark now, and the silver creatures are fewer here. I'm thankful for that, at least.

My mind wanders, shuffling between thoughts of my family, of Fie, of Breagha in the garden. A tingling sensation shivers across my scalp, and I turn to see someone staring at me from between the rocks.

Bubbles erupt from my mouth. A foolish mistake, as I nearly swallow water. But I am certain I saw the flash of someone here, a person, a pair of eyes, a smudge of mouth. I turn and come face to face with myself – hair dragging upward, face distorted by the uneven surface. My reflection, caught in a mirror, warped with age and brine. The last thing I expected to see here in the depths of the pool. Its silver frame is suckered with barnacles, and the glass is streaked with black. It is like a mermaid's glass, positioned upright against the rocks.

My lungs burn. I have wasted time. But I cannot turn away from the mirror. I grip it, and it is not as secure as it seems. I lift it away from the rocks to find a hollow behind it.

Inside, pale in the dark water, is a bone.

I snatch the bone and return the mirror to its place. I'm not superstitious, not like my father, and I don't believe in mermaids, but it seems as if the mirror belongs here, that it has a purpose, and I do not want to disturb it.

As I swim past the mirror, I knock it accidentally with my foot. It tumbles forward. My impulse is to catch it, but with the bone in one hand and the lamp in the other I cannot. My fingers brush the barnacled frame, but I cannot grasp it. I am certain, as the mirror sinks into the depths, that I see a face staring back at me, two large eyes and a pale mouth, distorted by shifting coils of shadow. But as I turn away and begin to kick towards the surface, I reason that it was only my own reflection.

There is no time to look at the bone, to wonder what body it once belonged to. My lungs beg for me to swim faster, but

I pace myself, aware of my ears and blood and what could happen if I rise too quickly.

The water grows lighter. I am almost there.

I burst from the pool, which glitters in the brightening light, and spreads out silver all around me. The water beyond the surface is very dark and ominously deep, and I am propelled by an urge to get out, get away, before anything should drag me under.

Lady Erskine very nearly snatches the bone from my fingers.

'Good,' she says, the most praise I think I'll ever get out of her. She clasps the bone in both her palms and peers into the cave formed by her fingers. She seems to whisper something into it, and her eyes are bright, triumphant. The nape of my neck itches as I watch her.

As Lady Erskine tucks the bone away into the pockets of her dress, I set the lamp aside and pull on my jumper. I rub my arms to bring heat back into them and shake out my numb feet. Already, exhaustion is creeping in. I was in the water for a long time. Even my heart feels cold.

She does not wait for me to warm myself, so that I have to hobble after her, bones aching from the cold and needles spiking up into my heels with every footstep. Although the sky has lightened, the shadows thicken the further we get from the clearing. Lady Erskine's dark dress is nearly impossible to see. I am torn between an intense concentration and a desire to plop down and rest my eyes for a moment. I imagine it's the sort of feeling you might get just before you drown.

I stop. Blink. And she is gone.

22

THIS IS NOT MY PLACE, this forest of narrow pines and shadows. I am not at home here where I cannot see the horizon or even much of the sky; snatches of the dawn between the dense branches are hardly a comfort. Walking into town from the shore makes me jumpy with a sense of suffocation. But the forest is far worse than the town. There is hardly a breath between pines, and I feel them looming above me in all directions, bearing down. I should have kept hold of the strange lantern Lady Erskine gave me for the dive, but I was too worn out to even think of it when she took it after the bone.

I breathe deep, fill my lungs. Amid the scent of pine and earth mingles the smell of the sea. I remind myself that it is not far away. I grip my knife firmly and follow the narrow path.

The pines rustle. A flurry of sticks crack all at once. I peer around me, but the trees are so close together that the dawn light doesn't penetrate beyond the first row of branches. The foxes will still be out, and there must be many here, prowling the estate. A fox, I think. Surely.

I continue forward, hoping that at any moment I'll see a break in the trees. But there is more of the same, dark trunk after dark trunk. Wherever Lady Erskine has gone, she is nowhere in sight.

A long, hollow hooting sound weaves among the trees. Not from any bird I know. It is a mournful sound, almost like a cormorant's call but more sustained, more breathless. My skin prickles, but I do not stop walking. I'm not afraid of a few forest beasties.

When I hear not only the cracking of branches and the shifting of leaves but also a huffed breath, I turn and face the source of the sound, squaring up to it, willing for whatever creature follows me to show itself.

Nothing does. Not for ten long breaths. Nothing. Now I feel foolish as I press forward, but my instincts are on high alert now. I listen for patterns in the sounds around me, and I am certain that what I hear is no animal but the footsteps of a human. The mournful whistle sounds again. Whoever is in the forest with me seems to give up any attempts at stealth. Leaves crunch to the rhythm of steady footsteps, and I have to swallow down the urge to run. I am deep in the forest, deep enough that running is not an option. And anyway, I know I wouldn't, even if running was the best choice. Instead, I grip my knife and wait.

Someone laughs. A man's voice.

'That's enough of that,' I say, channelling my younger self, the girl who was afraid of nothing.

I am shocked when a face appears among the shadows. A white-grey horse peers at me from between the branches of the pines, and I recognise it as the horse I saw on my first day here. The creature's eyes are bright and grey, and its muzzle is dark. All I can see of it is its head, which looks suspended among the trees. There is an unnaturalness about it that I cannot place, and not simply because of its sudden, unexpected appearance in the forest. It looks, from what I can see, like a typical horse, albeit a striking one, with a gaze more human than animal. Perhaps this is what is most strange about it – the horse's eyes, which remind me somehow of the young woman's from the portrait I passed yesterday morning. There is no fear gleaming in the creature's irises, but there is that same longing, that sense of being out-of-place. It stares at me without blinking, and an urge wells up within me. I almost drop my knife, as a desire courses through me to lift my hand, to stretch out my fingers, to press my palm against the whirl of hair between the horse's eyes. As I am thinking this, gripping my knife tighter in an impulse to fight this strange urge, I notice that the horse is dripping wet. Water drops from its black lips. A trickle of water runs from a curl of its mane, along the ridge of its eyes, as if the horse were weeping.

As if it has just leapt from the sea.

The horse steps forward, slowly, gracefully, so I can see the whole of it. Its mane is dark and knotted but it does not look uncared for. Quite the opposite. It is a beautiful creature, impressively tall and muscular, with an enchanting pattern of spots along its flanks.

The horse stands motionless, only the slight movement of its nostrils betraying the life in it. The urge to touch it is still there, and I lift my free hand, though I wouldn't normally make a habit of stroking wild horses. Certainly, I shouldn't make a habit of doing so now, not here, when I sense this place has no interest in seeing me well.

Someone clicks their tongue. Out from the pines steps a man – young, dressed oddly in a fur-topped cloak and full riding gear, despite the summer warmth. His dark eyes are unfriendly, and I immediately dislike the way he holds his chin up as he walks.

'I wouldn't touch,' he says. 'She's not as good-natured as she seems.'

'Neither am I,' I say.

He grins wide; I'd quite like to slap it off his face. 'You're lost,' he says.

'I'll find my way.'

'You won't. You've been walking in circles.' His gaze darts to my knife, which I'm still holding in front of me. 'What are you hunting?'

'Nothing, if you're lucky,' I say, bluffing, of course. Though I can't bring myself to harm even an insect if I can help it, I'm finding I need to supress a growing urge to strike Innes Erskine in the jaw. Assuming, of course, this is Innes. I wonder how often all the Erskine siblings are together. I cannot imagine them in a kitchen, making breakfast, joking with one another or even sitting in companionable silence. This thought sends a pang through my chest, as I think of my own family.

'I came to offer my services to a girl in distress.' Innes steps forward with the horse still beside him, in a move that I know is meant to intimidate me. He's my height, though just, and the furs make him appear a strange mix of wild and distinguished. On a cord around his neck hangs the source of the mournful sound I heard. A whistle made from shell, I think. He looks like a lost prince, angry he's been expelled from his kingdom, banished to these dark woods. Innes has the mark of a bully, and I've never in my life been able to back down from a bully. For better or for worse, I'll admit.

The horse snorts, and I notice that it wears a thin silver bridle, so delicate it looks like spider's silk. Innes doesn't touch it but keeps a hand on the horse's withers. This is enough, it seems, to keep the horse close.

'A *what*?' I say.

He looks amused. 'Should I say seal killer? A seal killer who has lost her way in my forest.'

'My name is Kier,' I say, making a note of how he called this place *my forest*.

'That's right, you're Mother's bone diver.'

'You're Innes Erskine.'

'Did Breagha tell you that? She shouldn't be talking to you.' A look of irritation crosses his features, and I notice how dark his eyes are, framed by long lashes.

'She's a far better conversationalist than you are.'

He huffs and pats his horse. 'I think you're afraid.'

'Yes, I'm afraid of the forest,' I say. 'As any rational person would be.'

'Are you afraid of me?' he says, and I brace for him to move towards me, but he doesn't. In fact, his voice isn't as threatening as the words suggest. He seems to be asking me genuinely if I am afraid of him, and I think of all the times I've sat in the Corbie's Nest and heard the townspeople telling stories about the Erskines. They are monsters, the stories always come round to. That's why they never leave. But now I wonder what the real reason is. Because although every Erskine I have met has been strange, sometimes hostile, I do not think I would call them monsters.

Not yet, anyway.

The horse beside Innes raises its gaze to me, and I find it almost impossible to look away.

'No,' I say, remembering Innes's question. Almost embarrassed, I lower my knife. I don't sheathe it, not yet. 'I've lost my bearings, that's all.'

'So you admit that you need my help?' Innes smiles.

'Are you truly offering?'

Innes looks pleased. 'Yes, we'll lead you through the forest, *bone diver*.' He clicks his tongue and begins to walk. The horse pierces me with a long stare before moving silently after its master. I follow, trotting a bit to make pace with Innes so I don't have to walk behind the horse, which moves with an easy grace that shouldn't be possible in the forest.

'It's not your fault,' Innes says after a while. 'The forest plays tricks on everyone.'

'Except for you,' I reply.

'Not any longer. I've learned how to trick it back.'

'Like the sea,' I say eventually. 'You never know what mood she'll be in.' I sound like my father and, under most circumstances, this would make me proud. Now, it just reminds me, yet again, of what I've lost. The panic starts to bubble up again, all those questions – will this work? Is it worth it? Did I make the right choice, coming here?

Innes slaps the trunk of the nearest tree as he passes. 'These trees are alive with the sea, so maybe you're right.'

'Pine trees? From the sea?'

'Yes. Their roots drink seawater, and their sap tastes of salt.'

'Sounds like a nice wee story,' I say.

Innes shrugs. 'You've seen the caves. They're everywhere beneath us, so maybe it's not just a nice wee story.'

'Trees can't live on salt water.'

He looks over at me, raising a dark eyebrow. 'You're far from home, bone diver.'

'Not far in distance,' I mutter. 'But far enough.'

He clears his throat. 'You live in the village.'

'No,' I say. 'I live in a cottage beside the shore. I thought Calder would have told you that.'

Innes gives me an amused glance. 'Calder can't see the village from the cliffs, only the boats and the fishermen.' He pauses. 'And the seal killers. But you go into the village every day.'

'Aye, most days.' I sense Innes' restlessness in my silence. He wants to know more, but my mouth feels gummy. I don't know what to say. I could tell a story about what creatures might lurk the grounds of the Erskine estate, but how do I describe the high street or the fish market? What is there to say about the humble town hall and ceilidhs that fill the place with music? The Erskine estate, this forest and the Erskines themselves seem so far removed from the village – and, more than that, I feel like Innes doesn't deserve to know. How could I describe it all in a way that wouldn't sound provincial? He wouldn't understand. He wouldn't see it all the way I do.

I feel myself slowing, creating more of a distance between myself and Innes and his strange horse, which walks noiselessly beside him. Innes seems to be true to his word; I don't feel like I'm going in circles. I think I can smell the tang of the sea, and the panic starts to loosen its grip.

Up ahead, I spot a patch of nettles. I've always got one eye trained on the ground so I might avoid their stinging leaves. Me and nettles have never got on well. I remember well the day when I ran full pelt into a patch of nettles in our garden. I was four or five years old and not much taller than the plants. It was a hot day, too, so I wasn't wearing much. I ran into that patch and ran right back out, screaming that I'd been struck by lightning. Itchy, stinging lightning that raised red welts all over my skin from head to toe.

So, I don't like nettles and always make a point to avoid them even when, as now, I have must bigger concerns. Innes, on the other hand, troops ahead as if he's impervious to their stings.

'Wait,' I say, reaching out and lunging forward to grab his shoulder and pull him back. I get a fistful of fur before he spins around. There's a strange look on his face, a mix of surprise and discomfort and maybe a bit of curiosity.

'Nettles,' I say.

Innes' conflicted expression is replaced by a slow smile, and I half-expect to see sharp teeth flash between his lips. 'I'd expect a seal killer to brave a nettle patch,' he says.

'Better to go around if you have the chance.'

'Why not,' he says, and takes my advice.

Then, without warning, the forest opens up, and we are standing on the edge of it. I see the walls of the garden and Erskine Manor's spires piercing the sky. I sigh, releasing a long breath that I must have been holding for ages. Finally, I can breathe again.

'There we are,' Innes says, gesturing to me like a prince ushering his princess into a grand ball. A wild prince, draped in furs with a fierce horse at his side. I'm almost charmed by this vision and think how Fie would be utterly taken by it, the romantic that he is. 'Now you owe me something in return.' I think he might be joking, but he looks at me as intently as his horse, dark eyes flickering with fire. 'A favour for a favour, seal killer.'

Innes steps back and clicks his tongue, and the horse beside him retreats. Together they step back into the forest, melting into the shadows, and a moment later I hear the mournful call of his whistle.

Though I know the source of it now, it still leaves my skin prickling.

23

A WARM BRUISE OF A CLOUD settles on the horizon, and I know from one glance that soon it's going to unburden itself of a torrent of rain. So the house it is for me the rest of the day, despite my restlessness.

I've explored every inch of my room in Erskine Manor, and it's become more familiar to me than my bedroom back home. The room is filled with odd things, some completely unexplainable – a marble figurine of a herring wedged behind the dresser, a painting of the sea slathered in haar (that is: a painting of nothing but grey), a book on whale oil, another about the language of shore plants. Odd, interesting things that Fie and I could spend hours ruminating over, things I'd normally make silly stories out of. In fact, this whole place ought to inspire so many stories, but whatever joy normally sparks me to spin a yarn has faded. My mind won't let me. Instead, other thoughts creep in. Worries and unformed fears. Things that feel like they've dragged themselves out of the deep to gnaw at the back of my teeth. I feel them now, nibbling, as I sit on the edge of my bed and spin my knife in my fingers.

What would Fie say if he were here?

I didn't come here to hear your whinging. Get on with one of your stories. I'll make you a cup.

I wish someone would bring me a cup of tea. Not a cup of the thin, bergamot stuff the maidservant is always delivering to me, already cold, but a big cup just like Fie makes it – piping hot, too sweet, rich with milk.

But then – I think of Fie again. *You're whinging, Kier.*

All right.

I'm halfway to the door when something shoots out from underneath it. An envelope made of dark grey paper. I ignore it for a moment and open the door. No one is there, and the corridor is dim and still, quiet save for the distant sound of a ticking clock. Puzzled, I shut the door and turn to the envelope.

The paper feels expensive, weighty. I'm surprised to pull from it only a thin, single piece of paper.

Dear bone diver, someone has written. *Please join us in the dining hall at your earliest convenience.*

There is no signature and, when I turn the paper around, I find nothing on the back. I have the fleeting, giddy thought that it might be from Breagha, but the 'us' suggests not, or at least not only her. Is this an invitation to lunch? I assume it must be. I look around my room, at a bit of a loss, wondering if I ought to prepare in some way. Ultimately, I decide there's really nothing I can prepare anyway, except to keep my knife hidden in its scabbard.

Stepping into the hall feels like I am stepping into my own tomb, but I do my best to ignore the slippery sense of dread I've almost, but not quite, got used to in this place. Though it's the middle of the day, I could use a lamp in these dark corridors. There aren't very many windows here, and the ones that do exist are made from a tinted glass, giving the effect that outside it is always the gloaming.

Thank the sea I'm not having lunch in the kitchen today. Nothing is more soulless than having to eat alone while the maidservant stares silently on. I'm starting to think she watches with a kind of fascination as I work my way through terrible meal after terrible meal.

I'm not quite sure where the dining hall is, but I make a series of educated guesses to find it. I think I've been in this corridor before, but never have I seen the double doors at the far end opened. I don't think I've ever really noticed them, but now I do. They are so much like the large, front double doors of the manor house – black as jet, shining as if wet – and today they are opened wide. Through them, I see the dining hall.

It's not as big as the town hall, but not much smaller. A long, dark wooden table extends through much of the room. A black iron chandelier studded with guttering candles looms above the table. Paintings hang on the walls, three huge canvases, one for every wall, but these are only seascapes. No human subjects to stare mournfully at the diners. Though I cannot say the seascapes are much improvement; in each one the sky is dark, and the sea is peaked with stormy waves. In the nearest one, I am certain I see the shadow of a ship, hull broken, figures thrown or leaping to their deaths.

All of this I observe with only half-interest. What surprises me most are the four beautifully dressed people clustered at the far end of the table, each staring at me with bold interest.

There is Lennox Erskine, with her straight black hair and hard-edged fringe, standing with one hand resting against the tabletop. Seated in a chair beside her with his feet thrown up on the table is Innes. No longer dressed in his furs, he wears a formal suit with a jacket with long pointed lapels that I'm sure Fie would have an opinion of. Another young man hovers beside them, nearly hidden behind Lennox, and this must be Calder. He has a loose mop of black hair that almost covers his eyes and the disposition of an easily spooked horse. And seated across from Innes is Breagha, with her legs stretched long to the side as if she's astride a horse side-saddle. Her cane is propped against the table beside her.

The force of their stares nearly sends me bolting out of the room. The table is not set for lunch, and the room is heavy with quiet. I think perhaps I have misunderstood the purpose of this gathering.

'A prompt arrival,' says Lennox with a voice that is surprisingly deep and smooth. 'You have not kept us waiting long, bone diver.'

'Uh, that's good,' I say, feeling uncomfortable beneath their stares. No one looks as if they are going to say anything else, so I awkwardly add, 'What exactly are we waiting for?'

'Nothing, now that you are here,' says Lennox in her smooth, pragmatic way. She spreads something across the table, a streak of scarlet. It takes me a moment to realise that I am staring at five red ribbons, one of them noticeably shorter than the others. Although Lennox is currently unburdened of her bow, she still looks prepared to shoot me, if it should come to that. I get the sense that whatever this is wasn't her idea, but she is dutifully taking up her role as eldest. Though now that I see Lennox and Innes side-by-side, I guess they must be twins, and Lennox's oldest-sister persona is somewhat of a choice rather than fated happenstance. Certainly, it suits her better than Innes, who is picking his nails with a small silver knife, his feet still kicked up on the table. 'Because *some* of us are determined to talk with you even though I have forbidden it,' Lennox continues, 'we have decided you will join us for a game.'

Innes lifts his eyebrows, an action which Lennox makes a point of ignoring, as she arranges the ribbons into a straight line on the table.

'The game is called Hunter, and since you are a hunter yourself, you are well suited for it,' Lennox says. She looks around at her siblings. 'Afterwards, we will have a sense of you, and together we will decide if we ought to convince Mother to make you leave.'

'It's a *test*,' I say.

'Yes,' says Lennox, just as Breagha says, 'It will be fun.'

'We've never played with someone else before,' Breagha continues, looking delighted at the idea.

'Um ...' I start.

'The rules are simple,' Lennox says over me. 'Whoever selects the short ribbon is the Hunter, who must find and kill the prey.' She taps the short ribbon. 'Not only must the prey hide from the Hunter, they will be given a map, on which is indicated the rooms of the house they must collect one object from.'

'When you say *kill*—' I interject, earning a fierce glare from Lennox.

'If the Hunter finds you, you must wear the ribbon, and you will join her to hunt the others. To win the game, you must avoid the Hunter, collect the objects and return to the dining hall before any of the others.'

Once again, I am pinned by the stares of all four Erskines. My stomach growls faintly. My hopes for lunch are dashed, and now it seems I'm to play an odd, somewhat menacing version of hide-and-seek. Somehow, this situation feels even more unexpected than being asked to dive for bones.

'You should know,' drawls Innes, 'that those are *all* the rules. Do whatever you can to win.'

'Are you saying I should play dirty?' I ask.

Innes shrugs. 'Shouldn't be hard for a seal killer.'

Lennox clears her throat. 'So it's clear.' She sweeps the ribbons into her hand and arranges them in her fist so they all appear to be of the same length. 'Now, we choose.' Each of the Erskines reaches forward and plucks a ribbon from Lennox's fist. I'm the last to take mine and disappointed to see I've chosen one of the long ones. Looks like I'm prey.

Innes swings his feet off the table in what is obviously a show of disappointment. He's also selected a long ribbon.

'Oh!' says Breagha, holding up her short ribbon. 'You're all going to die.' She says this very cheerfully, looking round at all of us.

'Here are your maps.' Lennox hands everyone a piece of paper. They are hand-drawn maps of the manor house. In five of the rooms is drawn a thick 'x', while the names of the rooms are written in a narrow, looping script – drawing room, kitchen, silver room, Mother's room. I stare at that last one with a sense of dread creeping up into my throat. We are supposed to take an object from each room indicated on the map. It's not exactly appropriate for me to be sneaking into my employer's bedroom, but then what choice do I have? If I don't play this game, I'm certain Lennox will convince the others to have me sent home. And I can't have that, not until I've collected all the bones Lady Erskine needs.

'Good luck,' Innes says with his wolfish grin.

'You have three minutes before the Hunter can leave this room.' Lennox folds her map into a small square and tucks it into her pocket.

'Goodbye.' Breagha waves her short ribbon. I return her smile with a pained one of my own.

Innes stomps out of the room, followed by Lennox. I am just behind them when Calder comes up beside me, his breath warm against my ear. 'Breagha will kill you.' His voice is whisper-low and raspy like the sound of leaves tumbling in the wind. 'She always does.'

I turn to look at him, but he slides ahead of me and disappears into the dim corridor beyond.

24

THE SILVER ROOM IS NOT silver but variations of deep, glorious blues. The curtains, the carpet, the upholstery are each a unique shade of blue, but I can see why the room is called the silver room. Sitting on a dark chest of drawers pushed flush against the longest wall, a massive silver clock stretches to the ceiling. It is the sort of clock that does more than tell time, though I'd be hard-pressed to understand anything it's saying. I'm certain it is giving all sorts of information about the planets, the moon, maybe even the tides, assuming some of the little symbols represent waves. The sound of its ticking is brittle, filling up the whole room, despite the many soft furnishings that ought to absorb the sound. It's a fascinating, beautiful object but because it's gigantic, I have little interest in it.

The silver room is the first room I find on the map, and I am determined not to linger. Annoyingly, there is nothing immediately apparent that I can grab and pocket as part of the game. The clock looms down at me, ticking with seemingly greater enthusiasm, as I slide open the first draw beneath it.

Inside is only a book, which is too thick to be worth taking. The next drawer proves more fruitful; it's filled with pine needles and among these are scattered glass marbles. I pick one up, realising it's been tumbled smooth and muted by the sea. Fie would love this and, in fact, I think I'll take this with me when I finally leave this place.

I'm just sliding the marble into my pocket when I hear a distant tread. Making the quick decision to leave the drawer hanging open, I dash towards one of the floor-length curtains and haul myself onto the windowsill just as the door creaks open. I strain for the sound of a cane against the floor, but instead I hear a whispering that grows louder as whoever is here moves across the room.

'You must apologise,' the voice says, and I recognise it as belonging to Calder.

'I already have,' a louder voice returns. Lennox. So they have teamed up, it seems.

'Not to me. To the birds.'

Lennox sighs louder than her whispers. 'I will not be going anywhere near your absurd dovecot. It's rancid, Calder.'

'You have upset them when they are already worried.'

'What are they worried about?' Lennox retorts. Calder doesn't reply, and I hear the two Erskines moving about the room.

'There was no reason to kill her,' Calder says eventually, in a whisper I almost cannot hear.

'I had a very good reason. I was warning the bone diver. She needed to know that I am watching her.'

'You could have left a note in her room like Breagha did for the game.'

'A note is hardly menacing though, is it?' Lennox says. 'Ah, look. She was already here.' I imagine them both standing before the clock, observing the open drawer and its odd collection of needles and sea-tumbled marbles.

'She took a marble,' Calder says, sounding disappointed, and I guess the collection belongs to him.

'I will make sure she gives it back,' says Lennox, managing to sound both exasperated and protective of her brother. I hear the rustling of pine needles and the wooden grind of the drawer closing, and I count to thirty before I hop down from the windowsill. My lower back is tight from the awkward position and I am reminded why hide-and-seek is usually a children's game.

The next closest room on the map is the drawing room, but an intuition tells me I ought to try a different room instead. Calder and Lennox are likely to be in the drawing room, and although it's Breagha I'm really hiding from, I guess that sabotaging other players is a likely strategy for Lennox. To the kitchen then, which I'm hoping Breagha will be less familiar with.

The corridors leave me feeling exposed. Only the shadows, which are plentiful, provide a semblance of cover. Should Breagha appear from any of the rooms along the way, I'd be immediately found out. I am nearly at the kitchen, distinctly feeling like my luck is about to run out in any moment, when a sweet scent wafts by. It's familiar, though I don't immediately know why. Though it's sweet, it's not floral, something more akin to vanilla or brown sugar. Then, I realise. It's Breagha's perfume. She is here, or if I am very lucky, has just walked by.

I don't take another step. As if it would be enough, I press myself against the wall and wait. My gaze sweeps back and forth along the corridor, and my ears strain for any sounds coming from the kitchen. I have underestimated the strength of the shadows because I do not notice Innes coming down the hall until he is almost upon me.

In a move that is anything but strategic, I step forward as he nears, stopping him in his tracks.

Innes lunges towards me, a growl rumbling in his chest, but comes up just short of grabbing me by the shoulders.

'*Bone diver*,' he says in a rough whisper, clearly displeased.

'Breagha's in the kitchen,' I say, sliding away from the wall and a step further from Innes. 'I wouldn't go in there.'

Innes regards me with a throaty sound of suspicion. 'How do you know?'

'It's all in the details,' I say. I'm not going to admit the slightly mortifying fact that I recognise Breagha's perfume.

'Right, well, let's see if you're as good a hunter as you think you are.'

'In this instance, we're both prey,' I remind him.

He moves past me, and I make to hold him back, but he shoots me an irritated glance. 'I know a different way. Just follow me. We'll see if Breagha has caught anyone in her trap.'

Instead of taking me the way I know to reach the kitchen, Innes leads me through a door in the corridor that is all but invisible if you're not looking for it. The walls this close to the kitchen are bare of wallpaper and even much of the plaster has worn away. Innes catches me off guard by leaning against a bare patch of wall, which gives under his weight. We both disappear into a dark passage, which is only illuminated by a strip of pale light at the end.

'That's the kitchen,' Innes says.

'Who would ever use this passage?' I ask. It's dark, damp and smells strongly of earth in here. I can't imagine a scenario in which I'd rather scurry down this way just to save a couple of minutes.

'The servants like it,' says Innes. Recalling the silent maid, I'm inclined to believe him.

We reach the end, and Innes presses his palm carefully against the door to the kitchen. He dips his head enough for me also to peer through the crack in the door, so we can both see the room beyond.

All is silent, but after a moment, Lennox comes into view. She must have left Calder to his own devices, as there's no indication that anyone else is in the room with her. Innes allows the door to open a few more inches so we can see Lennox make her choice of object. I'm not surprised to see she's chosen a silver knife. She is half-turned away when suddenly the oven bursts into life. A roar of flame shoots out from the stone mouth, and Lennox hops backward, the knife clattering to the floor.

A delicate laugh winds through the air, and Lennox scowls just as Breagha appears to tap a red ribbon onto the space above her heart. 'You're dead,' Breagha says, delighted.

'How did she do that?' I whisper to Innes, meaning both the trick with the oven and the uncanny way she seemed to materialise out of nowhere.

'She knows the house best.' Innes shrinks back from the door, and I follow his lead. He holds a hand up, commanding silence. Eventually, he seems satisfied and relaxes. He taps the door open with his foot and steps into the kitchen.

'We're even, then,' I say, referring to the favour Innes claimed I owed him after he led me from the forest.

Innes snorts. 'I didn't ask for your help.'

'But you needed it.'

'Not my problem, bone diver,' he says, though at the same time he hands me a silver teaspoon. 'I'll collect when I'm ready.' With that, he pockets his own teaspoon and leaves the kitchen the way we came. I give him a couple of beats before I leave, too, though I don't use the dark passage. Something about it leaves my skin tingling.

The room I fear the most, of course, I leave for last. Part of me hopes Breagha will catch me before I need to find it, but I manage to steal an object from the drawing room without incident. There is only one room left on the map. Lady Erskine's bedroom. This time, I need the map to find my way. I've not been to this part of the house yet, and I realise when I find the wing in which the room resides why my instincts have told me to stay away.

The air that sighs down the corridor is noticeably colder and heavy with damp, as if the haar rolls down the length of it.

At the far end is a door I recognise.

I freeze, confused. How could I recognise it? I've not been here before.

My skin itches, my neck tingles. The nightmare. A cold hand in mine, leading me through the house. This was the door in my dream on my first night here. I recognise its mother-of-pearl sheen.

With blood roaring in my ears, I walk down the hall and because I have a Sealgair sensibility when it comes to approaching something that frightens me, I burst right through the door without allowing hesitation to creep in.

The room is dark, the curtains drawn. Blessedly, one of them isn't closed completely and I see the rain streaking down the window. Wind makes the curtains shiver. Outside looks miserable, but what I'd give to be out there instead of here.

There is nothing special about the room, but I am itching to bolt out of here. The feeling of wrongness is so strong, I can nearly taste it. It tastes like blood. Then again, so does the sea.

I need to find a small object, something that will not be missed. Nothing rests atop the chest of drawers or on the nightstand beside the bed. I peer under the bed, but that, too, is bare. A drawer, then. I slide the first drawer open, expecting to find it filled with clothing, as mine is. There is only one thing inside, something larger than my hand, and because it's not something easily taken, I shut the drawer without giving it more than a quick glance. But I stop with my fingers still on the drawer pull.

Slowly this time, I pull the drawer open again. A stone mortar and pestle sit inside. The pestle rolls as the drawer slides open, scattering something pale across the wood. I swipe a finger through the mortar. A white powder coats my finger. I raise it close to my eyes to see it better, but there is nothing more to see. A white powder. It could be anything, but I know what it must be. Bone dust. Lady Erskine is grinding the bones.

Why?

I think of the seal bones on the windowsill at home, of the small bone Dad gave to Fie when his own father wasn't talking to him. Fie still has that bone. He even keeps it in his pocket most days. I remember seeing him spinning it around in his fingers sometimes. My grandmother and my father believe that certain bones bring luck or balance or health. But I've never known them to grind the bones into powder. What could possibly be the use of that?

There is no time to investigate further. The doorknob twists. I throw myself onto the floor and scramble under the bed. It's a tight fit, and my hair catches on skelfs poking out from the bedframe. I am just tucking myself further beneath the bed when I see the door open. Lady Erskine's dark gown drags across the floor, trailing a silvered streak of water as she moves into the room. With my own breath held, I can hear her laboured breathing. It's such an unexpected sound that it takes me longer than it ought to realise what it means – Lady Erskine is holding in sobs. She has shown such little emotion in all our interactions, and I had simply thought she was a woman who never cried. Yet clearly she is agitated now; her movements are jerky and unpredictable. At first she seems set on something, striding across the room, but she turns back halfway towards the door, kicking the hem of her dress aside to reveal a long gash down the length of her shin. It is smeared with blood, which rolls down in beads that drip onto her ankle.

She turns and rushes towards the chest of drawers, and I am certain she has found me out, that she has noticed the door is not all the way closed, but instead of deftly swiping aside the bed skirt and discovering me, she yanks the drawer open. With a howl, she throws the stone mortar against the ground. It smashes apart, cracking in two and sending shards of pale stone scattering in all directions. A sharp piece knocks against my arm, making me flinch.

'It's not enough,' she says, her voice cracking with emotion. She stops to stand over the largest piece of mortar, and I'm afraid she will bend down to pick it up. Instead, I hear her suck in a long breath and, although I cannot see more than her legs, I imagine her composing herself. 'I need more.' Her voice is back to its usual cool tone. As she turns away, the train of her dress knocks aside the mortar. She disappears from view, and I hear the opening and closing of the bathroom door and a minute later the rush of water filling the tub.

I snatch up the piece of mortar that has landed beside me and drag myself out from under the bed. The water rushing through the taps is loud enough to cover the sound of my movements as I hurry to the door. Only when it is safely closed behind me do I take a proper breath.

More *what*? I wonder, but of course I know. It can only be one thing, can't it?

More bones. Lady Erskine needs more bones.

I am so absorbed in this thought that I do not hear Breagha until she is already tapping me on the shoulder.

'You're dead,' she says brightly as she presses a red ribbon against my thundering heart.

25

THE NEXT MORNING, I wake to the scent of rot. The last remnants of a dream linger, and there is a moment where I am uncertain if the scent is real or only the dying remains of something I've spun in my mind. I open my eyes, stare at the ceiling and let the dream fade. I suck in a deep breath and immediately regret it. The scent is very much from the real world. Holding my breath, I go to the window. Nothing there of note, only the unkept estate and the edge of pine forest.

I wonder where the Erskines are, and if they have convened yet about the result of yesterday afternoon's game. Breagha killed me, of course, but she killed everyone (so she triumphantly told me), and I was the last to die, the only one to sneak an object from Lady Erskine's room. No one asked me to return the objects I found, so I have the shard still, hidden in my own drawer, making me wonder.

Yesterday seems like ages ago, and now here is something else making my instincts flare. The scent of rot. It's a natural scent, not necessarily uncommon on the shore, but something feels wrong about it.

I breathe through my mouth as I move through the corridors, but the taste of it is worse than the smell. When I walk down the front steps of Erskine Manor, I try to imagine the caves sprawling beneath the surface. A desire thrums through me to sink into cold water, submerge myself into darkness. But I cannot for long lose myself in memories of my previous dives because the stench is even stronger outside.

Instinctively, I turn my face towards the sea. A breeze lifts my hair. Cool and northerly and suffused with the stink of death. The wind carries the smell from the sea, and I can taste it, thick as pea soup.

I press my knuckles against my nose and clomp reluctantly towards the cliff edge. On the way, I spot a little dark shape flitting between gorse bushes, making them shiver.

'Good morning, you,' I say, bending to give Dratsie a scratch on her head. 'Where's that smell coming from?' I ask her. 'Do you know?'

In reply, she scampers away, seemingly dropping right off the cliff face, but as I get closer, I spy her, nosing around the rocks in a dip at the cliff edge. Beside me, gorse bushes shake in the breeze. They are in full summer bloom with bold yellow flowers that normally would suffuse the air with a nutty scent, but today I cannot smell anything but what the wind carries from the shore.

I look down at the rocks and sand below and know immediately what is causing the stench.

Black kelp covers the sand where the tide has drawn back. Massive piles of it rise up in uneven clumps, and you can see where the sea has tried to pull it back but has failed. Long, glistening strips of it lie along the sand closest to the water, and the further from the sea's edge the thicker the layer of kelp becomes, growing into the heaps that press against the rocks. Birds swirl in eddies above the piles of seaweed, and even more trot across the rubbery tendrils, plucking cockles and muscles that remain caught among the flora.

I've never seen such a thing, such a massive collection of kelp. There was a storm last night, but I didn't think it was as powerful as this. Worry tugs at my mind. Apart from the seaweed, there is no other indication of a major storm. Usually, I'd expect the shore to be littered with washed-up branches, even tree trunks, smoothed by the waves.

Dratsie scurries out from a gorse bush, and I follow her along the cliff's edge. My gaze flits from the sea to the shore to the flat grass beneath my feet. I am looking for something but I'm unsure what exactly – a way to explain the worry twisting in my gut.

From over the edge of the cliff, I spot a groyne made of wood dark with age. It looks like any of the several groynes stretched along the coast that keep the shore in some sort of order. This one, though, is broken, the tip of it crumpled, like a giant took it in its fist. My gaze darts over it and away, but then I stop and turn to look at it again. Around the broken end of the groyne, the waves criss-cross, toss white crests into the sky before melting into one another. A broken groyne could explain the mass of kelp further along the shore. It would mean a change in the wave pattern, and even a small change on the shore can have huge repercussions.

I stare at the spikes of wood as if it were a puzzle. What is so strange about a broken groyne? Why does the sight of it leave my skin prickling?

Then I notice the gorse bush closest to the edge of the cliff. It's half-torn from the earth with its roots exposed and clinging to the ground for dear life. Beside it, the ground is disturbed. I crouch down and run my fingers over the soft grooves in the earth – five deep cuts into the mud, evenly spaced. I place my hand atop it, and the grooves line up near perfectly. It is impossible not to imagine someone, something, clawing their way up the cliff, dragging themselves onto the Erskine estate. Yet, of course, that's impossible. No one could climb such a sheer cliff.

I rise slowly, hoping reason will soon settle over me and burn away the prickling feeling that hops across my skin.

This far down the shore, I can see a line in the sea where dark water meets light. Before me, a dark stain blooms across the water. These are the Erskine waters, where no one dares go for fear the old superstitions are true. Fishermen love their superstitions, they live and breathe by them, and though ridiculous they may sound to anyone not accustomed to staking their life and livelihood on the fickle sea, I always knew there was a kernel of truth in every strange belief. From where I'm standing on the clifftop, I can see why we are afraid of the Erskine waters. Not only are they dark, rich as red wine, but they are rougher, too, and mist hovers in places. I look at those waters and think of the night I lost my knife – a flash of pale skin curving beneath the water – and I shake my head. My cheeks are clammy from the sea breeze. I press my palms against them and wonder what I am doing here. Was Fie right? Was I wrong to come here?

Something is in the sea, disrupting its balance, and I've left my mother to go out across it every day, pushing further and further to hunt enough seals to get us through the winter.

But then – I left them eight years ago, didn't I? When the curse took my future, all planned out before me like every Sealgair's. At least here I am working towards something, enough money to help us for months. If I can secure that, then I will feel worthy to go home.

What is the cause of the darkened Erskine waters? An algae bloom, perhaps, caught in a current that twists a certain way. There is a natural reason, though I'm not sure we'll ever know it. The storyteller in me imagines that the water is darkened with blood, that the foundations of Erskine Manor are built on bones, and these bleed black into the tide, staining the sea. I look towards the house. Every house has a history, doesn't it, but why is Erskine Manor's estate pocketed with sea caves, and why are these caves littered with bones? Where have they come from? The sea, maybe, because the sea likes to give up her dead when it pleases her.

'I don't understand,' I say aloud, though I've lost sight of Dratsie now, and I may as well be speaking to myself. Something *wrong* is in the sea. The thought chills me. The sea is everything to me, to my family, to everyone who lives along the shore. You would never call the sea predictable, but there is a certain sort of balance the sea maintains. It is the greatest force here, and if anything should tip the balance, warp the order of things, I worry what might happen. I stare long at the horizon, as if I might catch a glimpse of a boat. My family's boat.

Nothing breaks the silver-blue of the water.

26

LADY ERSKINE IS WAITING for me on the front steps of the house. She holds her arms behind her back and stares in the direction of the sea. When I come plodding into view, she doesn't react. Doesn't raise her arm in greeting, even after I do. She seems unaffected by the stench, while I'm still breathing through my mouth and trying to ignore the taste coating my tongue.

'Another dive,' she says by way of greeting.

'Aye,' I say, feeling stupid and provincial as soon as the word leaves my lips. Her only response is to step down onto the path and brush past me.

We skirt around the garden walls, and I manage to catch sight of the stone door, still open. The pines are still obscuring the view inside.

The forest sighs cool air, a relief from the stench of the rotting seaweed still blowing in from the shore. The breeze lifts my hair, yet somehow Lady Erskine's clothing is unmoved, as if she were encased in glass. I'm not surprised when she leads me into the forest. I do hope this time she doesn't leave me to fend for myself on the return. I'm not keen on owing Innes any more favours.

The forest, as usual, is disorienting. I swear the undergrowth is thicker than it was a day ago, but this is normal near Midsummer. Every year, the longest day sneaks up on me. The winters are so dark, so long, and it seems ages before the trees are in bloom. Every year, I blink and almost miss it – the weeks before Midsummer when the nights are slow to arrive and the earth bursts with green. Then, winter seems like a bad dream, a nightmare that never really happened. When the leaves on the trees are so full, and the flowers are blooming, it's hard to imagine everything stripped and darkened.

The pool is unique in the way they all are. It is hidden, snug among the pines, covered in a layer of needles and surrounded by stone marked by human hands. Looking from where I stand, it's impossible to tell how deep it is, but surely it's as deep as all the others. Lady Erskine doesn't bother to lift her skirts as she bends towards the water. She dips her fingers into the pool, and her lips move, whispering something, but as usual I cannot make out what she says.

The breeze quickens, raising the hair on my arms at its chill. I realise the stench from the sea is gone, and, oddly, it makes me afraid. The sea seems so far away now.

'Go on,' Lady Erskine says, as she steps away from the pool's edge.

I nod at her and undress and waste no time lowering myself directly into the water. Submerging yourself in cold water isn't the time for contemplation. I can do that sort of thinking when my fingers are numb.

The pool proves itself to be deep. Not as narrow as the others, but the darkness here is thicker, like it's painted on. The deeper I dive, the thicker the darkness, but only a few moments after the last light from above fades away, a new light appears. A pale blue luminescence fills the water. The rocks around me glow softly at first but more strongly the deeper I go. In all my dives on this shore, I have never seen such a thing. It's enchanting, and I wish I had breath enough to enjoy it. But I know the bone will be much deeper and already my lungs strain.

A bit deeper and the blue glow fades away. My impulse is to panic, but I don't let fear get the best of me. An instinct makes me close my eyes, and part of me thinks I may be going mad, but another part of me knows this is right – it is too dark to see this deep in the pool and with my eyes closed I unlock my other senses. Unexpectedly I think of my dream from not long ago, of the hand that led me through the corridors of Erskine Manor. My own hand feels guided, as my fingers roam across the rocks, dipping into the nooks and crannies.

I'm wasting time. There's nothing here. I haven't even reached the bottom of the pool, where bones are most likely to lie. But then I find something. Long and narrow. Lighter than stone and heavier than a branch of driftwood. As I wrap my fingers around it, I worry they are too numb to hold it, and I have a terrifying image of the bone slipping from my grasp, falling to the unreachable depths of the pool. But I manage to hold onto it. When I open my eyes, I see the pale shape of the bone in my fingers. A glow softens the shadows, just enough to take the edge off them. It's the same sort of glow that suffuses the midnight sky at Midsummer. I'm unsure where it's coming from, but I'm grateful for it.

I've got the bone, so I should start propelling myself to the surface. I've been in the water for at least a minute, judging by the stale feeling in my chest, and staying much longer is risky without reason. But in the new hazy light, I see something I hadn't before: *A*.

The letter is unmistakeable, carved into the rock. I brush my hand over it, moving aside the algae that clings to the wall, and more letters appear. I feel them beneath my fingertips.

Artair.

I know that name. How do I know that name?

Artair, the wall says back silently, and I remember. A young dark-haired man holding a silver comb, his eyes pools of ink. The young Erskine from the portrait hall.

My body reacts on its own accord, taking over because my useless brain is obviously not getting the signals. I'm running out of air. Instantly, I ball my hand into a fist so tightly that my nails bite into my palm. I turn and begin the swim up towards the light above.

I'm delirious from lack of breath, I think, as I rush upward through the water. Why is a name carved into the wall of the pool? What does it mean?

Soft sounds become harsh as a I break the surface. I tread water, strangely reluctant to leave the pool. Lady Erskine is where I left her, standing beside the pool with the train of her dress partially in the water, the fabric floating like lily pads, shifting as I make ripples with my movements.

'What did you find?' she says.

My fist is still beneath the surface. When I drag my hand from the water, I feel resistance, as if the bone itself is reluctant to meet the air.

I hold the bone up so she can see it. Both of us stare at it. It's the largest bone I've found. Not a scrunched vertebrae or a narrow rib, but a long yellow-white bone knobbed at both ends. My mind flits through the anatomy of a seal, thinking, thinking, which bone is this?

Lady Erskine takes the bone from my fingers even before I've hauled myself out of the pool.

'Ah, Artair,' she says, turning the bone in her fingers, pressing it against her cheek.

That name again.

What bone is this? I take a seal apart in my mind. Skin off first, blubber and muscle next. Then the bones, cleaned, boiled, white. I lay them out in my mind just as I've seen them laid out before, drying in the grass of our garden, warming in the sun. None of those bones in my mind's eye look enough like the one in Lady Erskine's fingers. A seal does not have a bone that long. A bone that makes me think of a narrow wrist. An arm up to an elbow.

'Thank you, my dear,' she whispers. Not to me, I am certain. To the bone she is tucking into her skirts. The bone. Recognition catches in my chest. It is not a seal bone.

The bone belongs to a human. I know now what the pools are. They are tombs.

27

I REALISE THE BONES MATTER. When I first arrived here, I thought asking no questions might be easy enough. I thought, what's the harm in diving for bones? Any creature involved is already dead. But Lady Erskine is not looking for the bones of creatures. The last bone was human, and while the others undoubtably belonged to seals, I cannot shake the unease I felt when holding that bone. And the name. Artair. When I recall Lady Erskine whispering that name, I think of each letter etched into the plaque nailed to the silver frame of the picture of the young man, one of the striking young Erskines whose faces peer at anyone walking down the length of the portrait hall. I am certain she said Artair, and now as I lie in bed, staring at the water stain on the ceiling, all I can think of is the young man's glistening gaze.

Why does Lady Erskine need the bones of dead Erskines? What would my father say? What would Fie?

I try to imagine a conversation with each of them, and instead I am pulled into an old memory, an unexpected one.

My mother's hands were rough from handling a knife and a spear. I remember that first of all – she had one hand on my arm, the other wrapped around my fingers as she helped me hold the spear upright.

'Are you sure this is the weapon you want?' my mother asked.

The question made me second-guess myself, and it made me angry. "Course it is,' I said. I first held a spear when I was eight years old and because I was ten, I thought I was already an expert. I resented her rough palms on my knuckles, her warm breath across my cheek, her scent – coffee and the musk of seal fur. I thought I didn't need her help. I was better with the spear than a club, and my mother's question made me indignant. I knew she would have chosen a club. That was her weapon. I wanted to be different from her, even though we were already so different.

'Make the kill, then,' she said. She took her hands away. 'If you're ready.' My anger brewed, hot enough to burn away the sense of disappointment and the twinge of emptiness.

I tried to make the kill, but a kill made in anger is rarely a good one. Only once ever have I done such a thing – tried to kill a living thing while my fingers were shaky with emotion. I won't forget what happened when I let that spear go. It sliced through the air, and it hit the target, but not as I had hoped. Aim for the heart or the head, and I hit neither. The seal writhed in pain, swinging its heavy body back and forth, trying to dislodge the spear. I froze. I panicked, and all I could do was stand there and watch.

Mum moved swiftly.

'Always trust your instincts.' She said this the moment she clubbed the seal to death. She always did it swiftly, in a single blow. Dad prefers a spear because he likes to hunt from the boat, but Mum always kills with the club if she has the chance.

The seal stopped moving. Mum put her foot on its belly and yanked my spear from its body. The rocks were so dark, already slick with seawater, that the blood coating them looked as harmless as water.

'Did your instincts tell you to throw the spear, Kier?' she asked. 'Or was it your pride?'

I took the spear from her. The sight of the dying seal had made my anger go stale, but I was still indignant and – worse – embarrassed. I wondered if she would tell Dad what happened and what he would think of me when he heard.

'No,' I said, not really answering her question, but she knew what I meant.

'Your instincts are a gift,' she said. 'A richer heirloom than even your knife. The knife kills but your instincts keep you alive.'

Always trust your instincts. That's what my mother taught me, and what she'd tell me now if she were here. Faintly, I find myself wishing she were.

Lady Erskine wants the bones for something, and every instinct in my own bones is telling me to stop looking for them, stop helping her, because I'm afraid of what that something is.

Mum would tell me not to ignore the misgiving I felt at holding that bone, not to run from Artair's lingering gaze.

Except she doesn't know what I have to lose. She doesn't know what it's like to feel powerless.

There is a blue glow around the curtains, suggesting the weather has shifted. I move directly to the window and push aside the curtains just enough to see out. A mist lays across the ground. Thick spools of it cling to the forest edge and in the dips of the hillocks that pockmark the estate. I realise, for the first time, that if I wanted to leave, I'm not sure I'd know how to. If I walked long enough, eventually I'd find my way through the forest, but I remember the way the pines seemed to narrow around me as I walked, how I continued to make the same turnings again and again. With the mist thick on the ground, as it is today, I'm not sure I'd make it through the forest without Innes' help.

I reach for the curtains, trying my best to close that thought with it, but freeze when I notice a stroke of white on the windowsill outside. Another hawthorn branch. I'm amazed it hasn't blown away. When I've got it safely in my fingers, something else makes me stop again, and this time my heart leaps into my mouth. At the edge of the forest, a glint of silver. Breagha's cane lies in a bed of pine needles just where the forest rises up.

The sight of it, discarded, makes me hot with worry. Something is wrong, and this is no uncertain instinct about bones and watery tombs. This is real and tangible and *right now* – Breagha is in danger.

Like the Sealgair I am, I don't hesitate.

28

MY GRIP ON MY KNIFE is firm, but my palm is slick with sweat. I move swiftly between the trees, my calves burning, my heart thudding. The forest is silent around me. My footfalls disturb the pine needles and the undergrowth, and blood beats against my skull with every step. I'm foolishly unaware of everything around me, as the forest flashes by. I don't make note of the turnings, the unique stones that could serve as markers. I just dash in the direction that feels right.

Scraps of mist float in the underbrush, sometimes lifting among the lower branches of the pines. Instinctively, I avoid them. The thought of walking through the cold, white wisps makes me dizzy.

Archie had said there was a mist that curled in from the sea.

My mother's rough hands come to mind again, and I think of my spear the moment before I threw it the first time I tried to kill in anger. That memory should have been a warning. Nothing is done well when you've lost grip of your emotions. And when I saw Breagha's cane, I ran into the forest without sense or plan, driven completely by a gut feeling. It's still here, churning and building on itself, the meeting of weeks of worry. Something is wrong.

My back is clammy with sweat. I keep walking, and for a while my fear for Breagha fuels me enough to let me keep up my pace. But I cannot do so for much longer, and when I see a statue I am certain I have seen before, I come up short. I suddenly cannot imagine taking another step. The wind is knocked right out of me.

Because this is not the first time the forest has swallowed me up, and I should know better. I should have known the forest wouldn't let me find her so easily.

The statue is a memorable one, not one I'd quickly forget. A man is submerged waist-deep in the dirt with nettles growing around his chin. Half his face is sloughed away, and the other half is so worn that what remains looks skeletal. It's difficult to say, but it seems he once had his arm outstretched, reaching for the sky as if trying to save himself from being swallowed up.

As I am. Swallowed up by this forest. I always thought it a possibility I might drown, given how much time I spend in the water. But I never thought I'd drown this way, sucked into a labyrinth of pines. This is worse, I think. Much worse than drowning in the water. There, at least, the calm comes eventually. Here, now, as I stare at the statue I've seen before, my heart whacks around my chest and this is the panic I'm usually so good at swallowing down – I am frozen.

'Where is she?' I say. I recoil as my palm meets the rough bark of a tree; I didn't realise I had reached out. My fingers are sticky with sap, and I feel ill, dizzy. I look around for mist and expect it to be rising among the undergrowth. There is no mist. Only the black earth beneath and the layer of pine needles that softens the sounds. A magpie chirps, and I flinch.

'A little help here?' I say to the bird, which seems to understand because it blinks each eye at me before hopping deeper into the forest. One of Calder's birds, I'm hoping, though I'm not yet sure how I feel about all that.

The forest doesn't give me much choice, so I sheathe my knife, and I follow.

The ruins trip me up, quite literally. I stumble over a half-buried stone, so small and worn, it's impossible to know what it once belonged to. But it's clearly not a natural feature of the forest, and, suddenly, I see what must have been visible for a while now if I'd known to look. More dark stones erupting from the earth, forming the corner of long-gone foundations. Statues, made of the same dark stone, with worn-away faces, leaning forlornly into the nearby trees. And, impressively, a staircase.

Carved from stone, flanked by two stone banisters and topped with an archway, the staircase anticipates something grand. The stone blooms with pale green lichen, and a crack bisects the archway – a threat, a deadly promise. It feels both expected and strange to take the stairs. A staircase is meant to be walked on. But a staircase without its walls – that feels wrong. I climb the steps and try to ignore the instinct to take up my knife.

The grand anticipation of the archway is wasted. It frames only more pine trees and scraps of grey sky. Nothing – except if I look more closely, I can see a pool. Mirror-still and black, covered in a fine layer of pine needles. Nearly invisible if you're not looking for it. But I knew to look for it, guessed by the way the other pools have always been surrounded by some old stone structure. Never anything as bold as the staircase, but there has been a pattern there. Again, I think of the latest bone. The human bone that Lady Erskine held against her cheek with an affection she seems to reserve only for the dead.

A disruption of the pool's pristine calm catches me completely off guard. A white hand stretches upward from the pool's centre, reaching with fingers kinked as if trying to grasp something, trying to hold tight to something that isn't there. It slips beneath the surface just as quickly as it appeared, and the pine needles shift lazily to cover up the dark space where the hand was, so that in a moment I'm standing there, heart stone-hard in my mouth, uncertain if I'd really seen what I'd seen. A ringing in my ears sounds too much like singing, like the ghost of a song, and I know if I wait here any longer and try to parse reality, I might lose it completely.

So I bound off the high platform of the staircase, making stairs out of the ruins below, even grasping the arm of a headless statue, as if it were a friend helping me down. And I run to the pool, kicking off my boots and shucking off my jacket all at once. The hand does not appear again, but I am certain, terribly certain, that I see a curtain of dark hair framing a face I recognise just beneath the surface. Breagha. She looks so much like she did when I saw her in the bath, as far as I can tell beyond the wavering of the water and the shifting of pine needles, with her eyes closed and a restrained yearning etched across her features. She is like a ghost just beneath the surface, there and gone, sinking out of sight, but I'm done hesitating.

I step back, suck in a deep breath, and I dive.

29

COLD. DARK. DISORIENTATION. All expected, and I'm prepared because of course I'm prepared. Because I've done this so many times, launch myself into unknown waters, that I do not panic. Even when the water fails to brighten, my eyes fail to the adjust to its darkness. As if somehow the meagre light from beyond the pines above cannot penetrate this particular pool. The water seems to be made of shadow. I shuck off the uneasy feeling and accept the situation – I can hardly see, and Breagha has sunk out of sight already, deeper into the murk, and I have no idea how deep this pool is, but surely it is as deep as all the others I've dived into, connecting eventually to a sea cave that must wind its way out to sea.

I see a pale streak that might be a hand, reaching still, and it's all I need. I propel myself as quickly as I can in its direction. With the dark water around me and Breagha still not in sight, it's easy to let the urgency unspool into fear. I wish I could take a breath to calm myself, but instead I do what I always do when I feel panic bubbling up during a dive. I look at my hands, watch their movements, think only of the next stroke through the water, then the next, the next.

I start to count the strokes. Seven before I finally see the outline of a person. I clamp my lips shut to keep from exclaiming in joy. I've found her.

The figure moves suddenly, too fast, right towards me. No curtain of dark hair. No pale limbs. But the large, black eyes of a seal, white whiskers, spotted fur that gleams even in the heavy darkness of the water.

The seal swims a circle around me, and I almost laugh.

Seals have always been this way with my family, more than anyone else in the village. They swim with us, bob their heads from the water when our boat passes by. They never seem afraid, even after we slaughter their friends. My father says Sealgairs have a special way with seals, that we've always had it, and it's what makes us such good killers, especially when we use our flute.

This seal seems as friendly as all the others, and the familiarity of being in the presence of seals again is so comforting that I almost forget the strangeness of it all. We are not in the sea. We are in a dark, deep pool in a pine forest. This is no place for a seal.

The bulk of the seal comes towards me, and I reel back in surprise. It comes close enough to brush against my shoulder and, as I reach out my hand to touch it, I see a long, jagged scar in its side, long since healed over and puckered pale.

My fingers meet the soft hide of the seal, and a memory takes me by the throat. I feel it all as if I were there again, standing on the boat alone, still thrumming with anger, as the knife shoots from my fingers towards the dark shape in the water that I am certain is a seal. It must be a seal, it must be a seal, it *must be* but why do I see a pale curve of a shoulder disappearing beneath the wine-dark water? Why, when I run to the edge of the boat and stare frantically into the water, am I convinced I see a woman sinking beneath the waves?

I shut my eyes and open them again, hoping to banish the memory, but it is still there, swirling around me. Everything else is swallowed by black. I hold out my hands. My numb hands. I hold them out, but I cannot see them. I cannot see my fingers as I hold them close to my face.

The darkness creeps in from all sides, chewing away at my vision, which erupts momentarily into a smattering of stars before winking out completely, shuttering into an inky black.

30

I AM NO LONGER IN THE WATER. I feel the ground beneath my back, and I realise I am gulping in air that smells of pine and earth, and my fingers are clawing into soft fabric. Silk. A clump of wet hair sticks to my cheek. It isn't mine.

When I open my eyes, Breagha is staring down at me, her face close enough to mine that her hair curtains my face. She is saying my name, and I am watching her lips, but her voice sounds distant. Water leaks of out my ears as I turn my head, and I can feel the pine needles sticking to me everywhere. I want to get up and physically shake myself off, flicking away any lingering remains of the shadows. But Breagha is here, so close, leaning over me, saying my name. She who didn't need saving, after all.

'I'm fine,' I tell her because she looks so distraught. I have never seen her this way, peeled back and vulnerable. My voice sounds distant; my ears are still thick with water.

Her eyes are wide, and she looks unconvinced as she presses her palm against my cheek. The words *I'm fine* don't make it past my lips again. Am I fine? Physically, perhaps, though I'll have to take stock once I can feel my toes again, but that memory, the way it choked me … it could have killed me. I could have drowned.

Breagha eventually sits back, giving me space to sit up on my elbows. Now able to see more than just what's right in front of me, I notice the pelt draped over her shoulders. It is not a jacket or a finished piece of clothing of any sort. I can tell by its ragged edges, and the smell – the thick, musky scent of untreated sealskin. Even with hardly any light making its way past the pine canopy above, the pelt glistens and glimmers.

'It's beautiful,' I say, ever the seal killers' daughter. I sit up further and brush my fingertips against the pelt. Breagha flinches, so I pull away, feeling uncomfortable. But I cannot stop staring at it. Even my own pelt is not as beautiful as this.

In reply, Breagha pulls the pelt from her shoulders. She holds it out with two hands. I catch her gaze for a moment to be certain before running my fingers over the skin. The centre, where the spine of the seal should run, is speckled in darker black spots. I follow the length of it with my fingers. A section of it is puckered, spider-web lines of white where the hair grows differently. A scar. I glance up. 'Where did you get this pelt?'

Breagha watches intently as my fingers move. Her lips are parted, but she does not speak right away.

'I stole it from my mother,' Breagha says after a long moment. Gently, she takes the pelt from my fingers. I want to resist. I want to feel it some more, but her movements are firm. 'I stole it,' she continues. 'But she stole it from me first.'

In a swift movement, Breagha twists the pelt and settles it back over her shoulders. I watch her eyes, which grow darker, wider, and I sense more than just her eyes changing but something else about her – something I cannot see. Though the sea is beyond the pine forest, beyond the drop of the cliffs, I feel it here with me, in this grove. That is what is changed about her – she feels like the sea, and I think of water all around me, the light from above, that calm, radiant stillness laced with death and fear and ambivalence, everything the sea is. Beauty with a depth to it that does not even hint at what it is capable of because you know, because you've seen it for yourself, how it will smash boats against rocks and drag people into rips, and so it glitters and shines with a beauty that could change in any moment. That is what the sea feels like, and all that I feel looking at Breagha now, as she dips her eyes, our gaze finally breaking, and tugs the sealskin to spread evenly across her shoulders.

Breagha Erskine as I know her is gone. Before me is not a young woman in a lovely evening gown with a silver-topped cane gripped lightly in her fingers. Before me is a beautiful silver-grey seal speckled with black, a pale scar on its side, staring at me with eyes I've seen before – huge, black, yearning. The seal twists its head to look at the pool, and it does not look back at me as it moves swiftly into the water.

I scramble to the pool's edge and look down into it. The shadow of the seal – of Breagha, of *Breagha?* – is gone within a moment, and the only evidence she was there are the circles of ripples atop the water's surface.

A flurry of pine needles falls from above. I look up and around and I have to remind myself that this is real. All of this is real.

We village people have always spun our stories about the Erskines. They are monsters, we said. Girls with glass skin, with sharp teeth, with long tails. We did not know them, so we thought the worst.

We were wrong. Of course we were wrong.

The Erskines are not monsters.

They are selkies.

31

The story of the selkie is my father's favourite. He likes it for all the reasons I don't – because it is a romance of sorts, and the girl leaves the boy for the sea. An act, I think, anyone in my family would do if given the chance.

The story starts with a boy on the shore, who discovers a beautiful girl dancing in the moonlight. He watches her, eventually working up the nerve to speak to her, but as soon as she sees him, she runs away. The next evening, with the moon still shining bright overhead, the boy looks for the girl on the shore. Again, he finds her dancing as the waves lap against her ankles. She runs away again, and the boy walks the shore alone, wondering if she will ever speak with him. He wants to tell her not to worry, that he is an honest fisherman, a hard worker, and he could give her everything she could ever need. He is about to turn away home when he sees something dark caught in the rocks. A sealskin, strangely warm. Thinking he ought not waste it, he takes the skin home with him. The next evening, with the moon just a bit smaller, shining a bit less brightly, he returns to the shore. This time, he sees the girl, but she is not dancing. She is weeping silently among the rocks. This time, she does not run away when he approaches. He asks why she is crying, and she explains that she has lost something very valuable to her and that without it, she will never be happy.

As soon as she says it, the boy is struck with a sudden certainty. The sealskin belongs to the girl, and if he returned it to her, he would never see her again. So he does not give the girl her sealskin. Instead, he offers her a warm bed to sleep in and breakfast the next morning, and eventually she accepts his offer of marriage, and they are something almost like happy.

But one day the boy leaves to fish and is caught in a storm, delaying his return. The girl watches the sea churn against the rocks, and a hunger blooms within her. Propelled by a sudden, frantic urgency, she searches the house from eaves to cellar and before the boy returns, she finds it – her sealskin, tucked away beneath the floorboards. Though she loves the boy, she does not hesitate. She thinks of nothing but the sea, and she runs straight into it, straight into the wild, violent waves, and as she pulls the sealskin over her shoulders, the boy, just returning, sees a seal leap joyfully among the white crests and he knows he has lost her.

In the end, the girl loves the sea more than she loves the boy, and the boy is left alone on the shore, watching the girl he loves disappear beneath the waves.

The girl is a selkie. Sometimes a girl. Sometimes a seal. But always a creature of the sea. Always longing for its currents and its depths.

My father loves the story because he thinks the boy a fool. Nothing is stronger than the pull of the sea. Nothing.

But that is just a story.

And yet ...

For a long time, I am alone. The whole forest seems to hold its breath. Certainly, I am holding mine. The pool, somehow, must lead to the sea. Will she find the way, called to the sea like the selkie in my father's story? Or will she return? I'm wondering this, and I'm trying not to ask myself too many questions because I feel that is a slippery slope that might lead me to a place I cannot return from.

What is real?

What does it matter?

A dark head emerges from the pool. Breagha as I've known her swims to the pool's edge. She holds the stone lip with her pale fingers and looks up at me with eyes that for a moment are completely black. But she blinks, and once again her eyes are rimmed in white as a human's ought to be.

'Are you surprised, bone diver?' she asks.

'You're a selkie,' I say, and I want to laugh, but if I start, I think I might not stop. Breagha is a seal. She is a woman, too. Something in-between.

'We all are,' she says, pulling herself smoothly from the pool, taking the sealskin with her. Though it must be heavy, sodden as it is, she has no trouble lifting it. In fact, she looks as vibrant as I've ever seen her. There's a bit of colour in her cheeks, and her eyes are shining. 'But only I know.' Breagha does not take the skin from her shoulders. She strokes it reverently as she speaks. 'Mother has hidden all of our skins. I have found mine, quite by accident. That is how I know who I am.'

'Your brothers and Lennox ... they don't know they can turn into seals?' I ask. I would expect a selkie to know who they were, deep down in their bones. Certainly, it would be obvious, natural, something they just know without having to be told.

Breagha shakes her head. 'How would they know? She's taken their skins.'

'Why?'

'So we will not leave,' says Breagha. 'We cannot go far without our skins. Innes has tried. It never works.'

I shake my head. 'Why doesn't she want you to leave? Why does it matter?'

'Because she loves us so dearly.' Breagha smiles, and I see the animal in her. She pulls her knees up to her chest and rests her chin between them. 'Truly, I don't know. Until I met you, I thought she was protecting us.'

'From what?' I ask.

'People like you.' Breagha's cheeks redden and before I can think what this means, she grabs my hand. She squeezes once, quickly before letting go. A tingling sensation remains that I try my best to pretend isn't there. 'You are not a monster like Lennox believes,' she says triumphantly, like she has won a game. She holds up her hand to emphasise the point.

'Oh,' I say, blowing out a long breath.

She considers me with her unblinking gaze. 'You're not special, are you?'

I laugh. 'No, I suppose not.'

'Everyone is like you?' She takes my hand again and turns it around in hers.

'Aye. I'm not special, nor a monster.' I shrug. 'I can't kill at all.'

She nods. 'That's right.' She releases me and, reluctantly, I pull my hand back. With her chin still resting on her knees, she looks at me for a long moment. It feels like swimming, looking into her eyes. 'Lennox and Calder and Innes, they don't know who they really are, and I don't want them to know, not until I find all their skins. Because once they know, they will hear the sea calling, and they will not hear anything else.'

'Do you hear it?' I ask, my voice lower.

Breagha looks down into the pool. 'Every time I go under, I think I may not come back again.' She pauses, and I think she might leap into the pool and be gone forever. My body is tensed to stop her if she tries – but what could stop a selkie from returning to the sea? 'I don't trust myself anymore.'

'But you *are* resisting it,' I say, thinking of Breagha in the bathtub. The sea calls to her, and instead she remains in Erskine Manor, a place that feels *wrong*, like it was dredged from the sea years ago and yearns to go back but cannot – and the best it can do is weep salt tears.

'What does she want with the bones?' I ask.

Breagha stares at me, unblinking. 'I do not know,' she says slowly. 'I have always known her to be wanting something, but

I do not know what. To return to the sea, I think, but there is nothing stopping her, unless someone has stolen her skin, too, but who would have done that?' She hesitates.

'Your father?' I try, thinking of the story, the boy who stole his wife's skin and kept it hidden so she wouldn't leave.

'No,' she says too quickly. 'Not him. He is gone.'

I don't ask, but of course I want to. Who is her father? Where is he? Is he somewhere still on this estate?

I stare at the now-still surface of the pool. 'I don't ask questions. But I think ... they *are* human bones. The last one was. The others belonged to seals.'

'Selkies. Other Erskines.'

'Yes,' I say. Of course they are. 'The portraits in the hall. Who are they?'

Breagha lifts her shoulders. 'My family. I've never met them. All of them are dead.'

'Are they your aunts and uncles?'

She shrugs. 'Yes, I suppose. She never says.' Breagha presses her lips together, looking pleased. 'I am glad you know the truth.' She strokes her sealskin. 'With you, I feel like I am swimming.'

I start to pick the needles off my wet clothes, as an excuse to break her gaze, but my cheeks are hot with joy.

'Bone diver' – Breagha's voice is quiet now – 'will you help me? Will you look for their skins with me?'

I look at Breagha Erskine with her selkie skin wrapped around her shoulders, and for the first time since I arrived here, I don't feel alone. 'Yes.' Of course. I think I'd do anything she asked. Fie would be having a right laugh at me if he could see me now. I'd deserve it, for all the grief I gave him over Liv.

She shifts, letting the skin tumble from her shoulders, and she holds a hand out for me to help her rise. 'Good.' Her eyes are bright, mischievous. 'In return, I will lead you safely from the forest. It doesn't like you much.'

'Aye, all right,' I say, laughing, and take her by the arm.

32

I DON'T REMEMBER MY DREAMS, but when I wake the next morning, I taste blood. I sit up and press a finger against my lip. I've bitten my lip while I slept, and a streak of scarlet comes away on my skin, which still smells of the sea.

The sea. Breagha. I rub my eyes furiously to rid them of sleep. Yesterday ought to feel like a dream, what with all that happened, but I know what I saw. I know what is real, and all of it was – Breagha in the pool, the sealskin across her shoulders, her seal self. This place is just as strange as everyone in town has always imagined it to be and yet nothing at all like what they could imagine. Selkies. The Erskines are selkies and I have agreed to help Breagha find their missing skins.

The bedroom door creaks open, and I nearly jump straight into the air.

The maid stands in my doorway, dressed in a fresh dress with her pale hair pulled back taut. She stares right through me and steps into the room with a tray of tea things in her arms.

She is arranging the teapot, cup and plate of what looks like a slice of yesterday's cold meat pie onto the small table when I say, 'Good morning.' She does not look up. 'What's your name?'

Nothing, and then she is turning away and, without thinking, I grab her wrist. It is clammy and deathly cool, more like the skin of a fresh-dead corpse than a living woman. I only touch her for a moment. She shakes me off with a sharp twist of her wrist and bares her teeth. No sound escapes her lips – she is silent, as usual – but her expression for a moment is like an animal's. I remember the silvered edges of her face as she tilted her head back and bit the head off a toad.

My fingertips tingle at the memory of the maid's skin even after she's gone, and the scent of mud lingers in the air where she stood. I pour myself a cup of tea, but before I can take the first sip, there is a knock on the door.

'Come in,' I say, guessing it's the maid who must have forgotten something, though she has a tendency to barge right into my room without knocking.

When the door opens, Lady Erskine stands at the threshold. She does not come in but appraises me with an expression of mild distain. I must be a state compared to her, with my bedhead and crumpled pyjamas in stark contrast to her smooth hair and silk gown. Why does she always look like she is ready for an evening of cocktails and fancy ballrooms? Why bother dressing up when you never leave your old, damp house?

'I am requesting another dive,' she says, in what I think is her attempt at being polite. At least she isn't demanding it, though she may as well be. I'm not going to snuggle back up in bed and pretend she isn't here, though I'll be honest, I'm sorely tempted.

'I'll get changed,' I say, and she nods, stepping back into the hall and letting the door drift closed.

A few minutes later, I'm more presentably dressed and we're both stepping out onto the front steps of Erskine Manor. The haar is thick this morning. Even under the blanket, I felt the chill of it and am not surprised to see it lying thickly across the ground.

Without a word, Lady Erskine leads me into the forest.

The mist is thicker here, clinging to the ground and obscuring the undergrowth. It feels even more like winter in here, the mist giving the effect of a blanket of snow. The chill of it seeps into my boots.

As I watch Lady Erskine ahead of me, I wonder at the fluidity of her movements. There is no doubt that she is a selkie like her children. Being a selkie herself, knowing the sea's call, what reason would she have for denying her children their skins? Maybe I am making connections where there are none, but I think of the bones – the selkie bones – and wonder if these things are tied to one another. I wish I knew what Lady Erskine was using the bones for.

Though it's difficult for me to keep my bearings about me in the forest, I sense that we are going a way we have never gone before, deeper towards the forest's centre. More stone structures appear from between the trees, and these seem less worn than others I have seen. When Lady Erskine eventually stops, the place she takes me to is so clearly a tomb that a grave-yard chill whispers across my skin. The pool is demarcated with an unbroken stone border and, crouching beside it, fingers lightly dipping into a pool, is a stone figure. The head is bent towards the water and the outstretched hand is eager, wanting, reminding me of the gazes of all those dead Erskines in the portrait hall. Letters are inscribed in the stones around the pool, but most are too worn to make out.

'I have been here many times.' Lady Erskine brushes her fingertips against the bent neck of the stone figure. Her silk dress drips into the pool, shifting the pine needles that float atop. 'I am certain there is a bone remaining within. I need you to find it.'

So Lady Erskine has been collecting bones herself, perhaps long before my arrival. A silly flush of pride warms my chest at the thought that I am a more skilled diver than a selkie. Maybe, or maybe Lady Erskine just doesn't want to risk her own neck diving in the treacherous pools.

Let's see what this pool has in store for me.

As I sink into the water, I think of the monsters I once thought roamed the dark unknowable sea and imagine them winding circles beneath me. Dad told me, when I was a bairn, that it was right to fear the sea. That to fear it was as natural as breathing, and anyone who didn't fear it was either lying or completely mad. At the time, I was convinced my father was afraid of nothing. I thought, perfectly literally, that he could do anything, and that even the sea monsters were afraid of him and his spear.

I sink, remembering the look in his eyes the day I opened the shutters to reveal the sea. So I am afraid of the dive. Why shouldn't I be? I was afraid of the sea when I made my first kill. I was afraid of the spear when I first held it. So I sink and twist in the water and propel myself downwards.

The bones are always deeper. In fact, it seems that with each new dive, the bones become harder to find, testing my lungs to their limits. I try not to show any weakness to Lady Erskine, who I doubt would take kindly to it, but every time I lower myself into the cool water of a pool, I wonder if this will be the dive I finally come up empty-handed.

For this dive, I have no lantern. It's late morning, but even so the pool darkens quickly. Soon, I can hardly make out my hands in front of me.

Slowly, like the sun coming up on a winter morning, light fills the pool. It doesn't grow stronger than a soft glow, but I can see my hands now, and the edges of the pool, hewn rock carven with designs. The lights swirl through the water. They are the colour of the Merry Dancers, which can sometimes be seen on a dark, cloudless night, waving their flags of blue, purple and green across the sky.

The urge to kick myself back to the surface takes hold of me, but I ignore it. Go deeper. The bones are always deeper.

I scour the walls, but they are mostly void of nooks and crannies. Any one I come across, I inspect thoroughly, hoping I will find a bone tucked inside, just as I did during the dive in what I now think of as 'the mirror pool'.

The nooks are always empty, the walls mostly flat and bare. Down I go.

The bottom of the pool comes hazily into view. Much of part of the circular wall is crumbling away, and a pile of rubble spills out into the pool's centre. I only have enough breath to glance at it before I have to kick myself back to the surface, faster than I would like.

Lady Erskine regards me without a word when I emerge gasping from the pool.

'Not yet,' I say between breaths, and she hums acknowledgement but nothing more.

This time, I go down quickly, swimming straight for the rubble at the bottom. The rocks, made from the same stone as the manor house, are impossibly heavy, even beneath the water. It takes far too long to shift even one and by the time I do, revealing nothing, I am out of breath again.

I try three more times before I'm afraid my muscles will simply stop working and I won't have the strength to come up a fourth time.

'What are you doing?' Lady Erskine looms above me as I cling to the pool's edge and begin to haul myself up over the side.

'I need a break. And preferably a good lunch.' I try to find purchase on the stone, but Lady Erskine steps to the side, her legs and skirts blocking me from lifting fully out of the water.

'You need to find a bone.'

Shocked into silence, I look up at her. Her expression is stony and serious, the calm before a storm. Does she really expect me to keep diving? I haven't even had breakfast, the water is icy cold, and I think I barely have the strength to walk back to the manor house. I can't keep diving. To do so would be very risky.

'Go on,' she says.

I laugh, a strangled sound. 'No, I can't.'

Lady Erskine clicks her tongue. 'You will dive until you find a bone.'

'No, I will rest because I'm *only human*.'

She tries to block me again from leaving the pool, but I push past her.

'Return to the water, bone diver.' Her voice is raw, laced with something I have never heard before. Her expression is thunderous. She points to the pool. 'Find me a bone or I will make certain your father never hunts again.'

'What?' I croak out. She only smiles, and it's a blade to my heart. Is her threat a real one? Could she harm my father?

I do not doubt she *would*.

And that's enough to send me sliding back down into the water. I let the cold zap the anger right out of me; I am in no state to be driven by emotion. Lady Erskine has threatened my family, and I cannot take the risk her threat isn't a false one. I have seen this woman kill a fish and return it to life. She is a selkie, and perhaps something more.

There is only one thing to do – return to the rubble at the bottom and hope I can shift a stone fast enough, hope even harder there's a bone this time.

I reach the bottom, grateful for the lights, which still dance and shimmer around me. I have to act fast, but also I need to choose wisely. I will only have enough time to move one stone before I run out of breath.

As the Merry Dancers shift from indigo to blue, I see a glint of something among the rubble. I dart towards it, taking a tarnished chain into my fingers. I tug it, revealing a jewelled pendant. It seems the bodies are always left with an object of importance.

Too bad I'm looking for bones, not treasure.

I let the necklace slip through my fingers, but it's made my choice for me. I push hard against the stone its partially trapped beneath. It shifts, making a muted grinding noise. I put all my strength into shoving the stone away and am rewarded when it eventually moves, rolling to the side and causing a small avalanche of stones to tumble along with it.

That is when I see a welcome stroke of white.

A skull, a perfectly intact human skull grins at me from the gloom.

I never thought in all my life that I would hold a skull in my hands and feel such a surging of relief. Even with only one hand to propel myself upwards, I make good time, buoyed by my incredible find.

After I break the surface, I gently place the skull at the edge of the pool. Its yellowed surface glistens.

Lady Erskine laughs, a shocking sound in the gloomy forest.

'Ah, what a find.' She holds up the skull, resting in her palm, and stares into its empty eye sockets as if she wants to kiss its lipless mouth. 'You have done it, bone diver.' She looks at me as I climb out, the violence gone from her eyes, replaced with delight. Her cheeriness, as she stands there with a skull in her hand, makes me want to bolt.

Fear roots me to the spot as she approaches me and takes my hand in hers. She gives it a squeeze, a cool echo of Breagha's greeting when we first met, but this time, I am struck with an unease that makes me dizzy. 'Oh, you will be rewarded,' she says.

When she walks into the trees, I do not follow her. I realise I am more afraid of Lady Erskine than I am of the forest.

I sit down at the edge of the pool, leaning against the stone figure as if it were a friend lending a shoulder, and take deep breaths to calm my nerves. I am so shaken and exhausted, I do not realise that I am no longer alone until a darkly clad figure steps from the trees.

Calder. How long has he been watching?

'I want to show you something,' he says in his stiff, quiet way.

'All right.' Slowly, I rise. 'Is something wrong?' I ask, and it seems like such a daft thing to say because of course something is wrong. All of this is wrong.

He nods once. 'This way.' I know in my gut that he will lead me to the sea.

33

CALDER AND I REACH THE edge of the nearest cliff and, just like that, the mist is gone. Further along the shore, lights dance. The village. My village, that I left behind. The threat of the estate is still behind me; the mist is still there. One step back, and it will swallow me up. But before me, the sea is oddly calm and steel-grey. It seems to be holding its breath, playing a game, lying in wait. I do not trust it. I've never trusted the sea, of course, no matter how much I love it, but right now it scares me. Its endless, quiet stillness. The soft roaring of the waves. Something is not right. I feel it right through my bones.

Calder points down the shore, away from my village, where the dark Erskine waters spread like a stain. Something sits there.

It's a herring drifter. I recognise the shape of her, and I think of all those fishermen gathered in the Corbie's Nest. The boat is too close to the shore, and her crew should know better. The coastline here is riddled with rocks.

She drifts gently on the still water, and the more I stare at her, the more the unease grows in my stomach.

Something is not right.

Calder steps forward, right through a cluster of prickly gorse, and I am so absorbed in the sight of the boat, I don't realise until he's dropped from view what has just happened. Calder has walked to the edge of the cliff and disappeared. My heartrate kicks into a gallop and I rush to the edge, stepping through the gorse just as Calder did. He will already have fallen – he'll already be gone – and I brace myself for what I will see on the shore below.

'This way.' Calder's low almost-whisper nearly sends me tumbling into the gorse at my back. I curse and splutter as Calder, standing on the third step of what appears to be a stairwell carved from the cliff face, blinks up at me with a curious expression. 'We will take the stairs,' he says, a bit late if you ask me, and begins to descend.

I curse a bit more as I follow him, my heart still knocking around like a trapped bird. 'I didn't know there was a way down to the shore.'

'You were not looking carefully enough.' Calder takes easy, deliberate steps, not without caution but clearly he's taken this way many times. I'm uneasy, every step I take shaky with anxiety. The stairs are well made but old, carved right out of the rock of the cliffside. Surely, over time, some of them will have eroded, and any footfall could be the one that sends everything crumbling.

We reach the final steps and walk onto the shore, and the singular moment of relief I feel is immediately whisked away.

In all the time we were descending to the shore, the schooner barely moved. The stream tide is hardly flowing, and for some reason the crew are not manning the sails. In fact, when I move close to the water's edge to get a better view, I cannot see a single person aboard.

'I have to see it,' I tell Calder.

The boat rocks gently. The tide licks the shore. My head is stuffed full with a pounding pain, a warning. I ignore it and take off my shoes, my jacket. Three long breaths and I slip straight into the sea.

Even now, the beauty of the water around me takes me by surprise. It must always be this way, glittering and magnificent, but it seems especially so. Though everything around me is beautiful and the movement of my body through the water feels like flying, I am afraid. The kind of fear I felt the day I saw the dead seal on the shore with Fie and when the seaweed piled high against the sand.

All I hear is my own breath and my liquid movements. I am close enough now to get a better sense of the boat's size. It should hold a crew of seven. I ought to be able to hear their voices now. Laughter puncturing the air. Maybe a voice, singing, one of the songs my mother sings when she's gutting fish. The water slaps against the wooden sides, and that is all.

Something moves against my leg. I panic, more than I ought to, more than I would normally admit to anyone, and let out a shriek. I swim a few strokes forward erratically, sending white spray into the air, getting me that much closer to the boat that it's suddenly right there before me, blocking out much of the sky.

I haul myself onto the boat and earn a few skelfs in my palm for my effort.

No one else is here.

'Hello.' My voice is quieter than I mean it to be. I can hardly get the word out of my throat. The boat creaks. Nothing moves.

I walk all along the deck, even go down into the hold.

No one is here. Not a soul. But they were here – there's evidence of that. A couple of discarded jackets. A knife gleaming, caught in a crack between two planks of wood. A small sealskin sack, the very kind my father makes, and a half-eaten herring sandwich inside it. They were here, a whole crew of fisherfolk, and now they are gone.

The wind blows, lifts my damp hair. *Tick, tick, tick.* Water drips from the hem of my trousers. I shake my ankle to make it stop.

The only place I haven't checked are the nets. I haul the first one up a few inches out of the water, and I'm astounded by the weight of it.

The nets are full of fish.

Even in murky water, deep as shadows, I see the glint of scales, of silver-rimmed eyes. The nets are bursting with herring. I lean over the edge of the boat and breathe in the scent of brine, fish and the sharp tang of blood. I plunge my hand into the water, feeling for the cool scales of a fish, finding one and working it out through a hole in the net. It doesn't squirm, but I don't expect it to. That dread is beating a rhythm against my temples.

Once the fish is in my hand, I stand there, palm up, with the fish's guts spilling onto my fingers. *Tick, tick, tick.* This time, it is blood that drips against the planks. The white underside of the fish is slit, cleanly as if by a knife. I take the fish in both my hands and open it, pulling back both sides of its slit belly. A perfect, clean line just like my mother makes.

I throw the fish into the water and find another one. Just the same. A long, clean cut across the pale length of it. Another one is the same again, and another. All the fish are dead. There is no creature in all of the sea that could do this.

Behind me, the mist still hangs above the cliffs. But somehow I can still see Erskine Manor. Black bricks against the white mist. Spires thin as knives.

A whole crew of fishermen has vanished. Their nets are full of slaughtered fish. And I know, just as Dad knew, that something is not right with the sea. I look at Erskine Manor, which seems to look right back.

I can pretend that what happens here, and the dark things that happen on this shore, are separate from the town. That Lady Erskine's walls that keep her children within are enough to keep the village safe. But there are no walls in the sea, there are no barriers, only the shore which is always changing. My family are up along that shore. Tomorrow when the dawn breaks, Mum will set out on the sea again, going further and further to find the seals that once would sun themselves on the small islets to the north. The seals have gone, the fish have gone, and I cannot help but feeling that all of this is a trap. That we are being lured here to the edges of the Erskine estate. The sea ought to be unexpected. It ought to be unpredictable and ambivalent, but this feels deliberate.

When I return to the shore, Calder is waiting.

'It's empty,' I tell him. 'There's no one there but nets of dead fish.'

He nods as if he expects this. 'Something is killing my birds.'

'Not something natural.' I think of the perfect clean slices through silver flesh.

'No,' Calder agrees.

We stand together for a long while, both watching the empty boat, which drifts gently through the water, as if it has not a care in the world. I want to do something, but I feel stuck. What am I in the face of the great mystery of the sea?

The tide is creeping forward. I look down to see water flush around my feet. Finally, the numbness from my swim to the boat is wearing away, and I crave my boots and jacket. I search for them at the water's edge, hoping I had the foresight to toss them closer to the cliff, when a bundle of something catches my eye.

It is just like the seal I saw with Fie, but this time, when I approach, it does not reveal itself to be merely a seal. It is, in fact, a human, and the sight of who it is and what has happened makes me turn around and retch. There is nothing in my stomach, so I choke out sour bile that stings my throat and soaks into the sand at my feet.

The maid. She is dead.

More than that.

She lies on her back, eyes open and wide. Her pale hair, darkened by sand, has come undone and splays around her head. A long, scarlet gash runs from her neck to pubic bone. Instead of twists of meaty guts uncoiling from within, streaks of silver wriggle and squirm.

When I'm recovered enough to stand, I go back to be sure I wasn't imagining it.

The maid is cut wide-open, and inside a thousand tiny fish thrash in a sickening display of silver and scarlet.

'Calder.' My voice is hoarse, and I barely squeeze out this solitary word. When he doesn't reply, I look up, searching for him, thinking in a quick, irrational flash that maybe he is next, maybe he will be lying on the shore in a heap.

He hasn't moved from where he is standing and only gives a mild look in my direction.

'The maid,' I explain, and he blinks at me. I look back, but she is gone.

A shout of frustration dies on my lips. 'Where is she?' I ask, my gaze frantic along the shore. The tide must have dragged her away with its silver fingers. There is no sign of her.

'It's fine.' Calder turns away. 'We will have a new one tomorrow.'

34

Bone diver.
Bone diver.
Somebody is whispering in my ear. Water drips down the side of my neck, rolling down the curve of my shoulder.

'Wake up,' a voice says, and it is not the soft, whispering voice from my dreams.

I have to claw myself out of the dream – the corridors again, the clammy hand in mine – so that my reaction is painfully slow before I come to realise that someone is standing beside my bed.

I keep the knife in its scabbard under my pillow and, in one motion, I grab for it and swing it out in front of me. Whoever is there lets out a long, impatient sigh.

Innes. My eyes adjust, and I begin to see the details – the rough fur around his shoulders, his dark hair lifted away from his forehead, black eyes flashing in annoyance. He looms above me and is damn lucky I couldn't throw the knife at him if I wanted to.

'What the hell are you doing here?' I spit out, scrambling off the bed but not letting my hand with the knife drop.

'Did you forget you can't kill?' Innes says, eyeing the knife.

'Never said I couldn't maim. Maybe, if I got lucky, you'd die from your wounds.' I lower the knife. That's a lie, but Innes doesn't need to know that. 'Maybe curses have loopholes.'

Innes' brows come together. His expression has become unreadable, and I'm finding I prefer the irritating smug look he usually wears. 'I hope so,' he says.

'Right, well, you could have knocked,' I say. I wave a hand at him to move back. He complies, still wearing that unreadable look. 'Why are you here?' I ask.

'I'm leaving.'

'Good. Good for you,' I say, but I don't feel as flippant as my words. 'Come to say goodbye?'

Innes' gaze catches on my sealskin, which hangs halfway out from under the disturbed covers. 'Where did you get this?' Innes says. I watch him carefully, wondering if I can spot some sort of recognition in his eyes. Does he know he has one, too? One that could change him completely? For the first time, I wonder what it must be like to be Innes Erskine. To never have left the estate, to have a mother like Lady Erskine and a twin sister like Lennox. What would it feel like to have a secret other life that you know nothing about, that could change everything you know about yourself? Jealousy. I feel a pang of it. I realise that I wish I had something like that, something that could change me without me having to try. I can't help it, and I think of Fie. I've not got one ounce of courage compared to him.

'A sealskin,' I say eventually. 'My sealskin. Every Sealgair is gifted one on the day they're born.'

'I've never seen a seal,' Innes says, still staring at the skin. 'They won't come into our waters.'

How odd.

'They're lovely creatures,' I say. 'Full of life and bright joy. They trust us, like we're one of them.' I'm staring, too, lost in the glimmering sheen of the sealskin. 'That's why killing them feels the way it does.'

'What way?' Innes says, looking up at me.

'Like power,' I say.

Innes stares at me, and I let him break the gaze first. 'You're leaving with me.'

I laugh. 'You're not leaving.'

'I am.' Innes fingers the whistle he wears on a cord around his neck. 'This time is different. This time I have you.'

'That forest hates me.'

'It listens to me,' Innes says. 'I can get us to the gatehouse.'

'I'm not leaving. I have to stay until Midsummer.'

'You owe me a favour, bone diver. If you're afraid of getting lost, I'll make sure you don't. Get me through the gate, and you can do whatever you want.'

He's right. I do owe him a favour, and if I've given my word, I keep it. But I'm not Innes Erskine's ticket off this estate. He needs his selkie skin, and I can't offer him that, not yet. Breagha asked me not to tell the others about their skins, so what am I supposed to say to Innes now? I don't think I have a choice.

I have to let him try, at least. 'How can I be sure I'll make it back through the forest without you?'

'My horse will take you back.'

I laugh. 'Oh, aye. It'll take me back through the forest and then right to the bottom of the sea.'

Innes looks hurt, but it only takes a second for that look to be replaced by one of anger. Quick to spark. 'She won't.'

I hold my hands up. 'Okay.' A pause, as Innes continues to smoulder in my direction. 'I take it you want to leave now?'

'*Aye*,' he says, widening his eyes in what must be an imitation of me.

I snort. 'It's hardly dawn, you know.'

'It is the only time we can go. Everything is softer in the space between.'

'You mean the gloaming?' I ask, as he turns away. 'What's softer, exactly?'

'Meet me outside,' he says as he gets up and leaves.

I let out a long sigh and brush my hand across my sealskin. Not that damn forest again. It's the last place I want to go. For a moment, I don't move, focusing on my breath, anchoring myself to the present. The sealskin catches the soft light from the window, and I have an urge to scoop it into my arms. Instead, I tuck it under the covers, wishing I was corried in next to it.

I meet Innes at the edge of the forest. He stands in a strip of shadow where pine needles litter the ground.

'Ready,' I say.

Innes doesn't reply, only shrugs and turns around, not waiting for me as he plunges right into the pines.

We step into night. The air is cooler, suffused with the scent of dirt and pine sap. I expect Innes' horse to appear alongside him, but for a long while, it's just us two, alone with the birds and small creatures that make the undergrowth shiver as they scuttle by.

'Where are you gonna go?' I say to Innes' back. I wonder what sort of fur is around his shoulders. It looks most like a dog, a grey wolfish one, and I imagine it might well be – maybe there's some truth in those stories, about creatures going missing around the Erskine estate. More than one person in the village has claimed to have lost a dog to the great pine forests, but Fie and I have always guessed this was just a way for adults to cover up an old dog's death.

'Through the gate,' he says, not looking back at me. I ignore the proliferation of nettles around us and walk faster so we're shoulder to shoulder. He shifts to the side a bit and is clearly uncomfortable with me being so close. I also move to the side to shorten the gap between us. Trying to keep the mood up.

'Yeah, right, I got that,' I say. 'I mean, once you're off the estate. Where are you going?'

He looks at me with a brow-knitted expression that clearly reveals how stupid he thinks I am. 'I'll go as far as I can.'

I consider raising a few practical points about money, food, shelter, that sort of thing, but as I'm trying to feel less oppressed by the pines and the growing sense of disorientation, I don't bother bringing them up. Innes is tough. If he ever made it off the estate, he'd manage, I'm sure, though I don't doubt much would be a shock for him. What would he think of a pub like the Corbie's Nest? I imagine him sitting at one of the nicked-up tables with a crew of fisherman sucking down pints around him, and the image is mostly comical. Innes, like all the Erskines, doesn't feel to me like he belongs in this time, as if he's a relic of an era long ago lost.

'When you're out,' I say after a moment, 'do me a favour, okay?' That warrants a glance in my direction. 'Get yourself a fish supper from the chippy two doors down from the tailor shop. Ask for extra salt and vinegar.' I hesitate, imagining I can smell that chip shop, the heady warmth that rushes at you when you open the door, the particularly satisfying mingling of scents when the rain is coming down outside and you've got a paper-wrapped bundle of fish under your arm nearly burning your skin, and it's like a wee bomb of vinegar and heat against the chill. 'Add some mushy peas while you're at it,' I say, just to complete the image.

'Mushy peas,' echoes Innes, in what might be awe.

'No guarantee you'll like it, but you might as well go for the whole experience first time out.'

'Fish supper with vinegar,' he says, maybe to himself. 'Chippy by the tailors.'

We fall into silence. The air almost smells like that chip shop, and it helps me feel better about the trees around us, which seem to be pressing closer and closer to one another, the shadows between them thickening.

'Go on, then,' says Innes suddenly. He doesn't look at me but stares intently ahead. 'What ought I eat for breakfast?'

I clear my throat. 'A *full* breakfast. Bacon. Fried eggs. Sausages and cooked tomatoes. Hash,' I say, getting inspired. 'Have you ever had potato hash? It's best to fry the potatoes in the bacon fat, then add whatever spices you like. Goes great with a runny egg.' I pause, thinking of all the breakfasts I've ever had. Sometimes we eat a full breakfast at home but only if Dad and I are feeling inspired enough to go through the trouble. Usually, since we live so close to the shore, we eat fish. Often mussels or cockles. I remember the bucket Mum collected the day Dad came back from the accident. They'd have eaten cockles for days after that, and not just for breakfast.

Innes doesn't say anything, but blethering has warmed me up, and it's the only thing keeping my fear of this place away, so I keep going unprompted, telling him about pickled herring, scallops with butter, and sausage and mash. Somehow, I'm no longer blethering about food and I start to tell him about the town, giving him a vivid description of each of the shops along the high street. The butcher, the fishmonger, the grocery. The tailors.

'My best friend, Fie, he's a tailor, and he makes beautiful clothes. He made a wedding dress for the butcher's daughter. There's going to be a ceilidh in the town hall on Midsummer Eve.'

'What's that?' Innes asks. He hasn't noticed that we're walking almost shoulder to shoulder now.

'A ceilidh?' I try to hide my surprise. The only way you wouldn't know about ceilidhs is if you spent your whole life in a cave – which, I suppose, is about the same as being confined to one large, damp house and its estate grounds. 'It's a gathering,' I explain. 'People get together to tell stories and play music and if it's a wedding, it'll be more formal with a ceilidh band and a caller, and everyone dances.' Innes stares at me like I've told the most egregious lie. 'The band usually has a fiddle and a squeezebox, at least. The caller announces the different dances and guides people through them.' I hesitate because Innes isn't jumping in to ask anything. The silence feels deep, so I go on. 'There's a lot of drinking involved.'

'I would not know the dances,' Innes says.

'You wouldn't need to,' I say. 'The caller explains every dance before it starts. And there's always a few old couples who have been dancing for years and know all the dances by heart. They love to teach what they know.'

I think back to all the ceilidhs I've been to throughout my life. All the times I've spun through the dances, grinning so hard my temples hurt. Everyone getting progressively sweatier as the night goes on, with jumpers tossed onto tables and ties undone, and eventually the floor is covered in a layer of spilled drink and anyone with a weak heart is draped on chairs at the edge of the dance-floor, watching everyone else make a fool of themselves when they try to dance the basket. I like my time alone, and I don't need much more than my family and Fie, but it's at a ceilidh when I feel how important community is.

How all of us are tied together. It's a good reminder, and those memories stick with you, even if they do all blur together as much as the dancers do when they strip the willow.

The Erskines know none of that. They just know this house, the forest, the cliff's edge and the sea. Even though, when I first arrived here, I thought this place was huge and impressive, but to stay here your whole life – that would make even a grand place feel small.

'Everyone's invited,' I say. 'But I can't go. It's on Midsummer Eve, and I'll still be here.'

'Collecting bones,' says Innes.

'Aye,' I say. 'But you could go.' I elbow Innes. Immediately, he recoils and shoots me a deadly stare. But after a second, he softens and we return to our easy walk, side-by-side. 'What a thrill that would be for everyone, especially folk our age. I know a few people who would be particularly eager to eat you right up.'

'What do you mean?' he says, and I think he genuinely has no idea. I must have forgotten who I'm talking to. For the first time, Innes Erskine feels human.

Of course, he isn't. But he doesn't know that.

'Ah, well,' I say. 'It'd be easy for you to find a partner.'

Innes narrows his eyes at me like I'm making a threat.

'But,' I ask tentatively, 'what is it that you're really going to do? Once you're through that gate?'

At this, I'm certain something shifts in his expression. I am certain, when he opens his mouth, that I'm going to get the truth. But a magpie shrieks, and we both look away. The bird flaps erratically between the trees before coming to rest on a stone chimney.

The southern gatehouse. We both stop and stare at it.

There is the wall and the wrought iron gate.

'Do you have a key?' I ask, eyeing the gate and the rusted lock.

'No,' Innes says. 'I forgot it.'

'All right, I'll give you a punt, then.'

He gives me a withering look. 'You cannot climb over the wall.' He holds up a key. 'That was a joke,' he adds with a mild expression.

'I didn't realise you were doing those now,' I say.

Innes stomps forward to the gate and grabs one of the bars while he slides the key in the lock. It takes a good shove for the heavy gate to swing forward and, as soon as it does, I act without thinking. I step right through onto the path beyond.

Suddenly, I am acutely aware of where I am. Of where I'm *not*. The air here is changed, crisp and laced with pine-scent, but different. I suck in a great breath of it and revel as it fills my lungs. I am out.

The road stretches before me, and all it would take is a few steps in the right direction and I know I would not stop. I would soon be running, getting as much distance as possible between myself and Erskine Manor. I would run straight back home. I would not stop until I threw open the door to my family's cottage and stood there in the kitchen, and Dad would run out to greet me, yanking me into a huge hug and berating me for ever leaving. I would be back. I would be home.

I blink, and the vision fades away. There is a road before me. I could take it, but something roots me to the ground. Even if I went home, nothing would be the same. It wouldn't be as I imagine it. And more than that – if I went home, I would be abandoning them all. I would be leaving Breagha to search for the missing skins on her own. I would be choosing to let Innes remain trapped here, never having had the chance to find out who he really is.

Innes stares at me from edge of the forest. He says nothing, and I can tell from his expression that he does not expect me to return. He expects me to walk away and never come back, and I am so close, so close to doing that, but I don't. I can't. I *won't*. Not until I get them all out with me.

'Mushy peas,' I say. 'You have to try them.'

'What?'

I reach my hand out to Innes. 'Let's go,' I say. 'Let's get you out.'

He stares at my hand, and he hesitates. I wonder what he is thinking. Of his siblings, maybe, of everyone he is leaving behind. The moment passes, and he flashes me one of his animal grins before grabbing my hand.

Just as he takes the first step, Innes turns to look at something behind him. The horse makes no noise, but it is suddenly here, stepping out from the corner of the gatehouse. Its gaze is pinned on me, and its black lips stretch back into a silent snarl. My skin goes clammy, and I have a vision of being held beneath the water, the whole strength of the sea churning above me.

'Innes,' I say, not breaking my gaze from the horse.

'Come with me,' Innes says. He stretches his free hand towards the horse. The creature comes forward, close enough to nuzzle its nose against Innes' fingers. Then it looks up, snapping its teeth at Innes, who reels back. I'm grateful I'm no longer the focus of the horse's attention, but I don't like the way the horse is vibrating with something that might be anger. It doesn't want Innes to leave. 'Fine.' Innes shakes out his hand, scattering a few drops of blood. 'You made your choice.' Innes turns back to me, obviously making an effort to look unaffected. 'Go on.'

And we do. Three whole steps away from the Erskine estate. By the third, I start to believe maybe Innes was right, that my presence somehow is enough, like we're breaking some sort of spell. I realise this is what Innes must believe, that with me he is breaking a curse, that I'm his loophole.

The fourth step shatters that hope. Innes sucks in a sharp breath between his teeth and he almost cracks my fingers with the strength of his grip. I try to tug him forward, but when he tries to take another step, he lurches to his knees.

I kneel down next to him, taking him by the shoulders. He's gone deathly pale, and I can feel a tremor running through him. 'Keep going,' he grinds out, trying to rise. He doesn't get more than one foot on the ground before he collapses again, and I'm half-holding him from falling in the dirt. It's hard for him to breathe; it sounds like someone is choking him, like an invisible force has its fingers wrapped around his throat.

'Go back,' I say, pushing against Innes' chest. 'Go back or you'll kill yourself.'

Innes shakes his head, his dark hair hanging over his eyes, but I'm stronger than he is. I push him backwards, and when he tries to sit up, to crawl forward, I loop my arms through his and drag him back towards the gate.

The horse is no longer silent. A growl reverberates in its chest, and it lifts its front hooves, one after another, in a restless, repeating pattern.

'Take him to the shore,' I say to the horse. Innes isn't quite unconscious, which is a relief, because he lets me haul him up onto the horse's back and has enough strength left to cling to the horse's mane. The horse hesitates beside the gatehouse. 'Go,' I say, looking into the creature's eyes. The horse looks like it wants nothing more than to tear me to pieces with its monstrous teeth, and for a moment I am convinced it will. It blinks one eye and swings its head. 'Get him to the sea.'

Whether it can understand me or not, it knows enough to get its master far from here and quickly. With a growl that makes my blood shiver, it pins me with a glare before swinging around and disappearing among the trees.

I stand alone at the edge of the forest. When I glance behind me, I realise the gate has shut, though I don't remember tugging it closed behind me. A cool wind breathes from among the pines and the sky cracks right open, spilling a torrent of rain. Beyond the bars, the dirt road quickly becomes mud. I turn away from the gate and head back into the forest, hoping this time it lets me get back to the house.

35

SOMETIMES, THERE ARE DAYS when the sun doesn't rise. Sure, it seems like it might, suffusing the morning with a hopeful glow, but then it just stops there. It gives up, letting the clouds roll in thick and low, and what you thought might be a nice day turns out to be a day of no-time, a day unmarked by changes in the light's intensity. A long, grey day. A dreich day, like this one, though this one is absolutely sopping wet, too, thanks to a storm.

A day like this is a good one for telling stories.

Too bad I'm alone in a malevolent forest, and the only beings who can hear my tales are the magpies that argue in the upper branches of the pines.

You'd think I've gone mad by the way I tramp through the undergrowth, telling stories aloud, as if anyone but the birds is listening. But I can't bear to let the silence unwind around me, and so I tell my stories as I walk.

There's the one about the boy and the giant worm, a creature so large its teeth become islands and its thrashing creates whirlpools. There's the story of a father who accidentally eats his son.

There's my favourite story about a clever girl who saves a prince from the faeries, cracking nuts along the way as if saving princes is just another hobby of hers. She doesn't break a sweat.

The stories fill the forest. I like to think they soothe it, like it's a beast settling down onto its paws to listen. If I just keep talking, it won't bother me.

I am starting to feel a semblance of ease when I hear laughter.

I clamp my mouth shut to listen. For a breath, I only hear the sounds of the forest, of the rain thundering against the leaves and the trees groaning in the wind, and I almost convince myself I am hearing things. Rain drips down my face and snakes its way down the nape of my neck.

Then, unmistakeably, I hear a low, throaty laugh that has my fingers rushing to grab my knife.

Someone is in the forest with me. *Something*, I think, because there was an unnaturalness about that laugh, as if a dog could chuckle. A sound that should never be possible, nor ever heard.

There's no point in standing here doing nothing. Whoever or whatever is here with me is hidden; I can only see trees and more trees around me, their branches whipped by the wind, obscuring anything that might be moving among them. Keeping my knife at the ready, I move through the forest. The stories are over. Now, my own breath sounds loud because of how much I am straining to listen.

Mostly, the forest smells of pine, but there are traces of musk and earth. All these scents have unfurled in the rain, and if I didn't dislike this forest so much, I'd probably enjoy it. As I continue to walk with a growing sense of urgency, I notice a new smell creeping in. This one is cloying, sea-like but not in a bright, fresh way. It is a rotten, fishy scent that has me sucking deep breaths through my mouth.

The laughter rattles again, and I am certain it is closer now, following me.

Branches snap. Something moves across the ground, *burrrr*-ing across the carpet of pine needles. I freeze, seeking out the source of the sound. A cluster of nettles shivers and, despite the rain blurring my vision, I see it – a massive muscular tail, covered in scales, shining like oil on water. It slides through the undergrowth, and I catch only a glimpse of it before it is gone.

Never have I wished more for the ability to kill.

My palm is slick from sweat, and I hike the knife up higher in my hand to keep my grip. There is nothing for it. I must continue forward.

Although I feel more like prey, my hunter's instincts vibrate with intensity. Everything around me, every detail, might be important, and as my gaze sweeps the forest, my mind whirrs, picking up a detail, discarding it, moving onto the next one. I am looking for any indication of the creature, any hint that it will attack.

The gashes in a large pine aren't easy to miss.

Five long scars that curl the bark. I remember the claw marks on the cliffside. These are much the same. I follow the marks like breadcrumbs, tree to tree.

Soon, the sounds of the storm change from an incessant pattering of raindrops against the undergrowth to a softer rumble as the rain hits the thick, unkempt grass before me.

Somehow I have reached the edge of the forest.

I stand, still tucked in the shadows, holding my breath. Where has the creature gone?

Laughter, and I have my answer.

The horrible cackle is far enough away but clear. I know the creature has left the forest. Surely, it is going to the shore. Surely, the shore is where it crawled from. It cannot be a creature of the forest, not with such a tail, not with that rotten, fishy scent it carries.

Surely, it is going back to the sea, but perhaps …

Erskine Manor breaks the horizon as I crest the nearest hillock. The house looks no less magnificent in the rain. In fact, it looks pleased with itself, its bricks sparkling like jet. A gust of wind pushes me forward, and I hear the windows of the manor rattling in their panes.

Would the creature head for the house?

If I were a real hunter, I would strike it down before it reached Erskine Manor. But the best I can do is follow it at a distance, hoping it won't see me. I need to know where it is going. I need to be ready to warn the Erskines.

Keeping near to the garden wall, I creep forward. My gaze is trained on the house, seeking any movement in that direction, so I am startled when I hear the laugh again, far too close for comfort. I step as quietly as I can through the pines and lift away the branches that hide the entrance Breagha and I opened a few days ago. Rain pelts the branches, making the needles dance. From between them, through the narrow gap in the stone door, I see a woman.

She is tall, thin, with black hair slick and heavy down her back. She wears a long, black dress and carries no umbrella. She is as soaking wet as I am.

My first thought: *Breagha*.

But she carries no cane, and her posture is different, more rigid. Lady Erskine.

I open my mouth to shout at her and am ready to break into a run when something moves at Lady Erskine's feet.

The creature's tail slides across the muddied ground, shifting Lady Erskine's skirts, moving in such a slick, mesmerising motion that, for a long moment, I am caught in it, thinking of nothing, frozen.

Lady Erskine's head turns, noticing the creature. I am so sure, so sure that I am about to watch a woman die but I only manage a strangled sound of warning, which the wind swallows.

Lady Erskine extends her arms, not in protection, but as if she is welcoming an embrace.

The tail twists arounds her ankles, twirling up towards her knees. She does not move, does not struggle, only waits patiently with her arms held open. The tail twists higher. I move the branches aside and am already moving towards the doorway because I have to do *something*, even if she will not, when two pale limbs encircle her shoulders.

The limbs are long and nearly white in places, though they are threaded through with lines of black. Veins, I realise, coursing with dark blood. The hands are almost human-like, but they are tipped in talons and rent Lady Erskine's silken dress.

What is this thing? Something from the sea, but something almost human, too.

I can see nothing more that this – the scaled tail still wrapped around Lady Erskine's dress, and the long, unnatural arms looped around her. Bile burns my throat. The scent is terrible, like something dead dredged from the sea.

Lady Erskine tilts her head up into the rain and laughs.

She leans forward, as if whispering in the creature's ear, and says something, but I cannot hear what. As she does so, I am certain that I see two bright eyes peering over her shoulder. They are like the eyes of a human. Greenish brown and understanding. The monster watches me and, with one hazel eye, winks.

36

When I hear the knocking, I leap from my bed, my knife already in my fingers. I slept with it unsheathed, which is stupid, but even with the comfort of the cold steel beside me, I only got a few scraps of restless sleep. All I could see when I closed my eyes was the monster, its long limbs wrapped around Lady Erskine, its tail crushing the feral rosebushes of the garden.

The rapping at my door sounds again, more forcefully this time. The vibrations rattle the chair I dragged across the room last night and pushed against the door. I cannot lock my door, and there was no way in hell I was going to stay here without some kind of barricade.

More knocking, angry-like and a voice, Lennox's: 'Open up, bone diver!'

Last night, before I dragged the chair over to the door and attempted sleep, I searched the house for the others, hoping to warn them. I found no one, not even Breagha in her bedroom. The house, for all I knew, was empty. Save for me, of course, stuck in a room without a damn lock.

The sound of Lennox's voice washes me with relief. I didn't realise how worried I was for all of them.

I knock the chair askew so I can open the door a crack and peer out. Lennox's scowl fills the gap. 'Is this yours?' she says. I have to yank the door open, the chair grinding across the ground, to see what she means.

What I see makes me almost tumble backwards.

'Kier?'

I am staring at my friend's familiar face, thinking I must be dreaming. This cannot possibly be.

But there he is, my best friend, Fie.

'Surprise!' Fie, who is really there, who is really standing in front of me, holds out his palms.

'You,' I say, shouldering the door open further, grabbing Fie and nearly suffocating him in a hug. 'You eejit.' I pull him into the room, and Lennox reluctantly follows.

'I found him in the forest,' Lennox says in her level way. She looks about the room with an unveiled expression of disgust. I notice she has her bow under her arm and a quiver of arrows over her shoulder. I guess she was doing some early-morning hunting, and that's when I notice that the rain has stopped. Through the window, bright light washes in.

I finally let Fie go.

He looks dashing in a very clean pair of brown tweed trousers and yellow top, very put-together compared to my current get-up. He doesn't look like he's just tramped through the forest, but I suppose he had a guide. Lucky bastard. Where was Lennox when I was alone in the forest yesterday?

I shake my head, still not quite believing that Fie is actually here. 'Why the hell did you come here?'

'I hadn't heard from you for too long. It's nearly Midsummer, Kier.' Fie's voice is angry. I should have felt the anger when I held him, should have noticed the way he didn't ease into me but stayed rigid. I didn't notice because my instinct was to feel relief – relief that he's okay, that he's here, even though he shouldn't be. But Fie's anger sparks my own, vexes me, and I'm right back in his shop the day I left for Erskine Manor.

'I told you I'd be gone until then. You didn't have to go looking for me. You didn't . . . you *shouldn't* haven't gone breaking into the Erskine estate.'

'I didn't break in. The gate was unlocked.'

Of course it was. Innes never locked it after the whole nearly-fainting, mad-dash-to-the-sea situation.

'What a stupid thing to do,' I say. 'I can handle myself, Fie.' I lift my arms out to my sides. 'I'm fine.'

My face feels red, and I bet it is. My words come out all rushed and breathless. I'm *so angry*. Fie shouldn't be here. Fie should be back home, in our village, in his shop. Safe and warm and love-drunk.

Fie opens his mouth to say something, but I'm faster. 'We always thought there were monsters here, and *we were right*, Fie. There are monsters here, and you nearly tripped right over one!'

'Who is this person?' Lennox asks, and I realise I'd nearly forgotten she was here.

'Right,' I say, half-turning away from Fie. I point at him. 'This is my daft friend, Fie, son of the tailor.' I gesture towards Lennox. 'This is Lennox Erskine. Eldest sister. Not quite a monster, and the least of our problems right now.'

'What is our problem?' Fie asks. He extends his hand to Lennox, who stares at it but doesn't take it. 'That monster I nearly tripped over?'

'Aye, so go on home, Fie,' I say. 'I'll personally escort you.'

'Yeah, I'm not leaving.' Fie looks around the room. 'You've gotta give me a tour first.'

'Absolutely not.' I grab his shoulder, pushing him towards the door. I realise Lennox has slipped away. I was hoping to rely on her as a guide through the forest, but I guess I'll have to track down Innes instead.

'Hey, why did she call you bone diver?' Fie asks, snaking his shoulder away from me.

I groan. 'Because I dive for bones. That's what I do here.'

Fie opens his hand, palm up, gesturing for me to go on.

'Literally, that's it. I dive for bones and Lady Erskine does something with them, and that is all I know.'

'You haven't asked her?'

What the *hell* is Fie doing here? All I can think about is getting him off this estate as soon as possible, and he's asking me about the damn bones.

'She told me not to ask, so I don't ask,' I say brusquely. 'We need to find one of the other Erskines to get us back through the forest.'

'There are others?'

My gaze skirts around the room, checking I don't need to take anything with me.

'My daughter said we have a visitor.'

Fie and I both look, surprised, towards the doorway. Lady Erskine stands there, wearing a fresh blue dress and looking as radiant as I've ever seen her. Her skin is practically glowing, and a healthy flush of pink graces her cheeks.

Of course Lennox would clipe on us.

'This is my friend Fie,' I say, the words sticking in my throat like pins.

Lady Erskine extends her hand, and Fie takes it. 'I know you,' she says. 'You're the tailor's son.'

'That's right.' Fie nods.

'I don't make it a habit of keeping the gates unlocked, but since you are here, let us have some tea.' She nods and turns away. 'In the drawing room.'

Lady Erskine is already in the hall before Fie and I realise what just happened. We spark into action and hurry after her.

'The tea's rubbish, I'm warning you,' I whisper to Fie as we leave the room. I'm fighting the urge to smile, and I see that Fie is, too.

37

THE SCENT OF TEA IN the drawing room is enough to hide much of the ever-present musty scent of the soft furnishings. Through the rising steam emitted from the teapots, I see the most unexpected tableau. Lady Erskine sits on one end of a long, blue sofa, and Fie is in the armchair beside her. I'm in the chair next to Fie and can hardly believe this is happening. My first and greatest fear was of the monster, which may very well be roaming the estate as we sit here, but I was also afraid of Lady Erskine – I doubted she'd take kindly to Fie entering her estate without asking, even though he technically didn't break in.

Instead, she is sipping tea from a dainty cup and smiling at my friend as if she invited him herself. In all the days I've seen her, she hasn't smiled so much as she is now. She is like a woman transformed.

What is even odder is the new maid. She is almost identical to the other one – the one I swear I saw cut open and wriggling on the beach – save for her hair, which is slightly darker. Everything else about her is the same – her movements, her blank expression, her flitting gaze and her silence. I almost believe she's the same woman, but I cannot forget what I saw. Something is very, very odd about all this, but if I fixate too much on it, I think I'll go mad. Anyway, I need to focus on what Fie is saying. I need to know how the town is faring.

'The storm wreaked havoc on the town hall,' Fie is saying. 'Nearly blew the roof clean off.' He looks at me, a disappointed curve to his mouth. 'Mairi'll be raging.' He glances at Lady Erskine. 'That's the butcher's daughter. She's meant to be married on Midsummer Eve, but they've had to cancel the ceilidh. There's nowhere else in town big enough for a gathering of that many people.'

'Nowhere else in town,' Lady Erskine muses.

There's a flash of movement behind Lady Erskine, something moving in the hall beyond. The door is open just a crack, and I'm sure it shifts open a bit wider. A rustle of green silk. I look away so as not to draw attention to her.

Lady Erskine sips her tea with a faraway expression on her face. 'Lord Erskine loves parties.'

I am certain I've misheard her. *Lord Erskine.* She hasn't mentioned him once since I've arrived here. No one has.

She sets her teacup down with a delighted clink against her saucer. 'We will have the ceilidh here. It has been far, far too long since we've opened the doors of Erskine Manor.'

Fie is literally gaping, his mouth hanging open. I doubt I look much more respectable.

Lady Erskine continues, undeterred by our expressions of surprise. 'My children will have new outfits, and you will make them.'

'Midsummer Eve is just a few days away,' Fie manages, and I can see his mind whirring, imagining how he'd conjure up four new outfits in such short notice.

Lady Erskine waves her hand. 'Start with something they already have but make them new. You are a fine tailor. I have seen what you've done.'

Fie's face goes pink, and I can tell he's chuffed, if not a bit frightened.

'Tell this Mairi that she will have her ceilidh, after all. I only ask that she supply the band. I will handle everything else.' Lady Erskine looks positively delighted at the prospect. She rises and looks directly at me, gracing me with a smile that makes me shiver. 'You can tell her she owes a debt to Kier Sealgair, my bone diver.' With that she's gone, leaving behind only the scent of her tea and a long, electric silence.

38

THE SOUND OF THE CLOCK ticking away in the silver room is loud in the hallway, even before I open the door. I rap twice, as a courtesy, and slip inside.

Calder stands awkwardly, with his arms slightly extended at his sides, not far from the notable clock. He wears a deep-green suit, glinting with pins, and stares intently at the clock. Fie darts around him, pins flashing in his mouth. Fie looks up at me as I come in and holds up a finger while mumbling something from between the pins in his mouth.

'Take your time.' I plop onto the nearest settee to wait.

Fie works his magic with intense concentration. I've always liked watching him work. It really does feel like a kind of magic, the ability to transform cloth and thread into a suit or a dress. His creations always seem to transform the wearer, too, drawing out new elements of their personality, revealing something previously hidden. He was born to do this.

'Lift a bit,' Fie says, tapping the underside of Calder's arms.

Calder blinks, looking bewildered and unsure of what to do with himself, but he complies.

Fie darts a glance at me. 'You've only been gone a short time, but things have changed.'

'What do you mean?' I ask. I lean forward onto my knees. 'My family?'

'Is fine,' Fie says. He shakes his head. 'There's something ... The shore feels strange ...' He trails off, and I know how he feels. I've been having that same feeling for weeks. 'One of the boats didn't come back. The *Silver Stuckie*.'

'The crew?' I ask. The *Silver Stuckie* must be the boat I found with its nets filled with dead fish.

'Another boat picked the crew up further north, on the edge of the Erskine waters.' He hesitates. 'Most of them.' He gives me a long look. 'Everyone is on edge these days. Liv says she can feel it in the pub. They're afraid to go out on the water. These are people who have lived their whole lives on the sea, who aren't afraid of anything.'

'The balance is shifting,' says Calder, causing Fie to jump.

'What?' I ask.

Calder blanks me, returning to staring intently at the clock.

I can tell Fie wants to say something, but he's waiting for me. It's so nice, and so strange, to see his face. I've missed him, and the days we've been away from each other have felt like months, but I'm still angry. I know it's a stubborn, stupid anger, but I can't let it go. Feels like the anger is a sticky mass in my gut, and there's no easy way to get it out.

Fie presses his lips together. 'Your family needs you.' There it is.

'This is how I'm helping them.'

'By running away?'

'By making myself useful.'

'You're always on about *being useful*, Kier. Do you really think that's what your dad cares about right now? Do you think any of us care about how *useful* you are?'

'You might think they don't care, but they do.' I don't tell him about what my mother said to me before I left. It's something I've been trying to forget. 'I've gone off the path, and I can't find my way back, even though I've been trying. I've been trying and *trying*.'

'Why don't you try *not* trying?' Fie says. 'Why don't you stop chasing after something you lost, so that you can figure out what you really want?'

'I don't know how to do that.'

'Aye, you do,' Fie says. 'You're just making up excuses for yourself.' His eyebrows dip together, and I know he's had a realisation. 'I shouldn't have given you a hard time about leaving. I was afraid.' He rolls his eyes, like it's flippant what we're talking about, though we both know it's not. 'You know, I'm afraid of losing people because I almost lost my dad, but you were there for me, you always were, and when you said you were just going to disappear to Erskine Manor, I thought it would be even worse this time, that you wouldn't come back like Dad did.' He pauses, adds in a lower voice, 'It's been good for me, you not finding your path, because it keeps you close.'

I open my mouth, close it like a fish. 'I'm not looking for a new path.'

'You should be,' Fie says. He shrugs. 'Anyway, at least you've not been morosely walking the shore looking for driftwood. I don't think I could bear any more of that.'

I huff. 'I'm not morose.'

'Hmm,' he says.

'I'm not.'

'That's right, you're cursed.'

'I am!' I say, loud enough to startle Calder, who flinches.

We grin at each other. 'We done now?' I ask, looping my arm around his shoulder and pulling him in for a half-hug. 'With all the serious chat, huh?'

'Oh, aye.'

'They're going to cause a pure commotion,' I say, deliberately changing the subject. 'I don't think anyone is ready to meet the Erskines.'

'No,' says Fie, leaning back to look at Calder. 'They really aren't.'

39

Fie is gone. He left yesterday, burdened with the four outfits Lady Erskine has tasked him with tailoring by Midsummer Eve. It was hard to say goodbye to him a second time, but at least I know we won't have long to wait. Only three more days until the ceilidh.

When I arrived here, Erskine Manor echoed with stillness. It was full of shadows and secrets, and now it is bustling with activity. Lady Erskine has somehow procured a team of servants, men and women eerily similar to the usual singular maid. They are silent and flitting, but they seem to have an inexhaustible supply of industry. Now, I am never alone in the manor house. Always someone is bustling by, usually a servant, but sometimes one of the Erksines themselves. They aren't quite as hard-working as the servants, but they are clearly trying to make themselves useful. More than once, I've heard Lennox barking orders at the servants.

Personally, I feel a bit like a useless lump with all the activity around me, so I've escaped to the gardens, where at least I won't be getting in anyone's way.

In the full light of the afternoon, it seems hard to imagine what I saw here not long ago in the pouring rain. I look around for evidence of the creature, but what I do find – a crushed rosebush, broken branches – may very well be from the storm.

I'm leaning against the garden wall, sitting beside the oval pool and whittling an otter out of pinewood when voices lift around me. Breagha strides through the doorway like a queen, the tip of her cane catching the sunlight. Two servants follow close behind her.

'We are looking for ivy, but if you see any flowers in bloom, take note of them. Do *not* pick them now. We will come back on Midsummer Eve for the flowers, but the ivy will keep.' She notices me and her eyes sparkle. 'Hello, bone diver.'

The servants disperse. Breagha walks towards me, and I rise to meet her.

'It's an otter,' I say, holding up my half-formed thing. She didn't have to ask; I read the question in her eyes.

'Your little friend visits me. I have made a bed for her in the bathtub, but she is fickle. I never know when she will appear.'

'That's Dratsie.' I shouldn't be surprised that Dratsie has taken to Breagha, who has so much of the sea about her that she probably feels like home to an otter.

'I have taken up the task of the floral arrangements.' Breagha points with her cane in the direction of one of the servants, who is cutting ivy from the stone wall. 'I do not think a bride will be well pleased with gorse, so I have settled on ivy.' She presses her lips together in annoyance. 'For such a large estate, there is very little flora to work with.'

'There used to be roses,' I say, looking at one of the neglected rose bushes. It's just dried branches now, bristling with thorns.

'They haven't been cared for for many years. Mother doesn't like it here.'

Another one of Lady Erskine's lies, surely. She did not seem displeased to be here when I saw her with the creature.

'Why?' I ask, because I do not know how to tell Breagha what I know.

'This way.' Breagha takes my arm and leads me across the garden to where the bushes are so overgrown that they are almost as tall as trees. She pushes through them, guiding me forward, until we emerge beyond the bushes into a corner of the garden I'd never known to explore.

The ground is covered with nettles, which choke out any other plants that might have tried to take root here. Rising up among the prickly leaves is a folly or mausoleum, a round structure with columns and a statue in the centre. The roof is blanketed with moss and lichen, and the ridges of the columns are worn from wind and rain.

'That is why,' Breagha says, looking at the stone structure. She doesn't get close to it, but I'm curious, and I risk a tramp through the nettles to climb onto the circular platform. The statute in the centre is much like the ones I've seen in the forest. A woman sits with her legs folded beneath her, her head in her hands. Water laps at her ankles, swirling waves ushering her towards a sea that's just out of sight.

'What is it?' I ask.

'A tomb.'

'For a selkie?' I say, running my fingers over the stony waves. All the tombs I've seen here are pools, and it seems the bodies of dead selkies are buried in salt water, not earth.

'Yes. For Lord Erskine. My father.' Breagha stares intently at the tomb, an unreadable expression on her face.

'I'm sorry,' I say.

'I don't remember him.'

I nod, though I can't imagine what it would be like not knowing your own father. I'm not sure what I'd do without mine.

I'm not eager to stay in the mausoleum, and not only because I'm afraid I've made Breagha uncomfortable. There is something odd about this tomb. Why would Lord Erskine be buried in the garden when all the others were sunk into deep pools? Why deny him a watery resting place when, clearly, it's what selkies prefer? I sweep my gaze around the place, looking for a hint of who Lord Erskine was. The tomb is strangely devoid of personality, nothing besides the weeping statue to indicate who lies to rest here. Around the edge of the plinth on which the statue sits, I notice a pale line, the stone slightly lighter than the rest. Compelled by some instinct, I brace my hands against the plinth, just where the carven waves begin to swirl upward, and I push.

The statue shifts beneath my palms.

Not much, mere inches, but the movement resonates through my bones.

'Look,' I tell Breagha, as I push again, harder this time. I am rewarded with a scraping sound, as the statue and its plinth slide further forward. I heard rustling sounds as Breagha wades through the nettles.

She is beside me, her hands next to mine, and we push together.

Dark water shimmers. A chill rolls upwards, swirling around our ankles.

Another pool. Perfectly round, carved into the floor of the mausoleum.

A selkie tomb, after all.

'Why is it hidden?' I ask aloud, and my heart is thudding in my ears. Breagha's fingers find mine, and she squeezes so hard that I flinch. We must be thinking the very same thing, hoping for the same.

Without hesitation, I am slipping off my shoes.

'Be careful.' Breagha spins her cane in her restless fingers.

'I've seen worse,' I say, giving her a wink before I suck in a breath and dive.

Of course, the pool is dark, and my eyes struggle to adjust. It is small, not much wider than my arm span. I've hardly taken two strokes downwards when a murky shape appears. There is something spread across the diameter of the pool, something moving just enough for me to notice. My mind immediately jumps to wild conclusions, and I cannot help but recall the monster, with its long, skinless limbs.

But I am nearly there, just one stroke away, and instead of doing what my mind begs me to do – turn around and swim faster than I ever have before – I propel myself downwards until my outstretched fingers meet something more than water.

I know that feeling. I have felt it a thousand times. Perhaps, it is one of the very first things I felt the day I was born.

There is a sealskin between my fingers. Touching it ignites such a strong sense of being among the rushing waves of the sea that I momentarily forget where I really am. A small, dark pool. A tomb, hidden in an unlikely place.

Now I know why it is hidden away.

My eyes adjust enough for me to understand how the skins are held in place beneath the water. All three of them are attached to a metal pole, which is set into notches on either side of the pool. It is easy enough to yank the pole from the wall, but the skins are so heavy that the journey upwards, though short, is a challenge.

When I break the surface, I gulp in air and do not have voice enough to ask Breagha to help me. She understands, though, and moves swiftly. With surprising strength, she takes the pole into her hands and lifts the skins from the water. Three beautiful, shimmering selkie skins. They dangle over the dark pool, splattering drops of water. As fast as I am able, I am out of the pool and beside her, helping her set the skins gently onto the mausoleum floor.

'We found them.' My words are almost a laugh. 'Didn't we?'

Breagha nods. 'Lennox. Innes. Calder.' She touches each skin in turn.

'I'll go get them, if you want to stay here,' I offer. We have done it. We have found the missing skins, and before Midsummer, too.

'No. Put them back.' Breagha squeezes my arm. 'Wait until after the ceilidh.' She stares into my eyes, and it seems the green and browns of her irises swirl together. She breaks my gaze to look in the direction of the house. 'They should enjoy that first before ... before they may choose not to return.'

I try to hide my surprise with a nod and a downward glance. I thought she would be happy, but she looks sad.

'All right.'

The water is baltic, no less shocking as I lower myself into it again. I tug the pole and the dangling skins with me, setting the pole back on its perch beneath the water. Even in the shade of the mausoleum's roof, the selkie skins glimmer and shine. They are even more vibrant in the water, right at home.

Once the skins are in place, I do not immediately surface.

There is something tugging at my mind.

I swim downward, past the skins, and, with my hands outstretched, I scour the walls and floor of the narrow pool. Nothing but crumbling rock. Not a single bone.

When I eventually surface, I do not tell Breagha what I have learned. I do not know how to tell her.

Wherever Lord Erskine is, he isn't here.

40

THE MEAGRE CONTENTS of my dresser are spread out on the bed. It's very clear I hadn't planned to be attending a ceilidh during my stay at Erskine Manor. I've got a couple of jumpers, trousers that aren't suited for anything better than collecting driftwood along the shore, and old boots that certainly aren't worthy of a night out.

The ceilidh is tomorrow, which means this morning one of the new Erskine servants arrived with a precious bundle – the clothes Fie tailored for the Erskine siblings. I'm not so lucky and have to source my own attire.

'What do you think?' I ask Dratsie, who slinks between my legs. I reach down and scratch her behind the ear. 'What's the best of the worst options here?'

A *tap tap* at the door makes me turn. I'm expecting Lady Erskine, so my heart leaps a bit when it's not her but Breagha standing at the door. She's holding her cane aloft after using it to rap against the doorframe.

'What is "the best of the worst"?' she asks.

I gesture at my clothes on the bed. 'You tell me.'

She stands beside me and gives my clothes a once-over. She smells, as she always does, of the sea in a soft, clean way.

'Ah.' She slides her arm through mine. 'I will help you.'

Dratsie is delighted to follow us to Breagha's room. She seems to love it there, and I can't blame her. Everything about Breagha must remind her of the sea, of home.

'Here,' Breagha says, kicking the door closed as soon as we walk through and unhooking her arm from mine. 'I have already chosen something for you.'

I'm sceptical as she moves to her armoire. Breagha and I are nowhere near the same size. I imagine trying to squeeze myself into one of her dresses and have to banish the image that comes to mind quickly before I lose all my nerve and bolt back to my own bedroom.

I get close enough to watch her riffling inside and can see a cascade of beautiful fabrics. I think she must only ever wear dresses, given how many are hanging in her closet, and, anyway, I've not known her to wear anything else. Most of the fabrics are dark, black or a deep green, but there are occasional bursts of colour – cobalt and honeysuckle and burnt orange. It's the orange one she plucks out and holds out to me. The fabric flows over her arm and falls in a puddle onto the floor. I notice the gold threads woven through it.

'This is your colour,' Breagha says.

I do like the colour, but I shake my head. 'I'm a head taller than you,' I say. 'And a good bit wider around the everything.' I gesture at myself. 'I don't think it'll fit.'

'It will,' Breagha insists. 'Put it on.'

'Hmm.' I take it from her and am weighing it up in my hands, feeling the soft fabric, and realise I'm afraid. Not because I think it won't fit but because it doesn't feel like something Keir Sealgair would ever wear. I look up to see Breagha staring at me. 'All right,' I say.

I change in the bathroom, where there isn't a mirror, conveniently. Breagha was right; I slip into the dress easily. The fabric flows and is secured with a wrap-around tie that I can adjust to fit me perfectly. The arms are long so that the fabric brushes against my fingertips. I do a tentative twirl. I have to admit that it's very comfortable, which is usually about all I look for in what I'm wearing.

I'm hesitant to like it, but when I step out into the bedroom and see Breagha's eyes light up when she sees me, I think I'm warming to the idea.

'This is your colour,' she says, repeating herself but with even greater enthusiasm. 'Didn't I say it would fit?'

'You did.'

She takes my arm and leads me over to the corner of the room where a full-length oval mirror rests on a stand. She shuffles to the side and behind me so I can see only a sliver of her dark hair and the edge of her sleeve.

'Look,' Breagha says, but I don't, not really. I stare at my face so that the rest of me is just a blur in my periphery.

'I'll have to wear my boots,' I say. I crane my neck to look at her standing behind me. 'I don't reckon you have my size shoe kicking about in your closet?'

She laughs. 'No, your feet are huge, Kier.' I like the way my name sounds in her mouth. Long and soft, like the feeling of running my hand along a length of soft wool. 'The boots will be perfect.' She gives me another up-and-down glance. 'Perfect.'

'What about you?' I ask.

'Wait.' She presses her fingertips against my chest, just above my heart, and it's like I can feel them pressed gently against the beating organ itself. I don't think I'm breathing.

Breagha, with Dratsie trailing joyfully after her, departs for the bathroom. The door clicks shut, and I am alone. I turn to face the mirror again and look myself over. I don't recognise the person staring back at me. She doesn't look like a seal killer. Most importantly, most unsettling, is that she doesn't look like a Sealgair at all.

What would I be wearing if I were at home, if I had never left? A kilted skirt in my family's tartan and a shirt to match, nothing fancy. I wouldn't normally, under any other circumstances, wear a dress, and I wouldn't wear one this colour, either.

Slowly, I let my gaze wander away from my face and I look at myself properly.

I should hate the way I look. I should feel strange and uncomfortable in a dress like this, flowing and vibrant. But when I look at myself, I don't feel strange. I feel visible. I feel like a person that other people might look at and notice. I don't look like a hunter or a Sealgair or even the Kier who walked through the gates of the Erskine estate less than a fortnight ago.

Breagha's cane taps against the floor, and I turn to look at her.

'Oh,' I say.

She wears a green velvet dress, long-sleeved and full-length with no embellishments. Just simple, deep green velvet. The simplicity of it suits her perfectly; I notice everything about her all at once. Her dark eyes, her black hair, the curve of her neck, her fingers.

'Oh,' I say again.

She is smiling when she comes to stand beside me at the mirror. She loops her free arm through mine. 'Yes, *oh*.'

We are a sight together. Her in velvet, me in flowing silk.

Her in green, me in orange. Complementary colours, I think Fie would call it. Opposites that match.

41

Today is midsummer eve, when my father always says the air is thinner, changed. A day when anything could happen. The wedding ceremony must be finished because townspeople have begun to stream onto the estate. The new servants have cleared a path through the forest and act as guides, ushering guests from the gatehouse to the manor-house steps. It's a pure delight, watching the faces of the guests as they first catch sight of Erskine Manor itself. It is no longer forlorn, as it was the day I arrived. Now, in the soft light of the longest day of the year, it stands proud with its front doors thrown wide. Even in my room, the chill seems to have abated, as if the heat of more bodies has transported the entire manor house, finally, into summer.

I know I'm lingering on purpose, letting the house fill up with more guests and the ceilidh kick off properly before I head to the hall. Though the house is transformed, filled with life, worry still scratches at my mind. The ceilidh feels like a distraction, deliberately drawing me away from everything that has felt wrong about this place. Even my memory of the monster has softened, become more like an old bruise than a fresh cut, and I find myself wondering if I've simply imagined it all.

Though I'm wearing the orange dress, I take my knife with me, tucked away in its sheath, which I've slipped into the side of my boot.

A knock at the door pulls my attention away from the window. Breagha's face appears, as she pokes her head into my room.

'I urgently request your presence in the drawing room,' she says.

'What happened?' I ask, my mind immediately flicking towards my right boot, to the knife. I even start to reach for it.

'They will not go to the hall. I cannot get them to go.'

'Who?'

'Lennox and my brothers. She has turned them against me.' Breagha's expression is deadly serious, but my mind drifts away from the knife in my boot. This is a different sort of problem with a very different solution.

'You want me to talk them into going to the ceilidh?'

'Yes, as only you can.' She turns away and, of course, I follow.

All the Erskines are dressed in green. Not a young, bright spring-green but the deep bottle-green of seagrass. Lennox's gown is more complicated than Breagha's simple one; a darker green with a velvet belt around the waist. The dress is long and long-sleeved like Breagha's but is covered in elaborate beading. Both Innes and Calder wear dark green suits. Innes' waistcoat is chocolate brown, while his brother's is a shiny black.

Individually, they are striking. Together, they are like a tidal wave, unexpected and dangerous. The village is completely unprepared for the sight of them when they walk through the double doors of the Erskine hall.

If I can convince them to go.

Innes is irreverently draped across a settee, while Lennox stands behind him with her arms crossed over her chest. Calder is staring intently into the empty fireplace and doesn't lift his head when Breagha and I come into the room.

'You will not trick us into going to this party,' says Lennox before I can spit out an inspiring speech.

'It's a ceilidh. A wee bit different than just a party,' I say.

'With dancing and much drinking,' Innes says, obviously recalling our walk through the woods not long ago. He looks up and back towards his twin sister. She presses her lips together, shutting him down without a word, and he looks away to hunker back down into the sofa.

'What's wrong with a party?' I ask. 'You're already dressed, you may as well make an appearance.'

'There should be no party here at all,' Lennox says. She gestures towards the windows, from which drift scraps of conversation as guests make their way across the grounds. 'None of these people ought to be allowed onto the estate.'

'Are they not posh enough for you?' I ask, not able to help myself.

Lennox's eyebrows crumple in confusion. 'What is *posh*?' I open my mouth, but she beats me to it. 'Clearly, Mother is unwell. She has been acting strange lately, we have all noticed. She would not keep the gates locked our whole lives to suddenly throw them open one day for the sake of a stranger's wedding. There was a reason the gates were always locked. It was to keep *them* out.'

'The house smells different.' Calder doesn't look up as he speaks. 'And it is not so cold.'

'I like it,' says Innes, earning a cutting glare from his twin sister.

'Why is it that we cannot leave, but they can march through our front doors without a care?' Lennox continues, and I understand now why Lennox doesn't want to go to the ceilidh, to see the cavernous hall transformed. She is afraid. You would hardly know it, looking at her fierce expression, but I know what it's like to mask fear with fire. I know what it's like to stand at the edge of a pool, its depth unknown, and be terrified of diving in. It seems so easy just *not* to jump, but where is the joy in that?

All of them will be free soon. Free of this place, of their mother, who lied to them all these years, kept the world from them and the great, glorious sea.

This is their only chance, their last chance, at knowing what it is really like to be human. To be a part of a community that dances and laughs and gets drunk together.

After today, when Breagha presents them with their selkie skins, they may slip into the sea and never come back.

'I didn't take the Erskines to be cowards.' I shrug. 'Not showing up to their own party. You know, people in that hall think you're monsters. They spin stories about you, and all of those stories are wrong. Don't you want the chance to tell your own tale?'

Lennox narrows her eyes at me. She knows what I've just done, backed her into a corner by calling her a coward. But she knows I'm right. Staying here, hidden away in the drawing room, is a coward's move.

'It is like those dreams we used to have,' Innes says. He looks back at his sister. 'I still get them sometimes. I want to know what that's like. That feeling of going on and on.' I see him struggle to find the right words, and he lets it drop at that.

'You will not get that from a ceilidh,' Lennox says.

'I won't get it from sitting here.' Innes straightens and waves his hand at the room around him. A resolve settles in him, and he rises.

'Don't—' Lennox starts, but Calder interrupts.

'I like it, too,' he says. 'I've never liked the cold.' He finally looks up from the fireplace.

'Come on,' I say. 'Let's go, Lennox.' Suddenly, I laugh, remembering a song that feels made for this moment. '*Step we gaily, on we go,*' I sing, though I'm no good for it. It doesn't matter. We're on our way to a ceilidh. A little bit of terrible singing is a perfect primer. '*Heel for heel and toe for toe, Arm in arm and row on row, All for Mairi's wedding.*' I take Breagha's arm, and she beams, triumphant. '*Over hillways up and down, Myrtle green and bracken brown, Past the sheilings through the town, All for sake of Mairi.*'

'On we go,' Breagha says, matching my words but not the tune. 'On we go to Mairi's wedding.'

'Aye,' I say. 'On we go.'

When we walk through the drawing-room door, I know the others follow.

Long before we reach the hall, I hear the fiddle music. They'll have a full ceilidh band with a squeezebox and drums, probably a flute too, and of course the caller. Mairi, the butcher's daughter, has married into one of the wealthier families who live in one of the two-storey stone houses that have balconies that look out to shore. Even before the ceilidh had to be relocated to Erskine Manor, everyone expected it to be the grandest affair the town has seen in years, grander even than the Hogmanay celebration that ushers in the new year.

Though the silver doors to the hall are closed, the music flows out, getting louder and bolder the closer we get. Just as we are nearly there, one of the doors opens, emitting someone who stumbles out, already drunk, and gives the Erskines a surprised look before banging the door shut and bounding away. I can practically feel Lennox tense behind me.

'It's an experience, I'll tell you that,' I say. Before Lennox can reply, I open the doors with a dramatic flourish. 'You can't miss it.'

As soon as the hall doors are opened, we're blasted with the sounds of the fiddle and the squeezebox. Just as loud is the laughter and the whooping. Everyone, it seems, is here, squeezed into the hall, filling the place with the scent of beer and sweat and good times.

The hall is magnificent. Breagha's ivy clings to the walls, punctuated by the occasional bloom, softening even the dreary seascapes. The chandeliers sparkle with candlelight.

There is a moment where I feel both worlds at once – the tight air of the hall before me and the cool air of the manor house at my back. Then, I step through, the Erskines close behind me.

The Erskines survey the hall with their dark, intense stares. Compared to all the townies, they stand out like pretty pieces of sea-glass on the sand.

The music continues, the dancers are spinning, the caller shouting to be heard above the din, but everyone who isn't dancing is looking towards the door, their gazes as thick as syrup. They've noticed us.

The squeezebox exhales the end of the song. The dancers, seeing everyone's attention turned towards the door, stop dancing before the song finishes. The fiddler and the caller exchange glances, and the fiddler accidently strikes out a long squawk.

'Are they done?' Innes asks.

'Ah, no,' I say hurriedly. 'It's just the end of the song. They'll start up the next one soon.'

But no music strikes up. Instead, a hush falls over the hall.

42

THE SILENCE DOESN'T LAST LONG. This is a ceilidh, after all, and half this room is no doubt steaming with drink already. The initial shockwave of the Erskines' presence reverberates through the room then settles, like ripples on a pond, fading away to mere blips. The fiddle strikes up again, hardly cutting through the rising chatter, but then the squeezebox follows suit, and the caller is shouting to be heard as he begins to instruct everyone for the next dance. Hardly a moment passes before I feel anonymous again, or at least as anonymous I can be in a room full of people who have known me all my life. It feels easy, and I'm flush with pride, too, having convinced the Erskines to come.

I'm hardly in the hall before Fie rushes toward me. 'Kier Sealgair in a *dress*!' He waggles his eyebrows at me, holding me at a distance for a moment before scooping me into a hug. 'It suits you. *She* suits you.' He shoots a look at Breagha, who has her arm looped through Calder's. Their heads are dipped towards each other, their black hair mingling. 'Someone's going to snatch her up at this ceilidh, unless you do first,' Fie continues, to my obvious discomfort.

'You're looking sharp.' I give his suit coat and kilt an approving look. He does look sharp, in a classic but somehow very Fie way. He'll have made the suitcoat himself, and it's got all the little extra touches that define a Fie creation. Each polished button is different though they're all gold, and his lapels are narrower than a typical men's suitcoat. There's a dark orange swatch of velvet that curves around the nape of his neck, and this is echoed in a similar way on his cuffs.

Liv slips beside him, taking his hand and greeting me with a generous smile.

Together, he and Liv make a perfect picture. Her deep-blue dress complements the orange in Fie's suitcoat and the threads of orange criss-crossing his kilt. She's taken her hair down except for two locks, which have been braided and pulled away from her face.

'I feel underdressed,' whispers Fie, glancing at the Erskines.

'Hardly,' I say. 'You fit right in.' I clear my throat. 'I mean, you stand out, in the right kind of way.'

Fie laughs. 'If you say so.'

Someone rushes up to us, and it is the bride's mother, the butcher. She is dressed in a tight tartan dress instead of her usual butcher's smock, and her cheeks are ruddy with drink tonight instead of smeared with blood.

'Fie Gallach!' she shouts, yanking at Fie's lapels and pulling him into a hug. 'Mairi loves that dress. She won't be takin' it off ever again, I don't think.'

Fie says something that I can't hear because it's lost in the butcher's smothering hug. It's then that the butcher looks over Fie's shoulder and sees me.

'I've been told you have something to do with this miracle,' the butcher says, nodding at the whole of the hall before us. 'Everyone's talking about how the Sealgair girl got Lady Erskine to finally open the doors to this place.' She grins and hold out her hand to shake mine. Her grip is firm and dry, and she squeezes my shoulder with her free hand. I feel her gratitude in that gesture, and it fills me with an unexpected joy. 'Everyone'll be wanting Gallach gowns and ceilidhs in Erskine Manor from now on, but my Mairi's the first.' She winks, releasing me, before spinning off to join the next dance.

'Gallach gowns, huh?' I say, elbowing Fie hard enough that he stumbles.

'Aye, well, who wouldn't want perfection?' Fie's smile is so wide that I think he might split in two.

'Let's go,' says Liv, as the squeezebox exhales a long breath. In what is clearly a total shock to Calder, she loops her arm through his and drags him onto the dance-floor. He obeys like a lost puppy, shooting a panicked look towards Breagha, who laughs as Fie takes her arm.

'It's the "Gay Gordons",' I shout after her. 'An easy one!'

'We will not miss an easy one,' says Lennox, and she pushes Innes to follow after the rest of them. Suddenly, I'm standing alone, half in shock, grinning like a fool, as the dancers grab each other's arms across one another's shoulders and start to spin. There are the Erskines, among all the familiar faces I grew up with.

The beautiful thing about a ceilidh is you don't need to come with a partner; there's always someone willing to dance with a stranger. You don't even need to speak to anyone, and trying to is mostly futile, anyway. You're either joining in the dance or you're on the edges, getting a top-up of your drink, trying to catch your breath before you jump back in. There's little ceremony in joining a dance. Once a song ends, and another one starts, you step in the centre and follow the caller's instructions.

'Get in there, Kier,' someone says, pushing me towards the dance-floor. 'Benny needs a partner. Didn't know you to be one to stand there twiddling your thumbs.'

'Oh, aye,' I say, recognising the voice as belonging to Archie. 'I'm not.'

Benny is a soft-spoken man in his fifties who works the chandlery, selling supplies to the fishermen and sailors and some unexpectedly lovely candles that Fie likes to buy. He misses no beat when he sees me rushing up to him, and he takes my hand across his shoulder. We fall in line with the other dancers, who are moving together in a circle. 'Kier Sealgair!' he says. 'Surprised to see you here.'

'I love a ceilidh,' I say. 'Wouldn't miss it.'

'Good to have a Sealgair representative present,' Benny says, just as we turn and begin to march in the opposite direction. 'I'd think there's no seals left on this shore, what with how much your mother is out on that boat.'

'She's out now?' I ask, and I look around the hall at all the familiar faces, but Mum's face isn't among them.

'Aye, you didn't know?' Benny says.

'Of course she is,' I say, not really answering Benny's question.

The music ends in a flourish and all the dancers release their partners, spinning towards each other with a grin. I give Benny a half-hug, and he returns it with a pat on my back.

'That's me needing a break,' he says. 'Long night ahead of us, eh?'

I nod and laugh, letting Benny slip away to the side of the dance-floor, where everyone who isn't dancing is chatting and sipping beers.

The band doesn't give us more than a moment to catch our breath. They're right back at it, and I recognise the dance, which begins with a long, breathy wheeze of the squeezebox. A cheer rises up, a fan favourite: 'Dashing White Sergeant'. A few people rush from the side lines to join the dance, while a few folk sneak away from the dance-floor, knowing that the chaos of the next dance might be too much for their hearts. It's true that already I feel the sweat clammy on my back.

'Dashing White Sergeant' is a fast-paced dance, where groups of three dash about joining another group and forming temporary groups of six. You have just enough time to catch the gaze of your new group when suddenly you're wrenched apart and join a new trio, and on and on it goes until you've surely danced with every person on the dance-floor. It's the kind of dance that keeps you grinning and, by the end of it, your temples will be throbbing with the effort.

The caller gives us hasty instructions and then we're off. I grab the hand of the nearest dancer, someone grabs my other hand, and we're scurrying forward to join a new group of six. There's Lennox, who keeps her back very straight as she dances, but I see the small smile tugging at her lips already.

'You enjoying yourself?' I manage to say to Lennox before we're spun away from each other and a new group forms. I think I see her scowl, but I'm certain it doesn't last long.

As the song goes on, I catch sight of a dazed Calder being led by a lively elderly lady, and later Innes, grinning in a way I've never seen him before as he holds hands with a young man I recognise as a fisherman and regular at the Corbie's Nest.

The dance is a pure mess by the end of it, and I can hardly believe the band is still going strong, the fiddle scratching away and the squeezebox wheezing out the notes like an old man who knows this is his last dance on earth and wants to make the most of it. Everyone is soaked in sweat and breathing in gulping breaths. There is not a serious face among us.

Then the squeezebox lets out one long note, and everyone drops their hands from whomever they are holding, and we all turn to each other and exclaim at how exhausted we are.

Mercifully, the caller announces they will slow it down for the next one, a couples' dance. Immediately, I look to catch Breagha's eye, but I cannot find her. Couples begin to form on the dance-floor and, before anyone has the chance to ask me to join them, I slip away through the silver doors.

43

I'M IMMEDIATELY IN A different world, with the fresh air close around me, the music muted, the night smelling of leaves burning. I'm standing on the front steps of the manor house, and even so far away from the hall, I can hear distant fiddle music.

I take a deep breath and taste the sea. My mother is out there on the water, hunting for seals. I think I knew not to expect her at the ceilidh today, but it is still disappointing not to see her.

Part of me – honestly, a big part – thinks she's avoiding me. But I understand why she'd choose not to come here. The pull of the sea is strong, especially so soon after Dad's 'accident'. I feel a twinge of guilt, but I'm aware enough to let it go; my worry for Dad is different than hers. I can't go hunting for seals or slicing open fish. I can't kill, and so my fears can't be expressed in the same way as my mother's. My distress sent me to Erskine Manor, and look at what that led me to.

Someone slips their arm through mine, and I get a flash of a feeling – of the sea on a bright day, the water glittering and my body held by it, lighter, where nothing seems important except for this very moment.

Breagha's shoulder presses against mine, and her grip is fierce, like she expects me to pull away. 'I found you,' she says.

'I needed the fresh air,' I say. 'What do you think of the ceilidh? Are you having fun?'

'Yes.' I feel her twirl her cane and hear the soft sound of it on the steps. 'Some of the dances are too fast for me. They are doing now what is called "Weeping Willow". That is wild!'

I laugh. 'You mean "Strip the Willow".' I look into her eyes, and she's smiling back at me. 'That *is* a wild one. It's late enough in the evening, so I reckon someone is going to get thrown right off the dance-floor.'

Right on cue, as if by magic, we hear the crash of glass shattering, and a cheerful roar rises up. We both laugh, and I'm lost again in that feeling of just floating in the sea, being held in the present moment. Breagha leans her head against my shoulder. Without thinking, my body reacts without enough time for me to stop myself, and I turn and press my lips and nose against her hair, breathing her in.

'Kier,' Breagha says. She lifts her cane, pointing it up. 'There is a storm coming.'

'Can you feel it?' I say, surprised because the air doesn't feel close. In fact, it feels crisp and bright, a perfect, cloudless summer night.

'There is always a storm on my birthday.'

'It's your birthday?' I shift to look at her. 'You should have said!'

'Not yet.' She looks up into the sky. The daylight is still clinging onto the horizon in a strip of faded blue, brighter than the rest of the sky, giving the air a blueish haze. 'Tomorrow.'

'Soon then,' I say. 'Any minute, I guess.'

She nods, as if she somehow knows the time precisely. 'Yes.'

Her 'yes' dissolves into silence, but it's the sort of silence that is easy. Neither of us is in a rush to fill it, and we stand together this way, just watching the blue in the sky shrink thinner and thinner.

'Kier.' Breagha turns to me. Her expression is serious as she takes my hand in her free one and grips just my fingertips. 'Will you come with me to the sea?'

'What do you mean?' I ask, which isn't really what I mean to say, but it's the only thing I can think of.

'I think that if you come with me, you can bring me back.'

'What if I can't?' I ask, but I want to ask, *why me?*

'You will,' she says simply, and the look in her dark eyes is so full of trust that there is enough left for me to trust myself, too.

'I will,' I say, looking to the sky. The strip of light has vanished. 'Happy birthday.'

I am not sure if I kiss her first, or if she kisses me, but it is perfect.

44

My mind is buzzing with a new thrill that I don't know what to do with, but I like the feeling of it, making me light in all my limbs, as if my bones were hollow as a bird's. The desolate stares of the Erskines of old seem less potent as I pass down the portrait hall. With the house filled with music, it's easy to find my way, and soon I see the twin doors of the dining hall, thrown open to the yellow glow of the ceilidh beyond.

Breagha will soon be returning to the ceilidh to gather her siblings. Despite my attempts to help her, she insisted on going alone to the walled garden to fetch their skins. The stone statue hiding the small, dark pool where the skins remain hidden is heavy, but I've seen her strength, and I don't doubt she will manage on her own. I sense that this is something I should not be a part of – a private thing for Breagha and her siblings to experience together.

Breagha thinks I can bring her back to land, but I am not sure. I know how powerful the sea's call can be.

I don't want to think of it, only on the bright, lively present.

When I reach the ceilidh and imbed myself properly with a fresh glass of beer, I make a game of trying to spot the Erskines. Calder seems to have endeared himself to an elderly couple standing on the sidelines in their impeccable kit. The man has his arm around Calder's sloped shoulders and is clearly instructing him on the mechanics of the current dance. Innes is among the dancers, charging forth with confidence. Didn't I tell him he'd pick up the dances in no time at all? It takes me much longer to find Lennox, but when I do, I am delighted to see her hidden away in a shadowy corner, where she seems to be having a fabulous time kissing Mairi's wee brother. He's a handsome young man, but no doubt feels quite pleased with himself to have landed a girl as stunning as Lennox, an Erskine at that. What sort of stories will the townspeople spin now that they know who the Erskines really are?

Breagha was right. They deserved this night before she showed them the truth. Now, when she gives them their skins, they will have a true choice. Land or sea. Human or seal. At least now they have tasted a bit of what it's like to be human.

I am so absorbed in watching the party unfold around me, I nearly miss Lady Erskine's arrival. She makes no grand entrance nor announcement, only arrives without flourish into the hall. She is dressed no more or less elegantly than she usually is, in a long emerald-green gown and black lace gloves, but she is radiant in a new way this evening. Her cheeks are flushed and her eyes bright as she scans the room.

Someone follows close behind her, and at first I think she must have brought a servant with her, but then she turns to face him, and he comes fully into view.

The man is as dark-haired as she, but his hair is peppered with grey. Looking at him, I am overwhelmed with the same feeling that sweeps over me when Breagha is near – of sinking into the sea, washing away all colours but blue, grey and green. His resemblance to Innes is striking, and he carries himself with the same pride that Innes does when he's among the pines.

This can only be Lord Erskine.

Lord Erskine, whose tomb is tucked away in the walled garden.

Lord Erskine, whose bones are missing from the hidden pool.

He stares with obvious reverence into Lady Erskine's eyes and pulls her into a kiss. They are like new lovers, enthralled with one another's company, delighted to be together among a sea of strangers.

I look for the other Erskines, wondering if they will recognise this man as their father and what they'd make of him. But although no more than ten minutes have passed since I saw each one of them, they are gone now. I must have missed Breagha slipping in to tell them the news of their skins.

Lady and Lord Erskine link arms and walk a circle around the room. They point and smile at the changes to the hall, sometimes stopping to speak to someone or clasp a hand. They seem amused by the dancing and give instructions to servants as they pass. They draw no attention to themselves, are inconspicuous hosts. I realise the beer I've been clutching has gone completely warm, and I've hardly taken more than a couple of sips. I haven't moved from my spot on the edge of the dance-floor. Should I fetch Breagha? But would it be too late? Would I be ruining the moment when she gives her siblings their skins? And what would I say? 'Your dad isn't dead, he's just shown up at the party quite alive'?

I haven't made a decision, and soon it's too late anyway.

Lady Erskine catches my eye. She leans in to her husband, whispering something in his ear, and my palm itches. She has caught me.

As the lord and lady approach, I think that there is something wrong with his eyes. But there is nothing particularly unusual about his eyes, which are a hazel mix of grey and green. He looks at me in the intent way that all the Erskines do, and it feels like a challenge. *Yes?* he seems to say. *What exactly makes you afraid?*

Because I am afraid.

I am looking at a man who ought to be dead.

Let me add that to the stash of secrets I've collected here, alongside the bones and the selkie skins. Maybe they are connected, or maybe Lady Erskine is a collector of secrets, and I have just happened to find a handful.

'This is my bone diver.' Lady Erskine grasps Lord Erskine's arm fiercely, as if afraid he might slip away. When she speaks, she leans towards him, lifting on her toes to speak into his ear. 'Kier Sealgair, the seal killers' daughter.' She laughs. 'Isn't that amusing?'

'My pleasure, Miss Sealgair,' Lord Erskine says. He takes my hand, squeezing it once, and never breaking my gaze. 'I have always admired the Sealgairs. What single-minded purpose they possess. And when I hear their flute' – he smiles radiantly – 'I nearly leap out of my skin.'

'I will pay you handsomely, as promised, Miss Sealgair,' Lady Erskine says. 'Your efforts have exceeded my expectations.' She looks deeply at her husband. 'Lord Erskine is finally well again.'

'A party always raises my spirits,' Lord Erskine agrees. He nods once at me, still smiling, as Lady Erskine draws him away.

Their departure lingers like an aftertaste. My hunter's instincts are ringing alarm bells. I shift my foot, glad I can feel the presence of my knife against my anklebone. Trying to look casual, and not at all like my hackles are raised, I take a long sip of my warm beer. I cannot help myself – I watch them.

They move about the room again, greeting their guests. They speak for a little while with Mairi's mother and, afterwards, Mairi and her new husband. Lady Erskine is less brittle than I'd expect when Mairi pulls her into a hug. Genuinely, the lord and lady seem to be enjoying themselves.

The next dance is a couples' waltz. The lord and lady step onto the dance-floor, drawing the gazes of the entire hall. They are radiant beneath the glittering chandelier. A perfect match. Their presence inspires others, and in a moment the dance-floor is filled with couples waiting for the caller's cue.

The waltzes are my least favourite of the ceilidh dances because, as well as requiring a partner, they are slower and more deliberate. This is not a sloppy 'Strip the Willow'. Although the waltzes aren't as fun to take part in, there is still something mesmerising about watching the couples move across the floor, spinning and dipping in unison.

Lady and Lord Erskine twirl out of view, but I keep sight of the flash of Lady Erskine's emerald skirts between the other dancers. As the couples spin, they move around the room, creating the effect of a whirlpool of colour and voices, conversations snatched away as they dance past me.

Then I spot the lord and lady again. She is as bright as ever, but something is different about him. His head moves oddly, nodding from side to side as he dances. A strange quirk, I think, but when they twirl my way again, I am certain I hear his laugh, an inhuman guttural chuckle. He looks over his shoulder, catching my gaze, and I step back, knocking into a table behind me, making all the half-empty glasses set atop it rattle. His eyes are no longer grey and green but fully black.

Does anyone else notice? Can anyone else see what I do?

Lord Erskine dips, drawn downwards by the growing length of his right arm. Still smiling, he appears oblivious, but Lady Erskine's delighted demeanour has changed completely. Her expression is pinched with worry. She has seen it, too. With every spin, Lord Erskine is changing, his limbs growing longer, fingernails extending to points. He is becoming the creature I saw in the walled garden. The monster Lady Erskine held with such tenderness.

As my father says, there is a kernel of truth in every tale. Lord Erskine is a monster, after all.

The band plays and plays, and I can almost hear Lady Erskine willing them to stop. Her husband is changing, but she cannot leave the dance-floor while the dance continues. It would draw too much attention. The lord and lady's movements are no longer fluid. All the while she is holding him straight, directing him this way and that, he simply smiles. For the first time, I feel a pinch of sympathy for Lady Erskine. It seems only with her willpower alone does her husband manage to maintain much of his human appearance.

The other instruments gently cease playing, and only the fiddler continues, ushering in the end of the dance with long draws of his bow. The dancers scoop each other into hugs, some melting into kisses. Lord Erskine loses balance and crumples into one of the tables. Glasses scatter, shards of glass skittering across the floor. Lady Erskine pulls him into an embrace, feigning playfulness as she hides the truth. Some people laugh at the lord, who they probably think is just enjoying himself too much.

As Lady Erskine takes her husband's arm, trying to pull him away, he resists. He lifts his right hand, which even through the commotion of a new dance starting up, I see has become tipped with black claws. Lord Erskine's black eyes flicker to their human hazel. He stares at his twisted fingers and *sees*. I am certain he sees what he is becoming, but his expression does not shift into one of fear or shock.

No, he smiles.

He smiles as if he knows and is pleased at his transformation.

The moment shatters. Lord Erskine's eyes are clouded once again in ink.

Lady Erskine hurries her husband out of the hall, slipping away like a fish from a net – and, like the hunter I am, I follow.

45

THE ERSKINES MOVE SWIFTLY, but I have followed close enough behind them when they wound their way through the manor house that I can still make out their silhouettes ahead of me. Lady Erskine's slim figure always remains the same, but Lord Erskine is changing. His limbs have grown longer, his arms scraping the ground, and his head seems to have unwound itself part-way off his neck so that it tilts from side to side. I hear snatches of Lady Erskine's urgent whispers carried to me on the summer breeze. She is losing control. I can see it in the way the monster tries to tug her in this direction then that, and she must firmly guide it back.

They are headed towards the shore. As the roaring of the waves grows louder, so does my fear. Innately, I sense that Lord Erskine belongs in the sea, and that once he reaches the water, he will become something far worse than the shambling monstrosity he is on land. Surely, he is like a seal, a creature that is such a bumbling fool on land you'd be hard-pressed to believe just how graceful it can be in the water. Seals are fast, powerful and even dangerous beneath the waves. What will Lord Erskine become when he reaches the shore?

Lord and Lady Erskine reach the edge of the cliffs and disappear from view. I would think them fallen to their deaths, if I hadn't already thought the same of Calder, when he took the carven staircase down to the water's edge. Once I reach the uppermost step, I pause, undecided if I ought to wait for them to reach the shore before I descend. But Lady Erskine is so absorbed in directing the monster down the steps that I don't think she'll notice me creeping behind them.

Lord Erskine's laughter mingles with the song of the waves.

It's a horrible, eerie sound, mostly animal in its inflection, but a bit of the human is still there, still clinging on. What caused him to become this unnatural thing?

By the time I reach them on the shore, Lord Erskine is half in the water, and already it has changed him. Silvered by the moonlight, his skin is as clear as glass, revealing the tangled web of veins that run with black blood. His dashing suit is in tatters now, torn around his shoulders and neck. He stands as if he is pulled in two directions, his black gaze shifting from the shore to the sea.

Although my stomach roils in revulsion, Lady Erskine has not given up. She rushes into the water after him, reaching for his face, imploring.

'Come back to me,' she says, her words almost lost in the sounds of the sea. She wraps her arms around his shoulders.

Help me.

It's a whisper carried on the wind, an echo from my dreams. Lord Erskine's black eyes stare at me from over the pale curve of his wife's neck.

'*Finnian.*' Lady Erskine takes his face in her hands. She says his name like a burn tumbling over rocks, soft and rolling. For a moment, a spark of recognition flares in those black, unblinking eyes, but then his head tilts from side to side. His lips pull back, thinning, and his mouth widens, sucking at the air like a fish might. Without warning, his body twists and a clawed limb strikes out from the water, knocking Lady Erskine back and slicing a scarlet gash in her arm.

As she is flung around, she sees me, and I am certain she will be furious. I remember her ire when I rose empty-handed from the last pool. I remember her threat. But now, when she looks at me, her eyes grow wide and her demeanour softens, as if in relief. She is glad to see me. Water splashes around her knees as she hurries through the water towards me.

'Go,' she says, gripping my wrist with her clammy fingers. 'Find another bone, quickly.'

Her hair is plastered to her skull, her eyes sunken in fear. She is afraid of losing Lord Erskine completely. Behind her, moving with snake-like grace through the dark water, he sinks, leaving only the top half of his head visible. His black eyes stare beyond his wife, towards me. I feel as if I have swallowed ice. The monster looks on, unblinking.

Bone diver.

'Why?' I ask, ignoring the whisper that scrapes against my mind.

Lady Erskine's eyes flash with irritation, but she answers my question. 'Selkie bones have great power. Every one you found has brought him back to me, just for a time. Certain bones are stronger than others, and the skull ... I thought that was enough.'

I shake my head. 'Finding that skull nearly killed me.'

'We must find another bone tonight. He is changing too fast.' She grips my wrist harder and tries to pull me away with her as she walks towards the cliff. 'I will take you to another tomb. You will dive until you find one.'

But I do not budge. She is not strong enough to move me, despite her conviction.

'No,' I say.

'You must,' she says. 'We have an agreement.'

'I agreed to dive for bones until Midsummer.' I gesture around me. 'It *is* Midsummer.'

'You do not understand.' Lady Erskine's voice has softened, the venomous urgency gone. She stares out at the sea, and I follow her gaze. Lord Erskine watches still, but not as if he is listening. He seems to be biding his time, a hunter with all the time in the world to wait for the perfect moment. 'We made this house together, between our worlds, so we could live both lives as we pleased. By day among the waves and, at night, we would throw the most wonderful parties on the edge of the shore. It was perfect.' Her nostrils flare. 'A selkie's life is far longer than a human's. Together, we should have seen generations pass, but he was taken from me too soon.

An accident. A drunken guest in the walled garden. I rushed him to the sea as the life poured out of him and, as he breathed his last, I pleaded with the sea for help.' Lady Erskine's eyes narrow in anger. Her whole body tenses, remembering. 'But the sea does not give favours. The sea only cares for herself and nothing more, not even her loyal subjects. She seemed to help – he returned to me – but as the years passed, he began to change.' She lifts a hand towards the water, where Lord Erskine lurks. 'She has turned him into a monster, and I have done all I can to work against her. The selkie bones save him from slipping away completely.' She pins me with her stare. 'Every bone you find gives us more time. You must understand what it is like to lose someone you love. You must understand why I need you. Please.' She holds her hand out towards me.

She has meant to convince me with her story, and certainly I feel the grief steeped in her every word. But I cannot ignore my anger. She made a bargain with the sea, she made *this* ... this creature that is neither one thing or another, a monster that does not belong, neither in the depths of the sea nor in a great manor house on the shore. Lord Erskine was once a seal and a man, but he is neither now. He is the creature that has tipped the balance of the sea, eroded the livelihoods of the fisherman, corrupted the waters, and attacked my father on his boat.

And even if I wanted to, who am I to go against the will of the sea? Lord Erskine died. He died, and was it right for Lady

Erskine to bring him back to life? What are the bones doing but delaying the inevitable? Lord Erskine will never be who he once was. There are not enough tombs on this estate to bring him back.

'I can't,' I say, shaking my head.

Lady Erskine lunges towards me, water spraying from her hair and stinging my eyes. 'Come now, seal killer.'

'I am not a seal killer, nor a bone diver any longer.'

She laughs. 'Then what are you? A useless, useless girl who cannot kill.' She points at me, right at my heart. 'I made you this way.' Her eyes glint in the moonlight. 'I took the killing from you, and I can give it back, if you find me a bone.'

'*What?*' I say, but the word is lost in a flurry of commotion on the cliff.

The air smells suddenly and thickly of the sea, the deep, black depths of it. A wind lifts my hair, and with it I hear the hollow moan of a flute. A single note, held long and steady.

It is a sound I have heard so many times, but never has it filled me with fear.

The Sealgair flute. My mother is on the water, and she is calling the seals.

Several figures rush down the cliffside stairway. Four figures. Not until the first one reaches the shore do I realise what has happened. Four pairs of black, glassy eyes stare at me. Stare right through me.

In their arms, draped over their shoulders, they carry their selkie skins. Already, they are changing. I am too late to stop them.

The flute does not falter, and among its lilting I hear that whisper again.

Help me.

I look for him, but Lord Erskine has disappeared. His children rush past me and into the sea.

46

NOT NOW, I THINK. They cannot have the skins now. 'Don't go!' I shout, but of course they do not listen. Innes, with his selkie skin draped over his neck, is the first one to reach the water. As seawater splashes around his knees, he yanks the skin down, tugging it over his back. Between one step and the next, he changes. His shoulders curl, his whole body tipping towards the waves until a large one sweeps over him. As the wave rolls on, no young man emerges. Only a dark seal's back surfaces briefly before melting into the dark waters.

He is shortly followed by Lennox, and Calder behind her. They rush into the sea, just as their brother did, tugging their skins over their backs, transforming in the space of a breath.

Breagha is last to enter the water, and I rush towards her.

'Wait!' I shout, fumbling for Breagha's hand, as if I could ever stop a selkie's love for the sea. 'Breagha!' I shout. 'She will kill you! My mother will kill you!'

Breagha looks over her shoulder. Her eyes, too, are as black as a seal's. 'Stop them,' she says before she is gone.

When I turn back to face the sea, it is as if the Erskines were never here at all. The waves roll forward, uncaring, erasing all evidence.

Distantly, the Sealgair flute plays, and I choke down a frustrated sob.

'Stop them!' I shout at Lady Erskine, echoing Breagha's plea.

Lady Erskine holds her elbows, looking vulnerable in a way I have never seen her. 'No,' she says in a whisper. 'It is too late.'

A shape rises on the water, silvered in the moonlight. The *Silver Stuckie*. The boat without a crew. It is close enough to swim to.

It is my only hope.

47

THE ERSKINE WATERS ARE SO dark that I feel as if the sky and sea are confused, bleeding into one another as I swim. With every stroke I think of what lurks beneath me, those blackened limbs tipped with claws and the wide, sucking mouth. When my hands meet the hard, rough texture of wood, I waste no time hauling myself onto the deck.

I kneel on the boat and realise I'm shaking. I hold out my hand and watch it quaking for a moment before tightening it into a fist and taking a deep breath. I scramble over to the edge of the boat and look out across the water. In the distance, I see a disturbance in the wave pattern. It could just be a rock, but, in the low light, I cannot be certain.

'All right,' I say, looking around me.

The boat is a typical herring drifter, the same sort of boat my family uses, though ours is smaller and isn't fitted with nets. I waste a precious moment looking down into the net positioned on the port side to see it still laden with dead fish. The reek is incredible, worse even than when the black kelp was washed up on the shore not long ago. My first task is to release the net, which surely will slow me down once I get the vessel moving. It's not easy – I'm just one person, and this sort of boat requires a crew – but I manage it eventually. That done, I turn my focus on the engine. If that's still in working order, then I have a chance of catching my mother before she finds the Erskines.

I'm not a mechanic, nor much inclined that way, but like anyone who makes a living off a boat, I know the fundamentals of how this boat's engine works. It's even the same model as my family's, and looking at it brings a pang of nostalgia that only makes the task ahead of me feel more urgent. What would I do if my own mother killed the Erskines? What would I do if she drove her spear through Breagha's beautiful seal hide?

With a bit of tinkering, the engine starts. As it sputters to life, I let out a whoop, but that spark of joy burns out as soon as I turn to see a magpie perched on the boat's prow.

'What are you doing here?' I say. The bird's white breast glows in the soft shadows of night. 'There's nowhere for you out on the sea.'

The magpie shrieks and flutters its wings. I expect it to fly away towards the shore, but instead it finds a roost among the stays.

'Fine,' I say. The engine is running; I feel its vibrations in my legs. But when I steer the boat forward it slides through the water only for a handful of seconds before stopping abruptly, as if slamming into something solid. I try again and get no further. I try once more after turning the engine off and on again – this time, the boat moves forward for a good ten seconds before it stops. The engine clicks off.

'What's wrong?' I say, as if the boat could answer me. I stride to the prow, look over the edge. What did I expect to find? A damn iceberg? Nothing is there. Just the water.

'I need to go!' I shout down to the waves. 'They are out there with their sealskins, and my mother will find them. She will find them, and she will kill them – if Lord Erskine doesn't first.' I slam the heel of my hand against the prow. 'You have to let me go.'

I rush to the engine and although it roars to life, the boat doesn't move an inch this time. I feel the anger filling me up, making me want to scream. I had no time to begin with, and now whatever is left is slipping between my fingers.

I stop and breathe deep. I imagine I am about to dive. I prepare my body, my mind. When I return to the engine, a calm has settled over me. My hands move instinctively. I tap into old memories that lay buried with lack of use. I remember Mum and Dad bent over the engine, arguing as our boat sat stalled in the sea. Dad had one idea for how to fix it, Mum another – and wasn't Mum right in the end?

With my mind half in the memory, half in the present, I do what she did. The engine continues rumbling, but now, when I guide the boat forward, it lurches, quickly picking up speed.

The boat moves swiftly.

I look towards the mast. The magpie is gone. At some point, it must have flown away, but I never saw it go.

When I look back at the horizon, where the sea meets the sky, I see the outline of a familiar boat.

Mum.

48

Our two boats cautiously approach one another, prow to prow, before Mum smoothly directs my family's boat close enough to mine so that I can step aboard without fear of tumbling into the sea.

'That's the *Silver Stuckie*,' Mum says, when I step aboard. She's got a spear in her hand. For a moment, I panic, thinking maybe she's already found the Erskines, but the spear isn't bloodied, and I see no seal corpses hauled onto deck.

'Aye, the one that was lost in the Erskine waters,' I say. A stab of guilt shatters the joy I feel at seeing her. She's staring at me, like she doesn't know who I am. I did up and leave, after all.

'What are you doing here, Kier?'

'You need to turn back,' I say. 'You need to go home.'

'No,' she sighs, her voice sodden with disappointment. The weight of it could drag me right to the bottom of the sea. 'I need to hunt for seals. That's all I've ever needed to do, and we needed you, too, Kier, but you left.'

I hold out my hands. Empty. My knife is in my hilt, and it feels heavier than usual. 'I had to. I was no use at home, and

Lady Erskine gave me a job. She said she'd pay me enough to keep Dad off the boat until spring.'

'And did she?'

I open my mouth but can't answer. I feel like a fool.

'I'm not going back, not after I spotted those four seals just before you turned up. They were trailing the boat, practically throwing themselves onto my spear, and these were beauties, Kier, the sort your dad is always on about.'

'You can't kill them,' I say. 'You have to go home.'

'Kier.' Mum steps towards me, and I read the look in her eyes.

I shake my head. 'My head's clear,' I insist, and even to my own ears, my words sound fragile, brittle. 'I just need you to go home.' My voice breaks on the word *home*, and although I feel like sinking down onto the deck, I stay standing, hoping she will understand.

'You're not the sort to make a fuss for nothing, Kier,' my mother says. 'Tell me what's going on.'

I stare at my mother's face. Her expression is stern, like it always is, like she's afraid of nothing and no one. Dad is the storyteller. He's the one who likes to spin tales of sea creatures and monsters and selkie lovers. If it were his eyes I were looking into right now, I might have a chance.

You won't understand, I want to say, but I know if I said that, I'd be giving up. I'd be condemning the Erskines to death, condemning my mother to become a murderer. So, instead, I say, 'Do you know Dad's story about the selkie, the girl who puts on her sealskin and becomes a seal?' She nods, enough for me to go on. 'They're real. Selkies. They have the most magnificent pelts, and in the sea they look just like seals, except something is different about their eyes, in the way they stare back at you. The four seals you saw following the boat – I know them. They're selkies, and they're from Erskine Manor. You can't kill them, so you have to go back. You have to go home.'

She doesn't say anything, but I see her take a deep breath. '*I* have to go home. And where will you be?'

Before I can reply, the boat shudders, and we lurch forward, catching our footing. We launch into action, our instincts kicking in. My knife is in my fingers before I even realise I reached for it, and my mother hefts her spear, running across the deck in the direction of where the impact was.

That was a big lurch, made by something far larger than a seal. Not even a group of four seals could make the boat move like that. Lord Erskine has found us. And my mother, spear in hand, is running across the deck to face him.

I spin around to the controls and get the boat going again. It begins to move off and, as the wind picks up, I allow myself to feel a germ of hope.

Again, the boat rocks as something slams against our portside.

'What is it?' Mum shouts, looking into the churning water around us.

'A monster. The one that hurt Dad. We need to outrun it,' I say, but I think of those black eyes, and maybe there is no way to outrun a creature like this.

'No,' says Mum. 'We can kill it.' She turns to look at me, hope brimming in her eyes. 'We can kill it together.'

I want to do two things at once – grab my mother and pull her into a hug and tell her, *Yes, yes, let's kill this creature together*. And at the same time, I want to shake her fiercely by the shoulders and tell her that I would give anything to kill alongside her, I'd give anything to be a proper Sealgair, but I don't know what that means anymore, to be a Sealgair. Not for me, anyway.

'No,' I say.

My mother does not get a chance to do or say anything because, just as she turns to face me, a massive, scaled tail, dripping with seawater, catching the moonlight, rises above her.

It moves swiftly, twisting in a mesmerising motion, before slamming itself against the deck. Mum cries out as splinters of wood hurl all around her. She stumbles back just as the tail slides away and disappears beneath the water.

'What was that?' Mum says, breathless.

'Go home.' I grab my mother's arm. 'Lead the seals away. Don't turn around for anything.' I hesitate, the usual thought flitting through my mind – what can I do, the daughter of seal killers who cannot kill? – but I let it slip away. I have no use for it anymore. Now is not the time for doubts or wishes. Now, I trust my instincts, just as my mother taught me. 'Let me go.'

When she fumbles for my hand, I know she knows what I plan to do.

My mother, who was once a herring girl that could gut a fish in one clean stroke, holds my hand tightly and says, 'Aye.'

She gives my hand a squeeze. She doesn't protest, doesn't point out that I can't kill the creature, no matter how much I might want to. She doesn't ask the questions I'm sure she wants to ask. She lets me go.

'Get the breakfast started for me,' I say around the lump in my throat.

'You better be back in time,' my mother says back at me.

I walk to the edge of the portside. The monster has churned up the sea into a froth of silver and blue. The *Silver Stuckie* is already almost out of sight.

Just before I hit the water, before the rush of cold and the rise of panic, I hear my mother's words, almost whisked away on the wind, 'My brave girl.'

49

Absurdly, I am still wearing the orange dress. As I sink into the water, it billows around me like clouds of orange squid ink. But I quickly dive deep enough beneath the surface to where the water is strangely calm. Only for a few moments do I see the dark shape of my family's boat before it disappears, and though I look all around me, peering into the gloom of the sea, I do not see the creature.

Holding my breath, relaxing my limbs, my heart, to conserve the oxygen in my lungs, I wait.

I have not forgotten my dreams, of the hand in mine, leading me through the house; the voice in my ear, pleading for help. I have gambled everything on these dreams. Lord Erskine wants me, needs me, just as Lady Erskine did. If I wait, eventually, he will come.

A shadow appears among the shifting colours of the sea. It moves with effortless grace, powerfully quick, swimming directly towards me. I swim backwards, but there is no reason to. The shadow stops just in front of me, and I stare into the large, black eyes of a seal.

She is beautiful. This is her element. Beneath the surface, despite the gloom, her pelt is radiant, speckled with an iridescent sheen. She blinks at me before shooting off to swim circles around me. The water shifts, forming a wee whirlpool. We both surface together, as her momentum draws me upwards.

When the water clears from my eyes, the seal is gone. Instead, Lady Erskine stares at me with her dark eyes set stark against her pale face. Her black hair is slick against her ears, clinging to her neck.

'I see what you have done,' she says. I swear her voice is different, as fluid as the sea. The coldness that she usually wears like a shroud is gone. Her emotions are clear across her face; she is no longer guarding herself from me. 'Instructing your mother to lead my children away.' She pauses, her nostrils flaring. 'But this is only a temporary solution. They are free now, and together they will have no reason to return to the shore. The sea is open to them, and I have kept them closed in for so long that they will want to see it all. Eventually, they will grow tired of your mother's flute ... and he is waiting.'

'Lord Erskine.'

'Yes.' Grief fills her eyes. 'Yes, he will kill them. He has tried before, drawn by a twisted love. He forgets why he desires them. He only knows to kill. This is why I kept their skins hidden. Only until I found a cure for their father. Only for a short time, but time stretched on ...'

Ah, so that is why she hid her children's selkie skins in her husband's empty tomb. She could not let them into the sea, knowing who was out there, *what* was out there. The creature that attacked my father and the crew of the *Silver Stuckie*.

'Breagha found her skin, but I did not dare take it back. By the time I knew, she had already tasted the sea, already knew who she was, and taking it back would kill her. I feared her father would find her, but you found her first. You nearly killed my daughter, did you know that?' Lady Erskine continues. 'And so I took from you what you cherished the most.'

Lady Erskine reaches out her hand. A familiar sight, but one I had forgotten.

I know what will happen next.

So I let her do it.

She presses one finger against my heart. One single heartbeat, and I remember that night as if I were there now.

Driven by anger, I left the house long after sunset. I don't remember why I was angry, but I do remember *who* I was angry with. My mother – of course my mother. I felt often that she questioned me, that she was trying to impose her ways of hunting and killing on me. I felt such a deep pressure to be like her, unafraid, a killer right to her marrow, that compared to her, surely I was a disappointment.

Anger filled me up the night I took my family's boat on the water alone. Mum had warned me never to do so, which is why I took it without even thinking. I wanted to defy her, do something that she couldn't do. So I took the boat by myself, a fifteen-year-old girl filled with a false confidence.

I was so, so sure I would find a seal that night.

And I did. The most beautiful seal I'd ever seen. I'd been out on the boat hardly more than an hour when she appeared portside. At first, she swam alongside me as I drove the boat forward. The boat's movement through the water seemed to delight her, and she swam back and forth, appearing in one moment on my left, the next on my right.

As soon as I saw her, I knew I would kill her. A pelt like hers would garner a fortune. Already, I was daydreaming of hauling her carcass over my shoulders, her blood smearing across the floor as I dumped her, triumphantly, onto the floorboards of my parents' bedroom. Just like the seal my father had caught the day I was born. She was just as beautiful as that seal surely had been, perhaps even more so.

Eventually, I slowed the boat to a stop. It rocked on the waves. The seal popped her head out of the water and watched me curiously.

My knife or my spear? When I looked into her eyes, that's all I wondered. How would I kill her?

I choose my knife, of course. I was never as deft with a spear as I was with a knife. The knife, when I held it, was like a second limb, an extension of my hand. It was natural, powerful and perfect.

The seal blinked at me, and I laughed, startling her. Just as she turned to swim beneath the surface, her grey back rising, I threw the knife. It stuck into her side. Her head was already below the surface, so if she made a sound, I could not hear it.

My mother had said never to hunt when laden with emotion. Always hunt with a clear head, she'd told me. That way, you will be able to hear your instincts and listen to them.

Until the moment I threw the knife, anger had driven my actions. It was all I felt, and only when the knife stuck in the seal's side did I hear my instincts.

I had made a mistake.

I had thrown the knife too early and hit the seal's flank. A useless throw that only injured her. The water was too dark to see the blood, but I was certain I could smell it.

The seal twisted unnaturally, her head surfacing. Her nostrils flared, taking in air, and she looked at me with eyes that I was certain *saw* me. Something like guilt twisted in my gut; a feeling I had never felt before when on a hunt.

Then, she sunk beneath the surface, taking my precious knife with her. I thought for a moment that I saw a pale curve of flesh disappear beneath the water, but it must have been an illusion of the waves. I ran to the side of the boat anyway and peered into the water, willing the seal to appear again.

I thought then that I had lost everything there was to lose. My knife. My dignity. A new daydream wrestled its way into my mind; of me returning home, empty-handed, having to endure my mother's look of disappointment.

I was wrong. There was so much more to lose.

When I think back to that night, this is where the memory stops. I don't remember the moment I lost the ability to kill.

All I know is that when I returned home, I couldn't do it anymore. I was changed, and I couldn't change myself back.

But now, with Lady Erskine's finger pressing against my heart, I remember, and the old nightmares make sense now. A pale hand reaching through the dark waters, and a woman's face just beneath the surface. Her black hair floating around her like bladderwrack, and my own anger like a spark compared to the fire in her eyes. She reached up, fingers dripping with sea water, and pressed a finger against my heart.

Just as she is now. Only then, she took the killing from me. Now, she gives it back.

By the time I pull myself from the memory, Lady Erskine has already gone, but her final words to me still resound in my ears: *You must do what I cannot.*

The dark water settles around me, and I am alone.

I feel . . .

I feel changed.

As I take the knife in my fingers, I know it.

I know it in the way the knife feels in my hand. The knife is not heavier, not really, but it has a different weight to it now. Not the weight of expectation, of a dream dashed, but the weight of something I have not felt for so, so long. The stone-heft of power.

I can kill.

I know without a doubt that I could pluck a scallop from its sandy bed and let its soft body die in the cool air. I could crush a snail's shell with my boot. I could kill the spiders in my bed.

I could plunge this knife into the heart of a seal.

With that thought sinking into me, digging deep with its claws, I take a long breath of the sea air. I see my path unfurling before me. I do not stay behind in the mornings. I don't wander the shore, collecting driftwood, wondering when I'll be whole again, fixed. I join my family on our hunts. We kill together, united in a common sense of accomplishment, that elusive joy that is impossible to find elsewhere. The joy of killing, of bringing death, of controlling life.

I look back towards the shore, towards Erskine Manor. We are not so far out as it seemed beneath the water. Perhaps the tide is drawing in, relentlessly, quietly, tugging me closer to the shore. I hold up my knife so that it shines in the moonlight. The tip of it I press against the moon, as if I could burst it like a bubble. I want to see what I can do.

You must be a Sealgair again.

50

THE SEALS FIND ME, just as they used to, just as they have always found the Sealgairs.

Four slick heads pop up in the water around me. Their eyes catch the moonlight, bright intelligent eyes that aren't afraid. They are curious, and for a long moment all they do is watch me with my knife in my hand, as if I'm holding something as useless as a seashell.

One dips beneath the water. I see the arch of its back as it swims, and then its head emerges again, so close to me now that I could stroke it. I reach out, and the seal does not even flinch. It watches me and snorts, water spraying from its whiskers. My fingers meet the fur of its head. What a beautiful pelt it has. It's like a gift, like the seal is offering itself to me. It blinks, cocks its head, seems to say, *Go on ahead, take it.*

Though surely I am numb from the cold water, I feel warm all over. I realise the heat radiates from the knife in my hand. It spreads across the whole of me, sinking into my bones. How could I ever have forgotten what this was like?

The seals dart around me. Look at them – they are *happy*. And here I am with a knife in my hand, able and ready to kill.

Nothing else matters because when I kill these seals, everything will be right again. I will be a Sealgair, as I have always meant to be, and all the loneliness and heartache of the last eight years will feel like a silly, child's nightmare. None of it will matter. Nothing else does.

I know only three things. The knife in my hand. The black water around me. The seals, who ask me to kill them, who beg me.

'All right,' I say. 'Who's first, then?'

I am certain that the hand that grabs me, yanking beneath the surface belongs to a human, but when the bubbles settle, all I see is the dark bulk of a seal swimming away. I open my mouth, a rookie move, and swallow brine.

Treading water while choking is no easy feat, and I struggle for a few minutes, angry that I let myself get distracted, that I did something so stupid. Of course, it doesn't matter. The seals are still here, and my knife is ready.

Something brushes against my feet, something sharp against my shoulder, a little squeak in me ear. 'Dratsie.' She squeaks again. Surely her claws in my shoulder are drawing blood. 'You rascal, get off me.' I try to shrug her off, but she stays put. 'Aye, all right. You want to hunt?'

The closest seal is the smallest one. Its eyes are the biggest, round, black, hardly blinking. I choose this one to finally break the curse. This one will be my first kill.

Dratsie bites me. She sinks her teeth into the meat of my shoulder, and I scream. She has never bitten me before, not even a nip. 'You scamp!' I shout. It doesn't disturb the seals, but Dratsie chitters and darts away with a splash. I turn to look at her, to see her wee rascal face, when I catch sight of the dark shape of Erskine Manor in the distance. It makes my throat go tight and I wonder, *why*? What have I forgotten?

And I remember seeing the reflection of that house in a tidepool as Fie peered inside and pointed out a scampering hermit crab. I remember the way the stone walls seemed to be crying, and the mushrooms in the bathtub, the peeling wallpaper, the damp curtains. I remember the Erskines and the bones and especially Breagha Erskine, who was like the sea, in her green silk dress. I remember the ceilidh and the *Silver Stuckie* and my mother saying, *My brave girl*.

What am I doing? What have I nearly done?

I've lost myself in the allure of the lifted curse, of the knife in my hand, the potential that thrums through by bones now that I know I can use it.

But Lady Erskine did not lift the curse for me to kill her children. All this time, she was only protecting them.

She wants me to kill her husband. Because she must know, as I do, that there is no saving him. He cannot change back to who he once was.

Terror tightens my throat and gets the blood pounding in my ears, as I realise what has happened. The Erskines have lost interest in my mother's flute. She drew them away, but they have returned, drawn towards me.

That is not all.

The monster has come for me, too.

51

THE MIST ROLLS OVER THE SEA, stinking of brine, carrying an icy chill that seems drawn up from the water, which has darkened to the same bleeding black of the waters around Erskine Manor. *Wearing darkness like a cloak*, Archie had said.

The tail appears first in the black sea beneath me. Lengths and lengths of it, shimmering with the same sheen as a selkie skin. The face is next, pale in places where the skull is visible beneath the translucent skin, black where the veins run. The eyes have widened to orbs of jet, and the lips are bloodless, sunken.

He is beneath the surface, like a drowned man, but he rises quickly, his head breaking the surface and portions of his tail lifting from the water around me.

Lord Erskine smiles, showing sharp teeth, as seawater rolls down his face like tears.

His head whips around as a seal darts past him. The grin widens and his tail ripples, striking the seal. It is thrown backward, momentarily above the surface, before disappearing beneath the water.

I am no longer a *useless girl*.

Two more seals dart into Lord Erskine's view and, while they draw his attention, I take a breath and drop beneath the surface. I move quickly, knife extended, going for his heart, which I can see beating in his chest, a dark, pulsing fist.

Though he is not looking at me, he knows I am near, and one of his clawed hands reaches out, grabbing at my dress, ripping it. Beneath the water, the fabric makes no sound.

I lunge again, but again he claws at me, forcing me back.

To him, I am but a bothersome fly, distracting him from his real purpose.

Breagha appears beside me. Even without the jagged scar in her side, the scar I made with the very knife I hold in my fingers, I would recognise her. With slow-dawning horror, I realise she is trying to protect me.

Get away, I want to shout. *He wants to hurt you.*

But we are under the water, and I am a human. This is not my place. I cannot speak, and I am not as fast as either Lord Erskine or his children.

Breagha turns circles around me before shooting away, barely avoiding her father's claws. His tail pursues her, rushing through the water with impossible speed.

How can I possibly stop such a monster?

Lord Erskine doesn't bother to attack me, only glances briefly at me in a look of what might be amusement. The smile is still there, lipless and gaping, but chillingly human. And his eyes, too. They are hazel again. He stares at me and winks, just as he did in the gardens.

That is how I know.

Lady Erskine believes her husband is wholly a monster, driven by a twisted love. She believes he wants to hurt his children because he can no longer understand what it means to love them.

But those eyes belong to no monster.

The water around us is charged with energy, and it seems almost as if I can taste his desire. He wants death. He wants to destroy. He is the one who slit the belly of a thousand silver darlings, just because he could. No creature of the sea would ever do such a thing.

Lord Erskine wants pain, drawn out and pointless. He has enough of a man in him yet for that.

There must be a way for me to draw his attention.

Running out of breath, I break the surface. The moon grins at me.

Lord Erskine hunts for the pleasure of it. He hunts for the power. I know that desire; all the Sealgairs do.

Again, I dive. This time, I do not hover just below the surface. I dive deep, following the shapes of the seals as they do the same. Make him think I want what he wants. Make him think I am a seal killer again.

Now, I am more than just a bother. I am hunter, just as he is. There is nothing a hunter hates more than losing his prey to an opponent.

I follow the seals with determined intensity, just as I would if I truly wanted to kill them. For a moment, I am worried that this will not work, that Lord Erskine will not notice me, but suddenly something grabs my legs. The muscled power of his tail hauls me backwards, and the seals dart away.

Between one blink and the next, Lord Erskine changes. Before me is no longer a glass-skinned monster. Just as easily as Lady Erskine shed her sealskin, Lord Erskine's face and torso have returned to their human form. He is once again the charming man who hung on his wife's arm as she led him among the colour and movement of the ceilidh. He smiles at me, revealing even, white teeth. In his features, I see each of his children. I think of the life together they lost when Lady Erskine made her bargain with the sea.

Lord Erskine, his tail still curled around my waist and legs, thrusts himself towards the surface, and I am carried along with him. We both break the surface, though I am gasping, and he merely looks amused.

'Leave me to my hunt, bone diver,' he says in the same elegant voice he used at the ceilidh. The absurdity of this handsome man, conversing with me as the sea rolls around us, as his monstrous form curls hidden beneath the waves, is almost laughable. Perhaps I would laugh if the glint in his eyes weren't so frightening, so cold. This is worse than a senseless monster, worse than an animal, because he knows exactly what he is doing, and he enjoys it.

'I will need you yet. You think you have exhausted the supply of selkie bones the sea hoards, but you forget that a living thing has bones, too. Living, but not for long.' His gaze follows something behind me, and I know he is tracing the movements of a seal. Of a selkie.

So I have done this. This is what the bones have created.

Lady Erskine fed her husband selkie bones to draw the humanity out of him, but all the bones have done is make him this halfway thing. A monster with a man's mind, with a man's desire and intent. All this time, I have been fearful of the sea and the shifting of her balance, but it was my doing. I have been feeding something worse than a monster. And those were scraps of old bones. What would become of him if he had the bones of four selkies? What would happen to the sea, to everyone on this shore?

'Help me,' Lord Erskine says in a mocking whisper.

Help me. The voice grates against my mind. But it is not a plea to return him to his human self, as I once thought or hoped. Lord Erskine does not want to become human again.

Something tempting catches Lord Erskine's eye and his mirth shifts to hunger. Not far away, a seal's head bobs in the water. No, a woman's head, black hair slick with water. Lady Erskine. With shining eyes, she watches her husband, and I think she must see what I have seen. She must know what he has become.

In a blink, she is gone, but Lord Erskine is faster. His head and torso dip beneath the surface, and I am dragged with him, an afterthought. There is a moment when I think he will not catch her. She is an old selkie, a powerful one, but Lord Erskine was a selkie once, too, and seems to anticipate her movements. It is not long before he has his claws around her tail, yanking her back.

What can she possibly do to stop him?

Nothing, of course, and that is not her intent. She is distracting him. She is giving me a chance.

Lord Erskine takes his time, as his wife struggles in his grasp. He does not notice me.

I hold out my hand and look at the knife resting in my palm. All this time, I have not let it go.

I can kill again. I could slit his throat. That's how I could end this.

I could kill him.

Of course I could.

But my mother told me to trust my instincts before all else.

My mother would kill Lord Erskine without hesitation; my father would, too. But I am not my mother or my father. I am not a killer, but I am not a coward either. Perhaps I am something in between.

To kill, even something that ought to die, is to kill for the power. I could not kill Lord Erskine without feeling that familiar, aching pleasure that I once felt when I drove a spear through a seal's heart. I could not kill him and pretend I did not enjoy it.

My instincts say, *This is not for you to decide.*

This time, I listen.

I turn my palm over. The knife sinks. It is just a stroke of black in a dark sea and then it is gone, swallowed by the shadows of the depths.

I look up in time to see Lord Erskine release his wife's body, blood swirling in the water like a cloud.

The sea, I think. The sea doesn't care about Lady Erskine. She doesn't care if I make it to the shore, or if Lord Erskine kills his children. She doesn't care about my village. The sea, I imagine, cares only that she goes on. That the tides draw in and out, that sunny days are followed by the haar. The sea, if she cares about anything at all, cares only about balance.

Balance, which Lord Erskine threatens to disrupt. There are plenty of monsters in the sea, but none that kill for the pleasure and the power. Surely, the sea must know that as long as Lord Erskine swims within her waters, he will undo all she cares about.

I close my eyes, and I am certain I feel the stirring of a current. Something soft brushes against my elbow. Dratsie. My wee messenger, or so I hope.

He does not belong here, I think, fiercely pouring all my intent into the words. *He is not one of yours.*

I open my eyes. My lungs are bursting, I will have to rise soon.

The current I felt quickens, and Lord Erskine's tail unwinds itself from around me. He turns, his attention sudden and raging, and he reaches for me, the nails of one of his clawed hands scraping my arm, but something draws him backwards. A strong current that pulls him away from me. He changes quickly, his lips peeling back, his skin going pale, but his eyes remain human as he disappears into the gloom, his tail trailing after him long after his gaze is gone.

52

Choking on brine, I shoot upward, breaking the surface with a splutter. Something plops into the water beside me. Again and again, and I realise it is rain. Big, fat drops of rain. Storm rain. Suddenly, the air is thick, wet, electric-charged. I look up, and I can no longer see the moon. Wind skims across the water's surface, immediately raising little licks of waves, white-tipped and ubiquitous.

The big waves form quickly. It's astonishing how swiftly the sea shifts from calm to wild. I feel the water swirling beneath the surface. It's harder now to swim, harder to keep my head above the water as I'm bashed about by the waves.

With the knife gone, I have nothing left. The power that tricked me into a sense of invincibility dissolves away, and I am left fully aware of the weakness of my limbs, the weight of my bones. I have been treading water for too long.

The seals, the Erskines, love it. They twirl and spin around me. I suppose, they are home. They are exactly where they ought to be.

I am close enough to the shore to see the dark rocks, but if I manage to get near enough, surely I will be dashed against them. I am lifted up, and I know a wave is building behind me.

The last thing I see is Erskine Manor, perched on its cliff edge. I see it now for what it really is. A house on a crumbling rock. A fragile, old thing that does not belong to this world. The waves slam against the cliff that the manor house sits on. Huge chunks of rocks crumble away, swallowed by the waves.

Soon Erskine Manor will be dragged back to its home beneath these dark Erskine waters.

And I think, as I watch the cliff and the house collapse, that among the dark rocks and black water, I see a scaled tail. The waves have no mercy, and the tail disappears beneath a rush of white foam and carven rock.

I could laugh. For once, the sea listens.

53

I DREAM OF A BEAUTIFUL SEAL who saves me from the sea. Her pelt is soft, slick, against my cheek. As she moves through the water, my arms wrapped around her, I feel the strength of her muscles. The seal takes me to the shore, but when I open my eyes, a woman with black hair looks down at me. Her eyes are black, no irises, no whites.

'Bone diver,' she says, and although I try to reach out to her, open my mouth to speak, to tell her to stay, I slip backwards, falling into the dark.

Bone diver, I hear from a very long way away. I try to hold onto the words, to tether me here, but like everything else, they are gone.

54

THE AIR IS TINGED WITH the scent of salt and fire. Someone further along the shore has a fire going on the beach. We spotted it easily in the settling dusk, which falls earlier and earlier these days. I'm happy, though, to let the summer – with its short nights and bright midnight skies – slip away.

'. . . each one a slightly different shade of blue,' Fie is saying. As he walks, the pieces of sea-glass in his pocket clink together. He bends to pick up another piece, holds it up briefly against the sky so we can both see the rich, green glow between his fingers. 'That's a Kier piece,' he says, tossing me the glass. The scallops in the net over my shoulder rattle together as I reach out and catch the glass. Fie keeps the blue and orange glass, and I'm partial to the green, though I'm not sure Fie knows why I like this colour so much, who it reminds me of. Fie goes on, as if the sea-glass hadn't interrupted his conversation at all. 'Two are perfect. I've already started fitting them to the form, but I can't get the third one right. I've tried dying the fabric myself, but it's never right.'

'Better be right soon, cause at this rate, the dresses won't be ready for next Midsummer, let alone Hogmanay, and only two Gordon sisters will have a happy new year.'

Fie puffs out his cheeks in a long sigh. 'You can't rush perfection, Kier. Especially for a commission like this.'

'Look at you with your big city *commissions*,' I say, drawing out the last word with a grin. 'Soon you're going to be too big for this place. City people are going to be queueing at your door, trying to drag you back home with them to make their daughters' gowns.'

Fie shakes his head, but his smile stays put. 'This is just one. A friend of a friend of a friend sort of thing.' He shrugs. 'But how many dresses can I make before it's too late, and everyone forgets how good my suits are, too . . .'

Fie's words fade into the background, a cheerful hum, as I look out across the sea. I'm searching, of course I am, for a dark head. A seal's black gaze. My heart catches at the sight of a shape in the water, but it is only a rock.

'How about one step at a time?' I tell Fie, elbowing him in the arm.

'Right, right,' he says, tossing a piece of blue sea-glass into the air then catching it. He holds it up, squints at it, and I know he's thinking about that dress, about the next commission after that, and the one after. Or perhaps about Liv, who has no shortage of blue dresses these days; cobalt suits her beautifully, as does her tailor. It always seemed to me that Fie's path was set out before him, but it's not that simple, is it? He lets out a breath. 'Anyway, what are you up to later?'

'More of the usual,' I say, hefting the net of scallops.

Fie raises an eyebrow. 'Maybe skip the moonlight dive and join me at the Nest?'

Behind Fie, the moon sits in the sky, round and full, hanging above the ruins where Erskine Manor once stood.

'Tomorrow, okay? The sea calls to me,' I say, trying to sound flippant, but I know Fie doesn't miss a thing and, because he's Fie, he doesn't press me, he doesn't ask me again. He knows.

'Aye, tomorrow,' Fie says.

That night, I leave my bedroom light on before I leave the cottage so that as I walk along the shore, I can look back and see the familiar yellow glow. There is a light on in my parents' bedroom, too, and I wonder if they noticed me leaving.

What a feeling it is, knowing I can come back home, that I can always come back, no matter how much I've changed. We are all changing, now that the seals won't come.

Dad is still not well enough to join Mum and me on the boat. We don't hunt for seals anymore, but scallops are plentiful, and the Sealgairs have always been strong divers. Perhaps we're as good at diving as we are at hunting, we'd just never realised it. Mum and I have a healthy competition going, which Dad is clearly eager to join in on. Once the new year starts, he'll be back in the sea. A bit of bone dust in his tea every once in a while doesn't hurt, I suppose. Lady Erskine did give me something of worth, after all.

The rocks are wet; the tide has just pulled back. The moon hangs above me, slicking the edges of the rocks silver. A full moon. A harvest moon, the first moon of autumn. As I walk, my fingers reach for the knife on my belt, but there is no knife. Instead, in my pocket, is the Sealgair flute. It is all I have, and I hope it is enough.

Once I find a rock flat enough, I settle onto it. At my back are the Erskine cliffs. The water here is just as dark as it always was. Maybe it was always this way, long before Lady Erskine built her manor house on the cliffside.

The sea breathes against the rocks. The seabirds must be sleeping. When I begin to play, my flute is the only sound weaving through the air.

What are you doing here, Kier Sealgair, playing a song for the moon? I wonder, but my father's stories are in my bones, and I cannot forget what the young fisherman found beneath the full moon. The love of his life.

With my gaze trained on the sea, I play for a long, long time, long enough to see the tide drawing back, baring more and more of the rocks. Doubts settle in, curl up in my chest, make themselves at home, but I play anyway. I'll keep playing until the moon slips away and the sun comes up, if I have to. If I stop, then I will never know if this is enough.

A seal's dark head rises from the water, breaking the silver film of moonlight atop the sea. I will not look away from it and, at first, I try so hard not to blink that my eyes become sore, so I break all at once, blinking in a flurry all the blinks I held back. The seal doesn't slip away. It watches me, and the doubts feel smaller now. Still there, still settled in, but smaller, certainly. Maybe it's her.

And then the seal is gone.

I gasp, tear the flute away from my lips for a moment, but only a moment. I begin to play again, even though the seal is gone and the only movement on the water is the small, licking waves.

As she was when I first saw her, she is there all at once. She rises from the water with the sealskin in one hand. It dangles into the sea, making silver splashes as she walks towards the shore.

She is unsteady without her cane, so I rise to meet her in the water, offering my hand. When she takes it, I don't let go, and we stand together, knee-deep in the gentle surf.

'What a pretty song,' Breagha says.

'I hoped you'd like it,' I say, showing her my flute. I know she likes it, by the way her eyes grow wide, somehow wider than they already are, and she flashes a smile.

'It's too bad,' she says, 'that you cannot play it while you dance.'

With a splash, she drops the sealskin into the sea and loops her arms around my neck.

'Aren't you afraid you'll lose it again?' I ask her. I look down at the sealskin at our feet. Breagha has found what she was looking for. She is exactly where she was meant to be, and yet I should know better than anyone that there is no such thing as one path, one place, one dream. All of us are caught between, walking the shore between the land and the sea. Selkies, perhaps, most of all.

'Oh, no,' she says easily. 'With you here, I am not afraid of anything.'

I laugh, and I hold her, and we dance to the singing of the waves against the shore. We dance until the moon sinks and the sun rises and she returns to the sea, and I to the land, each of us where we were meant to be. But not quite, not exactly, both between.

Acknowledgements

When I wrote my first book, my son was (mostly) a baby; but he's a proper kid now and it's been so much fun to write a book with a kid who never runs out of ideas or creativity and is absolutely this book's biggest fan. So I have to first and foremost thank Harris for his enthusiasm for *The Bone Diver*, his tireless willingness to discuss the plot, his obsession with selkies, and his valuable input – you were right all along, buddy, a monster was exactly what the book needed.

The Bone Diver wasn't always going to be a story about selkies. For a while, I thought the book was going to be something very different, yet it never felt right. During the Edinburgh festival, my family and I were watching Janis McKay's show, *Wee Seals and Selkies*, listening to the fiddle music alongside Janis' storytelling, and I just knew what the book needed to be. Thank you, Janis, for the inspiration!

Thank you to Bob Pegg whose rendition of the folktale 'The Seal Killer' was so striking, I had to write a whole book about it. You can find the story in *The Anthology of Scottish Folktales*.

Thanks to the lovely Mary who introduced me to the song 'Mairi's Wedding' and the Scottish folk album *We Have Won the Land* by Rory Matheson; I listened to that album on repeat while writing this book.

Thank you to my family. Mom, massive thanks for helping me sort out the ending. Sarah, thanks for reading the early drafts and for your enthusiasm for Innes. Dad, Michelle and Jess – thanks for your constant support. Thanks to Charlotte for always being there for me.

Super special thanks to Braxton. You make my writing possible. And, of course, you're my muse, especially for this one. Because of you, I know so many wonderful Scottish words and phrases that made it into this book. (There's a lot that didn't make it in, but they're not quite appropriate to write here ...) Thanks for giving the book a good, Scottish read-through.

Thanks to my writing pals – Miriam, Alex, and the members of Funghouls. Thanks to the DeathWrites group, especially the SemiColons – Lynnda, Mary and Niall. You were the first people to read *The Bone Diver*, and your thoughtful feedback both made the book better and inspired me to keep writing.

Thank you to all the folk I work with at my 'day job' who have been hugely supportive of my writing – especially Helen for being such a wonderful person to work alongside and Scarlett for her unending supply of fab fantasy recommendations.

Robbie, thank you for joining me on this journey. I cannot thank you enough for your kindness and thoughtfulness. You're a brilliant agent.

Thank you to Craig for being a wonderful editor and a very big thank you to all the folks at Black & White who played a part in making this book possible – Hannah, Lizzie, Thomas, Tonje, and especially Ali and Rachel. Thank you also to Simon and Nicky.

To all the Edinburgh booksellers who make me so happy to be a part of this writing community, thank you for getting my books into the hands of readers. Thanks especially to my local indie, The Portobello Bookshop, the most beautiful bookshop with the loveliest staff. Thank you, Euan, in particular, for running stunning events. Having grown up surrounded by cornfields in the American Midwest, I still can't quite believe that I can walk to a bookshop anytime I like. I'm truly living the dream.

Finally, thank you to the folks at Tanifiki for creating such a welcoming space. I wrote most of this book at one of your tables with an oat milk flat white. Like I said, I'm living the dream.

ANGIE SPOTO is an American writer living in Scotland. She grew up near Chicago, lived in the Netherlands, and eventually moved to Scotland to get her PhD in Creative Writing at the University of Glasgow. She loves stories that are dark and surreal, strange and magical, and is inspired by writers like Ursula Le Guinn, Octavia Butler, Leonora Carrington, and Naomi Novik. She loves fairy tales, especially Scottish ones. She lives beside the shore with her husband and son.

@angiespotowrite on X and Instagram
angiespoto.com

'A powerful debut novel that explores serious, sensitive issues through a unique prism of fantasy.'
The Guardian

'A conceptually-explosive and vividly-rendered story that offers skewering insights into memory, grief, and desire. An anthem for our times.'
C J Cooke, bestselling author of The Lighthouse Witches

'Unforgettable and quietly devastating.'
Helen Marshall, author of The Migration